GRAVEYARD SHIFT

Books by Angela Roquet

Lana Harvey, Reapers Inc.
Graveyard Shift
Pocket Full of Posies
For the Birds
Psychopomp
Death Wish
Ghost Market
Hellfire and Brimstone
Limbo City Lights (short story collection)
The Illustrated Guide to Limbo City

Blood Vice
Blood Vice
Blood and Thunder
Blood in the Water
Blood Dolls
Thicker Than Blood
Blood, Sweat, and Tears
Flesh and Blood
Out for Blood

Spero Heights
Blood Moon
Death at First Sight
The Midnight District

Haunted Properties: Magic and Mayhem Universe
How to Sell a Haunted House
Better Haunts and Graveyards

other titles
Crazy Ex-Ghoulfriend
Backwoods Armageddon

GRAVEYARD SHIFT

LANA HARVEY, REAPERS INC.

BOOK ONE

ANGELA ROQUET

VIOLENT SIREN PRESS

GRAVEYARD SHIFT

www.angelaroquet.com

Cover Art by Rebecca Frank

Edited by Chelle Olson of Literally Addicted to Detail

ISBN: 978-1-951603-02-1

"Whatever we once were, we are no longer
a Christian Nation—at least, not just.
We are also a Jewish nation, a Muslim nation,
a Buddhist nation, a Hindu nation,
and a nation of nonbelievers."
—*President Barack Obama*

Finally, someone for everyone.
This one is for you, Mr. President.

CHAPTER ONE

"Suicide is man's way of telling god,
you can't fire me, I quit."
—*Bill Maher*

No one cared about Lial Gordon, but you might have never guessed if you had seen his funeral. A herd of socialites gathered around his grave. A silk handkerchief dabbed an eye here and there. A eulogy fit for the president was poetically read, and dozens of white roses were tossed with a dramatic and well-practiced sympathy.

Lial smiled and rolled back on his heels. He looked a little too smug for a dead man, but he was a dead man just the same.

"Pigs!" he snorted. "I don't know half of them, but there's no doubt why they're here. Everyone wants a piece of my money. Ha! Wait until they find out they've wasted a perfectly good Saturday for nothing."

Lial was in a much better mood than he had been four days ago when he came home early from his visit to New York. He was the president of a reputable bank and often took trips to meet his most valuable customers. Unfortunately, he had just lost one of his best. He was looking forward to sulking over one of his wife's casseroles, but soon discovered he wasn't the only man enjoying her cooking.

He entered his master bedroom to find his best friend, and vice president of his bank, snoring between his wife's legs.

Lial didn't wake them. He quietly retreated to his library to find solace in a bottle of aged brandy. Then, in a drunken stupor, he gathered the cash from his private safe, all of his wife's jewelry, and anything else of value he could smuggle out of the house. He loaded it all into the trunk of his Rolls Royce and left.

After an hour's drive, he pulled off onto a gravel road and followed it back to a lake surrounded by woods. At one time, the place had been special. He had gone fishing there with his sons when they were younger. Now, they only called if they needed money. Lial finished off another bottle of brandy while pitching bundles of crisp, hundred-dollar bills into the lake.

When he finished disposing of his riches, he got back into his car and drove home. Morning broke, and the sun glimmered into a rich dawn as he pulled into his driveway and found the traitors kissing goodbye on the front porch. They froze at the sight of him, and before they could compose themselves, Lial floored it.

He plowed the car right through the bay window and into the living room. The impact threw him into the windshield, where a piece of glass found his throat. He would have choked to death on his own blood, watching his wife and best friend run from the house, screaming like lunatics, if it hadn't been for the explosion.

That's how Lial Gordon died, and that's how he met me. Lial was pleased with himself. Not only had he taken care of his money and car, but now the house was worthless, as well. Not many are as proud as he was so soon after death.

"All right." Lial smiled and turned to walk away from the crowd of mourners. "Enough of this. I'm ready to burn in Hell."

The dead are strange. They always assume they can just walk into their afterlife. I reached for his shoulder and pulled him back.

"Hold still." If you had my job, you'd be grim, too.

I pushed my hand into the pocket of my robe and found my coin. Rolling it three times, I said the word, and we left the graveyard behind.

There is no tunnel with a light at the end when you die, just a reaper with a coin, like me. Maybe to a *human* the passage over resembles a tunnel. To me, it's more like a womb, and we're being pushed into existence elsewhere. Humans are always in that infant-like state of shock when they see Limbo City.

Lial's smirking good mood melted as we arrived. My world is very different from his. But I have to admit, my shock to his world when I got my first coin was just as bad.

The coordinates I had used pushed us out into the middle of the market area, shadowed by the towering architecture of downtown Limbo. Buildings crammed together down Morte Avenue, a collage of metal and stone. The old-world charm of cathedrals and temples mixed with New York-styled skyscrapers, imitating the human realm. Rusty streaks of light shot out from behind the city, strangling the illusion of a sunset. Limbo has no sun, but the fake light is welcomed by most citizens. Even the dead prefer to see what they're doing.

I sighed, wishing I had picked a different location. The market was an unthinkable place to be on a Sunday. Crowds of souls picked through an assortment of goods shipped in from the afterlives. The innocent items like phoenix feathers and vases autographed by Greek gods were arranged out in the open, but if you looked close enough, you could find someone selling vials of holy water or hellfire under the table. Both substances required a license to carry in Limbo City, but most vendors didn't care, if you paid the right price.

Crones hobbled by, gaudy amulets swinging from their necks as they waved their salt-crusted fingers to lure customers closer. A patron bumped a table of herbs, and a horde of pixies scurried to gather them before they hit the ground. A trio of saints lectured outside a white tent, stressing the importance of keeping faith in the afterlife to a crowd of fresh souls.

The harbor would be busy, too. It's always busy on the weekends. That's when the Sea of Eternity is the calmest. It used to be only Sundays, but less than a century ago, during the Colorado Labor Wars, two souls who had died in the Ludlow Massacre ended up working in the Three Fates

Factory. They convinced the employees to go on strike until they were given Saturdays off, as well.

The strike didn't last long. The factory is responsible for pulling souls out of the sea and reinstalling them in the human realm. After a few days, the Sea of Eternity had swelled up around Limbo City and threatened to swallow it. The Fates quickly agreed to give Saturdays off, and the factory began running again.

The Sea of Eternity used to be a river, but that all changed when humans began dabbling in science. More atheists and agnostics die every day. It's their souls that fill the sea, making my job even grimmer. It used to be easy getting a lot of souls to their afterlives. It used to take minutes, but minutes stretched into hours, and soon I fear it will become days. I don't get paid enough to waste that kind of time. Like I said, you'd be grim, too.

Taking Lial by the shoulder, I directed him through the crowd and down the main dock to my ship. He was my last soul for the day, and I was ready to set sail. I had twelve souls to take to Heaven, eight to Nirvana, and four to Summerland. Not too bad for a Sunday. Unlike the Three Fates employees, reapers don't get weekends off. But if we save enough coin, we can buy ourselves a vacation.

"What are you doing, Lana?" Josie, my sailing partner, stood on the deck of my ship with her arms folded. Tufts of black hair framed her oval face. The haircut was almost too short to be considered feminine, but she pulled it off with her delicate chin and ample pout. The fierce sweep of lashes around her eyes didn't hurt either.

She tapped her toe on the deck of my—well, *our* ship. We had gone in and traded our two smaller boats for something a little nicer and a little faster. A demon sold it to us, claiming Grace O'Malley had given it to him in exchange for some deed involving the possession of a queen. How fitting, that two lady reapers should purchase it. It had been a little too expensive for me to buy on my own. Besides, it was nice to have some company other than a herd of disoriented souls.

"Sorry, I know I'm late. We stayed for the funeral."

I hated being lectured. Josie was a better reaper than I was, and I didn't have a problem with that. What I did have a problem with, was her rubbing it in my face.

"No, what are you doing bringing that soul on our boat? I saw his file. He's a suicide and a non-believer. Where do you think we're taking him?" She tilted her head to one side and raised an eyebrow.

"By all rights, yes, he belongs in the sea. His soul is not nearly dark enough for Hell to pay us anything worth our time."

"But?" she snapped.

We hadn't been working on the same boat for very long, but her criticism was getting old. She always had to do everything by the book, like something bad might happen if she bent the rules. I didn't bend them all the time, and I never outright broke them...much.

"I like Lial here, and I have a coin I've been saving for a rainy day. Nirvana should take it. He's had a difficult life, and I think he deserves a little enjoyment before being sucked up by the Fates and spit back into that pitiful reality again." I yanked back the hood of my robe so she could get the full effect of the face I made at her as I pushed Lial on deck.

"Nirvana? You mean that Asian religion was right?" Lial's fear mutated into curiosity.

"They're all right. We just sort you humans by how well you measure up to your individual beliefs." You can't imagine how many times I've had this conversation.

"Then why are you taking me to Nirvana? Not that I mind," he quickly added.

"Because I think you deserve a vacation, and Nirvana's laws are easier to get around than Heaven's." I patted his arm and opened the door to the sailor's quarters.

My first twenty-three souls chattered among twenty new faces, Josie's catch. My stomach knotted. She had twenty-four souls on her docket that morning, same as me, all preordered by their afterlives. This meant four were in the hold. We never put souls in the hold unless we're taking them to Hell. Most Hell-bounds try to escape. Can you blame them?

I scowled, wishing I had reviewed Josie's list as well as she had reviewed mine. I hated making deliveries to Hell. Lucifer never gave me any trouble, but he had been on vacation lately. Gate duty had been turned over to Maalik, one of the Islamic angels.

Maalik had originally been appointed to watch over the Islamic hell, Jahannam, but with Eternity's growing demands, the rulers of Jahannam and Hell decided to adjoin their territories and utilize a single gateway.

Maalik made me nervous. He was too flirty and too pretty to be guarding the gates of Hell. I didn't trust him, and I didn't like that he was racking up so much coin with his ambitious work ethic. If he showed up in Limbo, I planned on hightailing it to Summerland until he left. I needed a vacation anyway.

Lial looked around the room. He was my most enjoyable catch of the day. I didn't regret staying for his funeral. Josie would get over it.

"I'll come find you when we get to Nirvana," I said. "Meanwhile, talk to James over there. He's a Buddhist. He can fill you in on how to get through the gates."

"Hey, uh, thanks," Lial whispered. "I don't know why you're doing this, but I appreciate it."

"Sure." I laughed. Granting little favors almost made my job worth it. I closed the door behind me and found Josie waiting.

"Do you even know how many rules you're breaking doing this?" she grumbled.

I folded my arms. "It's not a big deal. Like the Fates will even miss him."

"You're jeopardizing both of our jobs, not to mention gambling with a ship that I paid for, too."

"Lighten up. I'm going to change before we take off. Where's Gabriel? Didn't he need a ride?" I wanted to change the subject before she listed every rule I had broken since we'd started working together.

"He's late, as usual. Cocky jerk thinks the world revolves around him. He's probably still at Purgatory Lounge."

"I thought he quit drinking. He'd better sober up before we get to Heaven, or you know we'll get blamed for it."

"I know." Josie frowned. "You're redirecting souls without authorization, and now we're transporting a drunk of an archangel to make coin on the side. We might as well be demons."

"I'll go fetch him." I felt like a drink myself after Josie's little fit.

"If you're not back in twenty minutes, I'm tossing your refugee and taking the coin for your other souls," she warned.

"I'll be back in time. I just gotta change first. I'm not going inside Purgatory wearing my work robe." I looked down at the frumpy garment and sighed. While it looked good on Josie, it made me look like Marilyn Monroe's evil twin.

I headed for the captain's quarters before Josie could start another argument. She was a pain in the ass, but she was one of the few reapers I trusted.

Shuffling through my dresser, I found a pair of leather pants I had bought at Athena's Boutique. Athena had set up a nice little shop in Limbo after sulking for nearly a millennium over her decline of followers. It was doing her a world of good, and I was growing a rather charming wardrobe. A black tank top and my favorite pair of boots completed the outfit. I thought about doing something with my hair but decided I didn't have time. Josie was in a bad enough mood.

If I was late, I knew she would make good on her threat to leave.

I cocked an eyebrow at myself in the dusty oval mirror next to our bunk and made a mental note to give Josie back the tube of cherry lipstick she had loaned me. Anemic hooker was not the look I was going for. I combed my fingers through my black ringlets and left.

Limbo City was just as crowded as the market and harbor. The Fates' employees were busy shopping. Fresh souls happily filled the streets and sidewalks, only stopping for a moment to move out of my way. They knew I was a reaper, and it made them nervous. A reaper had brought each one of them over at some point.

The Three Fates used to recycle the souls on their own, but it made for tiresome and constant work. Some time ago, they'd discovered a way to keep a small fraction of souls in Limbo, and persuaded them to work at the factory in exchange for a grander entrance back into the human realm. I can tell every time I harvest a soul from America. More and more celebrities are sprouting up all over the place.

I passed the Muses Union House and Bank of Eternity before reaching Purgatory Lounge. Gabriel's musical voice spilled out as I opened the door.

"I haven't had this much fun since I told Joseph his fiancée was knocked up by God!" the angel slurred. He sat at a booth with two nephilim, fallen angel half-breeds.

"Gabriel! What do you think you're doing?" I plucked a feather from one of his wings, and he fluttered them in protest.

"Owww! What was that for?" he whined.

His drinking buddies eyed me suspiciously. Their wings were smaller, but their bodies larger. They weren't as attractive as real angels, but they were close.

"The ship is sailing with or without you, Gabriel. If you don't leave here with me now, you'll have to find a ride over later. I don't think Peter will be very pleased with you," I scolded him.

"Peter's halo's gotten a little fat these days. I tried to take him on vacation with me, but he doesn't seem to think anyone else is fit to man the gate," Gabriel laughed.

"I can't imagine why when archangels keep coming home drunk."

"Give it a rest, Lana. Josie must be rubbing off on you. You used to be fun. What happened?" He hiccuped and slid an arm around my waist to pull me down into the booth with him. The nephilim across from me gave a sheepish smile.

Gabriel was getting careless with his reputation lately. If another heavenly host spotted him mingling with the offspring of the fallen, he'd never hear the end of it from Peter. He'd be stuck with cherub tasks for a decade.

"I was just telling Bob here," Gabriel slobbered, "how I can do whatever I want because when people get to Heaven, who do they wanna see? Me! Right after Jesus and Mary, but still. I'm not gonna lose my job. I've been busting my halo for thousands of years. Thousands! I think I deserve a little fun now and then. Don't I, Lala?" His head rolled onto my shoulder.

Lala wasn't exactly a nickname. Gabriel only used it when he was tanked, which was about half the time.

I sighed. "Gabriel, Josie will leave us both here and take my commission if we don't go now."

"Fine, party-pooper. See you boys later."

The half-breeds nodded and went back to their drinks.

Gabriel left his arm around my waist as we made our way back to the ship. I didn't stop him because I didn't think he could walk upright otherwise. We got plenty of strange looks. *A reaper and an archangel walked out of a bar.* I almost had to laugh.

"About time!" Josie shouted at us from the deck where she untied the ropes holding our ship to the dock.

It was quieter now. Most of the reaper ferries had already departed for the afterlives. Gabriel spread his wings and flew up ahead of me. Feathers rained down as he ran into a mast and fluttered like a spooked chicken to catch himself.

"Don't fly on my ship while you're drunk!" Josie was still in a sour mood. She turned her hostile glare to me.

I grinned at her. "Told you I'd make it back in time."

"With the state he's in, I wish you hadn't." She turned away to pull up one of the sails. "A little help would be nice."

I stomped over to the next mast and untangled a web of ropes.

Once we were out of the harbor and the noise had faded behind us, I went to check on Lial. He was curled up on a couch next to James, who looked relieved to see me.

"Miss Lana, I don't know if I have enough time to prepare him," he said, nervously tugging the cuffs of his robe.

I nodded. "Just do your best. I'll take care of it when we get there."

I hadn't told James that I had a coin, and obviously, Lial hadn't mentioned it to him either. It wouldn't have done much good, seeing as neither of them knew how our coin worked.

Our coin wasn't just used as currency to make purchases. It held a doorway to the other realms. It would have been nice to just transport the souls to their afterlives with a coin, but if we did that, our boss would take it out of our commission. So we sailed the Sea of Eternity.

"I'm the king of the world!" Gabriel shouted at the head of the boat, nearly falling overboard. Only the flutter of his wings saved him.

"Gabriel!" Josie growled.

"He's already paid, so let's just get this over with," I said as she shot me another nasty look.

"Next time, we're charging more. I like order on my ship—"

"*Our* ship," I corrected her.

We were both possessive of O'Malley's boat. It wasn't every day that you came by a legendary female pirate's ship.

The sails were open and gently tugged us along toward our first stop, Summerland, my favorite of the afterlives. Not too crowded. Lots of nature to take in. It was a nice break from the bustling city life in Limbo. The pagans were friendly and didn't seem to mind the occasional reaper on vacation.

"You wanna go out for a beer when we get home?" I tried to smooth things over with Josie. Her scrunched up face lightened a little and then flushed.

"I can't."

"Look, I'm sorry for messing up your schedule."

"It's not that. I have a date," she whispered so Gabriel wouldn't overhear.

"Oh, really? With whom?"

"It's not a big deal." She toyed with the ropes of the nearest sail.

"Come on, who?"

She blushed and leaned over the railing. "Horus."

"Josie." It was my turn to lecture her. "You know he's just going to try to bribe you into sneaking more souls into Duat."

Duat was the Egyptian underworld, but its flow of souls had been steadily decreasing for some time.

"No, he won't. They get enough to keep them happy," she argued.

"When's the last time we made a delivery there?"

"He doesn't care about more souls. Osiris is watching over Duat, and Horus has been vacationing for almost a decade now."

"Just be careful."

It wasn't like Josie to go after one of the old gods. The laws were more lenient these days, but most of society still frowned on reapers dating outside the corporation.

"Hate to interrupt, ladies, but we have company," Gabriel sang out to us.

"What now?" Josie stormed off to the front of the ship with me close behind. We were an hour from Summerland, with three more stops to go. We didn't need trouble this early.

"Shit." I frowned at the horizon.

A ship approached us from the north. Clusters of dog-faced demons scaled the masts and sides of the black boat, and a dark-winged man stood on the main deck, holding a leash attached to a soul.

"Caim, that bastard. He's snatched a clairvoyant soul." I squeezed my eyes shut. The day just kept getting better.

Caim was enjoying his exile from Hell a little too much, especially since he'd left with two legions of demons. After his impeachment, he had gone underground for half a century. Now he was out stalking reaper ferries to loot souls.

"I'll get my bow. You'd better go find your scythe." Josie took off for our cabin.

My scythe lay next to the hatch where I had left it the last time I had to terrorize a group of Hell-bound souls down in the hold. There were thirty of them that day. Grim had given me an extra miserable lot after he found out I had snuck a boy, destined for the sea, into Summerland. The Hell-bounds were plotting an escape until my scythe flashed before them.

I grabbed my weapon and headed back to the front of the ship with Josie, who now carried her bow. She had a scythe too but rarely used it. The bow was a gift from

Artemis for delivering a message to her twin brother, Apollo. Artemis set up an archery shop after she saw what a hit Athena's Boutique was, but her brother still resided on Mount Olympus in Summerland.

"We should really get that soul back." I sighed over Gabriel's shoulder.

"I wasn't planning on getting that close." Josie's eyes widened with concern as her fingers twitched over the arrows in her quiver.

"You wouldn't have to," Gabriel offered. "Distract him, and I'll go over and get the soul."

"Do you really think you should be flying under the influence?"

"I'm an archangel. Give me some credit here."

Josie frowned and lifted her bow. "Fine. You ready, Lana?"

"Ready and armed."

I couldn't use my scythe long-range, but as soon as she let loose an arrow, the demons that could fly would be on us. I could see Caim's cocky grin now, and the sullen expression of the female soul he had captured.

"Go, Gabriel!" Josie shouted as she unleashed an arrow.

It was a perfect shot through Caim's wing. He twisted in agony and dropped the leash. Josie strung another arrow as I lashed out at two demons hovering above us. I didn't want them to land on our deck. We'd just had it washed. Demon guts were acidic and would burn holes in our ship if they weren't cleaned up right away.

Three more of the creatures appeared in mid-air, snapping and snarling. I swung to behead them, only missing one. It landed on the deck and scrambled toward Josie as she pumped Caim full of arrows. I lashed out, catching the creature's underside with my blade, and flung it overboard with a shriek. Sticky demon pieces splattered my leather pants.

"Lana! They're coming over the side!" Josie backed into me.

Four more demons clawed up the side of the ship and circled us. They were smaller than the others. Three sets of leathery wings scaled down their bony spines. One inched closer, dragging its talons along the deck with a squeal that rivaled a dozen chalkboards.

Josie cringed. "Now that's uncalled for." She lifted her bow and popped an arrow through the little devil's head.

The rest of the litter rushed us. Josie nodded to me, and we attacked together. She darted one with an arrow while I gutted another, splashing the deck with steaming gore. The last demon latched on to my foot just as Josie put an arrow through its head, pinning the toe of my boot to the deck floor in the process.

I sucked in a breath, anticipating a sharp pain that thankfully didn't follow. The arrow had wedged itself between my toes.

"Nice shot." I rolled my eyes and reached down to jerk the arrow free.

"Please, you've had those boots for nearly a century. It's time you invest in a new pair anyway." Josie took the arrow from me and stuffed it back in her quiver. "We're going to have to file a report now."

"I'll do it," I groaned. "I have an evaluation with Grim in the morning anyway."

Attacks on reaper ferries had tripled in the past week. Where Limbo City was the ultimate free world, the Sea of Eternity was an aged battlefield, just as hostile as Limbo was neutral. The attacks were the big news of the week, headlining on the covers of *Limbo Weekly* and the *Daily Reaper Report*. Channel Nine, *Council Street Live*, had even issued a cautionary warning to sea travelers and transporters.

Gabriel landed on the deck behind us. The captive soul trembled in his arms. I wondered if she could smell the alcohol on his breath. She stared at us as though trying to decide if we were any better than the creep we'd just rescued her from.

At a more comfortable distance away, Caim was busy yanking arrows out of his bloodied wings.

"Jerk," I muttered and wiped my hands off on my pants. They were ruined.

"So, where do we take you?" Josie cooed at the soul. The woman pulled away from Gabriel and looked up at him.

"It's okay," he said. "They'll get you where you need to be."

She turned back to us and smiled. "Do you travel to Summerland?"

CHAPTER TWO

*"Seeing death as the end of life
is like seeing the horizon as the end of the ocean."*
—David Searls

Funeral Home Chic. That's how I'd describe Grim's office. It was painted the most innocent shade of black with a matte finish. A pot of daisies sat on either side of his coffin-shaped desk. Awards and framed photos covered the three interior walls, while a glossy window overlooking most of the city swallowed the far wall. I could see the harbor, tiny in the distance, and wondered how much longer Grim would keep me waiting.

Grim was the mayor of Limbo City and owner of Reapers Incorporated. As if being mayor and owning the most successful business in Eternity wasn't enough, he was also the president of the Afterlife Council, and the only member with an indefinite term because no one else in Limbo had half as much power or influence.

Some thought that the Fates were powerful enough to take his place, but Grim had the Fates wrapped around his finger. He'd saved them from going out of business and helped them establish their factory in Limbo City. They were indebted to him and supported his position of power.

"Sorry to keep you." Grim's gravelly voice made me jump.

I turned to watch him walk into the room. He wore his usual slate gray suit with a black tie. His hair was shiny and neatly combed. He reminded me of a forty-something lawyer, even though he was well over two thousand. The lines around his eyes and mouth were the only signs of aging I could see, and they seemed to deepen as he looked me over. He cleared his throat and smoothed down the folds of his jacket before sitting.

"There's a position that will be available soon. Someone on the Afterlife Council strongly suggested you. Do you know anything about this?" He didn't seem pleased.

"No. What kind of position?" I asked, wondering which council member it could have been. I didn't know any of them well, and aside from shaking their hands after they were sworn in, I couldn't recall meeting one of them at any other time.

"That's not important. You'll get all the details when and if you get the job. Until then, your work will be closely reviewed. You should follow the rules if you have any desire to obtain this promotion or any promotion in the future."

"Of course." I couldn't help but smile now. Someone thought I was worthy of a raise. So what if it wasn't Grim.

He narrowed his eyes at me and leaned back in his chair. "You know, for as long as you've been working for me, it is very surprising that you're still a low-risk harvester. You've accumulated just enough soul violations to delay any possibility of advancement, but not so many that you would be considered for termination."

He folded his hands on top of his desk and sneered at me like an IRS auditor who had just caught wind of an illegal operation. Death and taxes, not only certain but cocky as ever. I squirmed in my seat.

I only knew of one reaper who had suffered termination, which is a fluffier way of saying he was executed. His name was Vince Hare. He got caught selling souls on the ghost market after reporting them CNH, Currently Not Harvestable. After that, anyone who reported more than two unharvestables in a year went through a meticulous investigation, during which, they were demoted to low-risk status.

I was already a low-risk harvester, even though I had never been considered for investigation. My soul violations were all classified as transfer errors, and since the souls in question were only destined for the already overflowing sea, I got off with a slap on the scythe.

Grim stared at me a few seconds longer, prolonging my anxiety as long as his schedule would allow, and then let go of his iron gaze and sighed. "Take tomorrow off. If you do happen to get this promotion, the opportunity for a vacation day will be suspended for an undetermined time."

I raised an eyebrow. Something wasn't making sense. Only high-risk harvesters had to worry about suspended vacation privileges. The importance of their work required them to be available at a moment's notice. They took care of the more important souls, harvesting them at the time of death rather than pre-burial like I did. A low-risk harvester like me never jumped that far up the totem pole.

"Ellen has your soul docket waiting out front." Grim gave me a nod and started going through his mail. I didn't bother saying goodbye as I slipped out of his office.

"Here you go, Ms. Harvey," Ellen chirped, handing me a sheet of crisp paper.

I pulled my clipboard out of my robe and fastened the page to it. There were thirty-six names, and nine of them were destined for the sea. Grim knew I hated dumping souls in the sea, but since I was being watched, now I had to. Part of me wondered if he hoped I would break the rules.

I turned back to Ellen. "I'm gonna need a report form, too. My ship was attacked yesterday."

"Oh, dear." Ellen took a sip of her coffee and opened a desk drawer. She shuffled through a pile of candy bar wrappers before finding a new pad of blank report forms.

The latest form revision condensed everything into two pages, which was fine by me. No one wanted to fill out eight pages of random questions, especially if there wasn't even enough damage to be compensated for.

"Do you need a claim form, too?" Ellen asked.

"No, we took care of the demons before they did any harm to the ship, and no souls were lost."

"That's a relief." She pulled a candy bar out of her purse and unwrapped it before blushing and setting it back down on her desk. "You can drop that form off tomorrow morning if you want."

"Yeah, sure." I clipped it under my soul docket and gave her a nod. "See you tomorrow."

"Have a nice day, sweetie."

CHAPTER THREE

*"We have enough religion to make us hate,
but not enough to make us love one another."*
—Jonathan Swift

"Let me guess, another funeral?" Once again, Josie met me on the deck of our ship with her arms folded. It was becoming a daily ritual.

"No," I sighed. "My evaluation didn't go so well, and there were thirty-six names on my docket."

I pushed past her with my last soul. He was a punk in his twenties who had overdosed on speed. He thought it was cool that he was going to Hell, but I put him down in the hold anyway. If I were being watched, I wasn't taking any chances.

"Oh." Josie's critical sneer melted into a frown as she followed me, waiting for all the details.

"It appears that I'm being reviewed for a promotion."

"What?" She didn't even try to hide her disgust. "You're joking," she said, putting her hands on her hips as her kitten gray eyes shifted into storm clouds.

"Grim's not happy about it either, so join the club."

"Then why is he offering you a promotion?" She still wasn't buying it.

"One of the council members suggested me." Hearing it aloud brought a smile to my lips.

Normally, I couldn't have cared less about a promotion. Hell, who am I kidding? I'd been avoiding promotions for as long as I could remember. Grim obviously had me figured out. I hated my job. But knowing that a council member had suggested me made me feel obligated to perform. Pride is a tricky little bitch.

"Which one?" Josie looked pained as she realized I was telling the truth.

"He wouldn't say. He wouldn't even tell me what the position was, just that I was being reviewed and that I should follow the rules."

"Oh." It was barely a whisper. "Well, congratulations."

She gave me a weak smile before turning to yank up a sail. I started on the next one over.

"I know you're a better reaper than I am, and I'm sorry you weren't interviewed."

"It's not that."

I could see the tips of Josie's ears redden as she turned to face me. She took a deep breath and let it out slowly. "It's just, Horus has been hinting that I might be offered a new position, and now I think he had it all wrong. I think he meant you."

"When were you going to tell me?" I snapped. I told her everything, and as soon as I could. Now I was feeling foolish and wondered what else she didn't feel the need to share with me.

"He said I should keep it to myself, that it was confidential."

"Right, and you don't bend the rules like I do. I forgot."

"Oh, Lana. I'm sorry. Really, I'm happy for you. Tomorrow's poker night. We can celebrate." She shrugged and went to pull up another sail.

"Lana Harvey?"

I turned around to find another reaper on our deck, Coreen Bendura. She was a second-generation reaper and proud of it. The last time we had spoken had been at Saul's memorial service.

Saul Avelo had been my mentor and a first-generation reaper who didn't carry around the holier-than-thou attitude most of the older reapers did. He was also the only reaper to ever die during a harvest. Coreen had been his first apprentice, and that was the only reason I had a shred of respect for her.

"Can I help you?" I would play nice. I was being watched, after all.

"Grim sent me to supervise you for the day," she said with a smile and lifted her chin. I don't know why she bothered. Being half a foot taller gave her plenty of distance to look down on me. She was waiting for me to refuse so she could lecture me on her seniority. I was glad for my meeting with Grim now. Had he not told me I was up for a promotion, I would have told Coreen to hitch a ride to Hell with someone else.

"Of course," I replied, mirroring her nasty grin.

"Docket please." She held out her hand, and I dropped my clipboard in it.

I would control my temper. She was going to press every button I had. It was okay, though. I knew where her buttons were, too. The fact that I was up for promotion had to be eating at her far worse than Josie. That alone kept me in check.

"Where do you keep your souls?" Her short, cropped curls stayed perfectly flat as she darted her head from side to side, looking around our ship with a disapproving eye. She could make all the faces she wanted. I knew we had a solid ship.

"Nine in the sea, twenty on board, and seven in the hold," I answered.

She looked down at me and frowned. "Do you mind if I verify that?"

"Be my guest." I fought the urge to point her overboard and instead waved my hand toward the sailor's quarters. She hurried off with her nose in the air.

"Lana, you haven't broken any rules that I don't know about, have you?" Josie whispered as soon as we were alone.

"Do you think I'm that stupid?" I snapped. "Grim told me I was being reviewed. You think I would do something that might get you in trouble when I know I'm being watched?"

"You really want me to answer that?" Josie laughed.

Coreen came out of the sailor's quarters and opened the hatch to peer down in the hold. She hadn't brought any souls on board with her, so I figured either Grim hadn't given her any for the day, or she'd had someone else take them. It was also possible that all her souls had gone into the sea. She was heartless enough to handle that much despair.

"Everything appears to be in proper order," she announced as she poked her narrow nose down in her record book to scribble a few notes. "We can depart whenever you're ready."

"Aye, aye, Captain." I gave her a salute and freed us from the dock. My mind was already racing with a dozen ways to make her wish she had never stepped foot on our ship. This was going to be fun.

CHAPTER FOUR

"It does me no injury for my neighbor to say there are twenty gods or no God. It neither picks my pocket nor breaks my leg."
—*Thomas Jefferson*

The streets of Limbo were peaceful come Tuesday morning. After Coreen's visit, I was thankful for the day off. The quietness of the city was mostly because the Three Fates' employees were working. The stores were open and empty of people. I had to force myself not to skip. When you're immortal, life's little joys tend to lose their kick over time. Shopping is one of the few things I still cherish, along with over-sweetened coffee and John Wayne movies.

A Roman god was out walking a lion, and a small parade of angels ducked inside Purgatory Lounge. Athena swept the stoop outside her shop, while next door, Artemis set up a display of leather quivers overflowing with bouquets of magnificent arrows, the fletching on each one unique and artfully detailed with polished gems and feathers of rare birds.

"Josie would love these." I sighed and brushed my fingers over their soft tips.

Artemis smiled. "They would make a lovely Samhain gift."

I had to be careful around the goddesses. They were old and wise, but their beauty made me forget sometimes. The average soul didn't stand a chance against them. They could sell holy water to a demon if they wanted.

"You know we don't celebrate your holidays." I stepped away from the arrows and ran my hand down the length of a leather hunting cape.

"Oh, that's right." Artemis paused and tucked a golden curl behind her ear. "What do you reapers celebrate?"

"Not much, really. The only annual event of importance we have is the Oracle Ball," I said, thinking how nice it would be if gift-giving became a part of the affair.

The Oracle Ball was a glamorous event in Limbo. It was like the Oscars for deities, and since it was hosted by my boss, I got an invitation every year. Grim's office was the tallest building in Limbo, and every year the ball was held on the roof.

Limbo hadn't always been a charming and orderly city, and Eternity's territories and borders weren't always defined. Despite what religions taught, it was actually humans, or their souls rather, that created the gods.

The soul is a powerful and mysterious thing. It's so powerful that it emits a substance that is the very stuff that created not only the gods but also Eternity itself.

When the afterlives first appeared in Eternity, there was no order, and they sloppily overlapped each other, causing a great deal of friction among the gods. It wasn't long before everyone in Eternity was at war. Millions were slaughtered before the gods finally called a meeting and signed a peace treaty. Territories were determined, and Limbo City was founded in the center of Eternity as its governing point.

When the War of Eternity finally ended, the Afterlife Council was created to ensure peace. They worked together and found a way to concentrate and confine the excess soul matter so the established territories wouldn't be disturbed by some new afterlife or god popping up unannounced. A yearly date was decided upon to remind everyone of the treaty and to distribute the accumulated soul matter, and the Oracle Ball was born.

"Too bad." Artemis frowned. "You know, that's this weekend. I haven't even bought a dress yet."

"I need to find one, too."

"I'm having a sale," Athena shouted to us.

It was a perfect day for shopping. The dressing rooms would be all mine.

"Apollo will be arriving tomorrow," Artemis whispered with a grin. "Does Josie have a date for the ball?"

"I'm not sure." I didn't know how close she and Horus were becoming, but I didn't want to make her the center of any goddess gossip.

"You should take her out to Purgatory tomorrow night. Don't tell her Apollo will be there. Let it be a surprise," she whispered lower to keep Athena from overhearing.

"Sure." I wondered how Josie had become so popular with the old gods lately. Was there something I had missed?

"I guess I'd better go pick out a gown." I looked over my shoulder at Athena, who blushed and ducked inside her store.

"If you see anything green and sparkly, tell her to hold it for me." Artemis laughed and went back to arranging her display.

It was cooler inside Athena's Boutique. The air was thick with perfumes—lilac and rose. Mannequins wrapped in tulle and lace danced and waved at me from their pedestals. Athena's sales had doubled after she enchanted them. I guess some customers liked to see how the gowns looked in motion. I found the models creepy and distracting. Last fall, I had commented on how soft a particular sweater looked, only to have the wooden dummy take it off and hand it to me.

Athena was busy hanging a sign in the front window to advertise her sale. By the time she closed, every dress would be gone.

"So, do you know if any more reapers will be coming in this year?" she asked as she stepped away from the window to inspect her sign.

"Six, under K."

"To K already? It feels like just yesterday that you arrived. How long have you been here now?"

"Almost three hundred years," I groaned.

Originally, Grim had been the only reaper, but since he played such a significant role in containing the excess soul matter, he was allowed to use a portion of it every hundred years to create more reapers. You could tell what year we were born, or made rather, by the first letter of our last names.

My last name is Harvey, meaning I'm an eighth-generation reaper. Josie's last name is Galla, making her a seventh-generation, born a hundred years before me. She pointed that out as often as she could.

"Any guess on who is being voted in?" Athena eyed me hopefully.

"Not a clue," I answered. So my boss ruled Eternity. I was just one of his underpaid peons. Like he'd ever tell me anything that important. Five of the ten council members were at the end of their hundred-year terms, and the new members would be announced at the ball.

"Do you have a date?" Athena was just full of questions. It didn't surprise me. She seemed to know everything, and you didn't get to know everything without asking a few questions first.

"No. I've been too busy to even think about a date."

"Maybe you'll meet a nice boy there." She always referred to us as if we were children. She had been around so long, though, I could see why. I wasn't sure of her exact age, but she was a goddess. Goddesses never seemed to age.

Athena's own serene beauty revealed none of the hardship or wrathful nature she'd experienced in her prime when she was known more for her war tactics than her weaving. Her legendary shield bearing the head of Medusa leered at me from its glass cabinet, high on the wall behind the register. Even though Athena had relocated to Limbo and passed her days more peacefully now, she wanted to make sure that no one forgot she was Zeus's first daughter and had a heroic past to prove it.

"How about something blue this year?" She turned to one of the racks and pulled down a dress. My breath caught. Thin black lace lined the strapless gown, above and below the bust, and then met in the back to form an elegant bow. An elaborate mass of vertical folds covered the bust, while the rest of the material flowed down to the floor in smooth perfection. A hint of black lace peeked out from under the gown. I had to have it. I could tell Athena knew from the pleased smile spreading across her face.

"Go try it on," she urged, laying the gown in my arms. I choked down my excitement and turned to find the dressing rooms. They were upstairs.

At the back of the shop, a spiral staircase led up to a balcony overlooking the dresses below. A dozen oak doors lined the wall behind the railing. I entered a room as big as my entire apartment and hung the gown on the door hook. The walls were a pale gold with a design of darker leaves in each corner. Beyond a jungle of mirrors, a plush couch rested against the far wall.

I slipped out of my jeans and tank top and pulled the gown over my head. Cool silk brushed my skin and came to rest just above the soles of my boots. It was a perfect fit. The royal blue brought out my slightly darker eyes and complemented the pearly undertones of my complexion.

I sighed in awe at my reflection and then frowned, wondering how much it was going to cost me. Athena already knew I would buy it. She was a clever woman. I had to have this dress.

I opened the dressing room door and stepped out on the balcony. "What do you think?"

"You look gorgeous," a masculine voice called back. Maalik waited at the counter with a smug grin.

"What are you doing here?" The words had spilled from me before I realized how hostile they sounded.

"Same as you, I imagine. Looking for something to wear to the ball." He laughed and plucked a mint out of a dish by the register.

Instead of the white robe I was used to seeing him in at the gates of Hell, he wore a pair of navy jeans with a matching vest, split down the back so his massive wings weren't smothered. They fluttered gently as his eyes flicked over me with amusement. He pushed a dark curl away from his face and began fingering through a rack of robes.

"Here we are," Athena sang as she bounced through the doorway behind the counter. She carried a robe to Maalik. It was the same royal blue of my dress. Crap.

"Don't you look lovely?" Athena sighed, turning her attention to me.

"How much?" I snapped. I needed to get out of there fast.

"Oh!" She frowned at my sour expression but quickly recovered with a smile. "Let's see. Its retail is six thousand, but with the sale, I'll cut it down to four, or," she added, seeing me flinch, "if you can make a delivery for me to Summerland, I could take it down to three."

"Deal." I resisted the urge to tell her I'd pay the retail price if she would find Maalik something that wasn't blue. I had been rude enough.

"And I'll buy it for you if you'll be my date," Maalik called out as I turned around. Okay, maybe I hadn't been rude enough.

"Sorry, I have a date." I forced a smile at him over my shoulder.

Athena raised an eyebrow, and then understanding my sudden mood change, she grabbed an emerald robe off a rack and shoved it at him. "This robe is nice, too. And it's on sale, as well."

"I think I'll go with this one," Maalik replied, his eyes still glued to me.

I ducked back into the changing room and slammed the door. This was just great. I finally got a day off, and I had to run into him. What was he doing in the city so early anyway? The ball wasn't until Saturday. He was probably expecting me to ask, but that wasn't going to happen.

I quickly changed and put the dress back on its hanger. So what if Maalik bought a matching robe? The dress looked too good on me not to buy, and I really didn't have time to shop for a different one now that I had to find a date, as well. I sure as hell wasn't going with him. Maybe I could bribe Gabriel into going with me. Of course, the fact that Gabriel was on my ship half the time I made deliveries to the inferno was probably the reason Maalik thought I had a soft spot for angels in the first place.

I sighed, draped the dress over my arm, and stepped out onto the balcony. Maalik sprang out of the next room. I jumped and threw a hand over my heart while he did a quick spin.

"How do I look?" he asked, stretching his wings as far as they would go before folding them against his back.

I remembered to breathe. "I don't think Athena's capable of making anything that would make you look bad," I said as flatly as I could manage.

"Is that your backward way of saying I look good?"

"Of course, you look good. You're an angel, and you're wearing the work of a goddess. How else could you look?" I darted past him and down the stairs.

Athena waited by the register with my bill. She gave a sympathetic smile as she charged my Bank of Eternity card.

Debit cards were a relatively new feature in Eternity. They made it easier to carry around more money, but you couldn't travel with them like coin. Our coin is like nothing from the human realm.

At the beginning of each work day, when reapers were assigned souls to collect, we were given one coin. The value of the coin could be seen not only in the color but also by the tally marks along the coin's edge. Each time we used the coin to jump between realms, the color changed and marks disappeared. A jump from Limbo to the human realm ranged between thirty and eighty marks, depending on the exact coordinates. When a coin lost all its marks, it became a base coin and had to be returned to Bank of Eternity for respelling.

Athena handed back my card. "I'll have Arachne leave the package on your ship Friday. It's just a few things I'd like to take with me for Samhain. Dad says he's gonna give my temple to Hecate if I don't show up for the festivities. Arachne will be watching the store while I'm gone."

From the myths, you wouldn't think Athena and Arachne were friends. It was rumored that they'd entered into a fierce weaving contest, and when the goddess lost, she'd turned the boastful maiden into a spider to teach her a lesson. Athena claims it was only a practical joke, that she let Arachne win so she could take her to Summerland as an apprentice, and that she left a spider in her place to tease the humans.

I signed the dress receipt and turned to find Maalik waiting behind me. He had changed back into his jeans and now carried the new robe over his shoulder. Confidence resonated off of him like a sticky, sweet cologne. He leaned in closer until I could smell the mint clicking between his teeth.

I took a shallow breath, trying to cool the heat creeping over me. This was why I hated pretty boys. He knew he looked good and that he was out of my league, but he rubbed it in my face all the same, even going so far as to assume I would fall over myself at the chance to be his date for the ball. The jerk. Staying a safe distance away and pretending not to notice him was the best I could do. But when he was this close, my common sense didn't just take a back seat, it was gagged and thrown in the trunk.

"I guess I'll see you at the ball." I tried to smile, but it felt more like a grimace.

"Save a dance for me," he purred.

He was far too cheerful to be the Keeper of Hellfire. I think I would have felt more at ease around him if he carried the solemn-servant-of-God aura around like every other angel I knew besides Gabriel.

Maalik gave a small bow and winked. I rolled my eyes and pushed past him, escaping back into the empty streets of Limbo. Suddenly, I didn't feel like shopping anymore.

CHAPTER FIVE

*"You can safely assume that you've created God
in your own image when it turns out that God hates
all the same people you do."*
—*Anne Lamott*

"Poisoned."

"Drowned."

"Stabbed. I win!"

Gabriel, Josie, and I sat around my kitchen table. On Tuesday nights, we played poker at my apartment. Gabriel usually crashed at my place when he stayed in Limbo, and Josie's roommate was busy studying to get a license for collecting high-risk souls in China. So my tiny apartment was the designated gathering place.

The round kitchen table was just big enough for the three of us. It was meant to seat four, but every time Gabriel had a good hand, his wings twitched uncontrollably. We were still working with him on his poker-wings.

Josie was winning tonight, but I had been letting her. I figured if I put her in a good enough mood, she might agree to go out with me Wednesday night so Apollo could surprise her.

The game we played was a modified version of poker. A Fates employee had taught us one night at Purgatory Lounge. I had liked it so well that I paid the Muses to paint us a deck with a reaper theme.

The hearts had been replaced with lost souls. Spades were transformed into scythes. Coffins took over the diamonds, and the clubs were now wilting daisies. My favorite card had to be the Queen of Coffins, displaying a sultry Bride of Dracula knock-off, posing like a pin-up in her earthbound grave.

Josie had dubbed the set our Death Deck, and together, we renamed the winning hands with forms of dying.

"My deal." Gabriel sighed as he gathered the cards and began shuffling. He seemed bummed tonight. Peter had probably given him some humiliating task as punishment for showing up drunk again. I hadn't asked him about the ball yet, but I knew I would have to soon. I didn't think I'd get another chance before Saturday.

"Hey, Gabe?"

"Hmm?" He glanced up from the table.

"Are you going the Oracle Ball this year?"

"Yeah, I guess I should since they're voting in new members of the council." He groaned and began dealing.

A cloaked skeleton was posed in the center of each card, our proud little mascot.

"Are you taking anyone with you?" I felt myself blush as Josie looked up and cocked an eyebrow.

Gabriel frowned. "Like who?"

I shrugged. "You wanna go with me?"

"Like a date?" He gave me a strange look and tossed his head back to sweep the curls out of his face.

"Just as friends." This wasn't going well.

"Since when do you feel the need to have a date for the ball?" Josie chuckled.

I had gone solo for the past twenty years at least. Josie and Gabriel both stared at me, waiting for an explanation.

"Maalik asked me to go, and I told him I already had a date." I hid behind my fan of cards.

"What?" Gabriel fumbled with the deck. "That snake! Ever since he got promoted to gate duty, I've been getting it thrown in my face. All I hear from Peter anymore is 'Maalik is responsible enough to watch the gate.' or 'Maalik doesn't drink. Why can't you be more like Maalik?' He makes me sick. He probably thinks you're my girl and is trying to whisk you away, just to prove he's better than me."

I peeked around my cards. "Does that mean you'll go with me, then?"

"You bet your pretty, little, soul-sailing ass I will." He smacked the deck in the middle of the table.

Josie looked from Gabriel to me and laughed before taking the top three cards.

"You got a date, Josie?" I asked, hoping she wouldn't say Horus.

"Nah, unless you want a threesome." She winked.

"My reputation's bad enough, thank you," Gabriel said as I took a card from the deck.

There was still one thing left to take care of. I was going to have to invite Gabriel to Purgatory Lounge along with Josie. If I didn't, she would know I was setting her up.

"What are you guys doing tomorrow night?"

Gabriel snorted and grabbed two cards. "I'm delivering the message of God to a man in prison around seven, but after that, I'm free."

"I told Athena I'd pick my dress up by eight." Josie smiled softly, probably as excited about her gown as I was about mine.

"Wanna meet me at Purgatory for a drink around nine?"

"Sure thang, darling," Gabriel answered with an obnoxious drawl.

I swatted his arm. A few years back, he had crashed on my couch after a night of heavy drinking. The next day, while I was at work, he'd distracted himself from his hangover by helping himself to my collection of western movies. Don't get me wrong. Seeing an angel impersonate John Wayne is quite hilarious...the first ten times. After that, I resorted to violent threats.

"What do you say, Josie? You up for a few drinks tomorrow?"

She tilted her head to one side and arranged her cards. "Yeah, I'll go."

"Good." I grinned. "What have you got?"

"Car Crash," Gabriel answered, tossing his pair down in defeat.

"Stabbed again," Josie cheered, laying out her hand of daisies in a fan.

I raised an eyebrow and placed my cards on the table, one at a time, four nines, and my lucky fanged queen.

"Electric Chair. Pay up, suckers." I had the answers I wanted. No need to play nice anymore.

CHAPTER SIX

"Men rarely invent gods superior to themselves.
Most gods have the morals and manners of a spoiled child."
—*Robert Heinlein*

Purgatory Lounge was packed. At least fifty souls and lesser deities swayed and bumped against each other on the dance floor to the beat of Rob Zombie's *Living Dead Girl.* The city's population had doubled overnight because of the upcoming ball, but it was nearing ten o'clock, and there was still no sign of Apollo.

Gabriel fussed with his sleeves. He was still wearing his work robe because the genius he'd delivered God's message to needed it explained in small words and four different ways. Josie and I had found time to change after work.

I wore black leather pants and a gray silk blouse Josie had given me along with the snotty advice, "The expression 'dress to kill' wasn't meant to be taken literally." My black ringlets were artfully piled atop my head, and I had exchanged the hooker lipstick for a glossy gray that matched my blouse.

Josie sparkled in a slinky, black cocktail dress and sky-scraper heels. Her short, black locks were sculpted into playful spikes, and a pair of feather earrings brushed the tops of her shoulders. She had gone all out. I didn't blame her. It had been at least a month since she'd come out for drinks with us.

We were seated at one of the booths across from the bar. The tables were made of weathered oak, and the benches were pews that the owner, a retired demon, had salvaged from a church as it burned down. You could tell by their blackened corners and sooty odor. The brick walls were plastered with fliers for the ball and posters of rock bands, illuminated by a web of red lights hanging from the ceiling.

I sat up taller to look around the room. A pack of demons huddled near the pool table. They didn't bother me here as much as they did in the other realms. If they put a talon out of line in Limbo, Grim would personally execute them. I'd seen him do it before. Other than the demons, I spied a cluster of angels, a Roman god and goddess arguing at the bar, and the rest of the crowd consisted of reapers and factory souls.

Josie rapped her fingers on the table, watching me scan the room for the tenth time. "Okay, Lana, give it up. Who's coming?"

"I'm just looking," I said.

"Right, and I visit Hell to ice skate."

"Josie?" Apollo's smooth voice carried over the chattering crowd. He had snuck in without detection. Soft, gold curls framed his smiling face. The woodsy smell of his leather pants and jacket let me know the outfit was new and probably from his twin sister's store. Josie jumped up from the booth and threw her arms around his neck.

"When did you get here?" she asked, laughing as she pecked his cheek.

"Just now." He tugged her closer and leaned down for a real kiss. When he pulled away, Josie looked surprised and reached up to tug nervously on her ear lobe, a cute little habit of hers.

"You know Maalik already, I'm sure." Apollo turned and waved for the angel to join us. I gritted my teeth.

"Hello, Lana." He was shirtless, wearing only a pair of black leather pants. His dark curls hung just past his shoulders, brushing a bare and muscled chest that immediately took my eyes hostage.

"Hello," I replied, remembering he had spoken to me. I had a hard time thinking around him, and he knew it. Hell, he enjoyed it. That was part of the reason I couldn't stand him.

"Not on gate duty anymore?" Gabriel snapped with a grin.

"No. I'm needed elsewhere," he answered.

Gabriel nodded and gently rested his hand on mine. Relieved, I scooted closer to him. I could think again. He was my savior.

"That's too bad," sighed Gabriel. "I bet you'll miss the income."

"I don't work for the income. I work to serve Allah. What are you drinking? I'll buy the next round," he added before Gabriel had a chance to think of a witty comeback. From his sour expression, I doubted he had one.

"Long Island," I answered first. I was going to need something strong if I was expected to put up with him.

"Water," Gabriel muttered. He was working harder on his image lately. I suspected Peter was keeping a close eye on him.

"I've got Josie's," Apollo laughed and tugged her away to the bar. She looked over her shoulder with a worried expression and mouthed *be nice* at me.

Maalik waved down a waitress and placed our orders, adding a cranberry juice. I had forgotten he didn't drink. Super. I was stuck at a table with two bitter, sober angels. Perfect.

"So." Maalik sat down across from us. "Will you be taking an apprentice this year?" His tone had switched from flirty to friendly as soon as he noticed my hand in Gabriel's.

"No. Maybe next time."

I didn't even want to think about an apprentice. Josie tested my nerves enough as it was. The idea of having an amateur tag along behind me for a hundred years wasn't appealing in the least. I could deal with Josie lecturing me on the rules, but a novice? Hell, no.

"This is the third generation after you. Grim hasn't asked you to take even one?" Maalik looked surprised.

"I don't think Grim wants me showing anyone the ropes. He's too afraid I'd corrupt them. I don't follow the rules as closely as he would like." I crossed my legs and leaned back in the booth.

"Now, darling." Gabriel donned his John Wayne voice. "You're an excellent reaper. They should let you make your own rules."

"Rules are made for a purpose." Maalik lifted his chin. I'd never heard him sound so justified. It made me wonder if he was being serious, or if he was just trying to agitate Gabriel. "This city wouldn't exist if it weren't for the rules the gods agreed to follow in the peace treaty," he added.

"Yeah?" I shot back, "and I wouldn't exist if it hadn't been for Grim breaking one of those rules."

He gave a small nod. "True, but he broke it with permission from the council. If he hadn't, he'd be dead right now, and so would you." His face was blank, but his words had a bite to them. I shivered.

Gabriel stood. "Well, I guess I don't have to worry about you breaking any rules while I'm in the can, then. I'll be right back, sweetheart." He pulled my hand up to kiss the tops of my fingers and grinned before strutting away. He was enjoying this way too much. I just hoped he didn't take it too far.

"I assume he's your date for the ball?" Maalik smiled at me, his chocolate eyes sparkling with mischief again.

The waitress appeared with our drinks, and I gulped down half of my tea before answering. "Yes."

"He seems very fond of you."

"And I'm very fond of him."

"Funny, in all the times I've seen you two together, I would never have guessed you were a couple." He grinned knowingly, but I wouldn't give up that easy.

"I may bend the rules, but I still take my job seriously. It would be unprofessional to display our affections while working."

"Does that mean you are a couple, then?"

He had me there. Lying isn't a talent of mine. Where was Josie when I needed her? She knew how to twist the truth to say whatever she wanted.

"He's my date for the ball, and he's staying the night with me. Is that enough personal information for you?" I snapped.

His flirty grin drooped. "I'm sorry. I didn't mean to upset you."

"Yes, you did." I scowled at him.

Gabriel plopped down next to me before realizing something was wrong.

"What'd I miss?" He looked from me to Maalik.

"I'm ready. Let's go." I took Gabriel's hand and stood. "Goodnight."

"Goodnight," Maalik sighed.

"Where are you two going?" Josie asked, tilting back her martini. She and Apollo had finally made it back to the table.

"Home, home on the range," Gabriel sang and pulled me closer.

"No way! I never get to go out, and Apollo's here. You can't leave now. We're going to dance and play pool and drink shots."

"Next time, I promise we'll stay until they kick us out. I just had to get you here tonight so Apollo could surprise you." I grabbed my leather jacket off the back of the booth and folded it over my arm.

"I knew you were looking for someone," Josie laughed.

"Come over Friday, and I'll make you dinner," I offered. She seemed content enough being with Apollo.

"Okay." She gave me a quick hug before chasing Apollo out onto the dance floor. When I glanced back, Maalik was gone. Gabriel took my hand and led me out of the lounge.

"Your place or mine," he teased in a sultry voice.

"You really don't like him, huh?"

"Was it that obvious?" He swung our held hands up in the air.

"You don't plan on being this giddy during the ball do you?" I was being reviewed for a promotion. I didn't think it would help my chances if two angels went at it with me in the middle, especially in front of all of Eternity.

"I'll be subtle," he whispered close to my ear and slapped my ass.

"Gabriel!" I popped him on the shoulder. "I mean it. I'm up for promotion, and Grim's watching me like a hawk."

"I'm just kidding, Lana. Geesh! You're going to be worse than Josie at this rate."

"You're an archangel. You're supposed to be worse than both of us put together. How is it we've become the good influence on you?"

"I have my suspicions." He winked at me. "Peter's paying you. Isn't he?"

"Get out." I chuckled and gave his shoulder another punch.

CHAPTER SEVEN

*"Pale Death with impartial tread beats at the poor man's
cottage door and at the palaces of kings."*
—*Horace*

Josie leaned back on my bed and set her container of Thai noodles on her stomach. I'd said I would make dinner, but I should have known better. It was the day before the ball. We were swamped at work, and Athena's *package* took us another hour to unload at Summerland's gate. *Just a few things* had turned out to be about a dozen trunks, heavy enough to make me wonder if there were a few dead bodies in them. After getting off three hours later than usual, we decided to grab some takeout instead.

Grim had worked out a deal with the Fates so that there was a minimum number of souls to harvest on the day of the ball. It made it easier for everyone to prepare for and travel to the Oracle Ball, but it also meant we had to work extra hard the day before.

"Today sucked," Josie said out loud what I was thinking.

"I have a feeling tomorrow won't be much better."

"Yeah," she sighed. "We'll probably have a huge lot of souls that all have to go to Hell."

"That sounds like something Grim would do." I stuffed my chopsticks down in my container of noodles and yawned as I leaned back on my couch and propped my ankles up on the coffee table.

My apartment was a mess. The kitchen table was covered in back issues of *Limbo Weekly* and the *Daily Reaper Report*, so we ate in the living room *slash* bedroom. I had a studio apartment. The rent was cheap, so I didn't mind.

"Who do you think they're voting in this year?"

"I don't know," Josie said. "I asked Horus, but he doesn't seem to know either. I wonder if he'll be voted in. Isis is leaving this year."

"From the way you've been talking about him, I was sure he would ask you to the ball." I smiled, still glad he hadn't.

"I don't think Horus is interested in me. I thought he was at first, but the more time I spend with him, the more I get the feeling that he thinks he's too good for me." Josie laughed, trying to brush it off, but I could tell her feelings had been hurt. "It doesn't matter, though." She hopped off my bed and faced me. "Because Apollo is taking me."

"I knew he would ask you. He's so much nicer than Horus, anyway."

"You have to see my dress! I'll be right back." She darted out of my apartment and down the hall. The elevator pinged. We lived in the same building, but her apartment was a floor above mine. I went to fish my dress out of the closet before she got back.

Even with a tiny apartment, I did have a nice walk-in closet. The souls who worked at the factory only stayed in Limbo for twenty to thirty years, but reapers lived here considerably longer. You can acquire a lot of clothing in three hundred years, especially if you like to shop as much as I do.

"Isn't it great?" Josie bounced back into the living room, holding her dress up over her chest. The top was a strapless suede corset. The skirt flowing out beneath the corset was a rich cream color, covered in layers of sparkling tulle cut into leaf patterns just above the hem.

I smiled. "Artemis helped you pick it out, didn't she?"

"How'd you guess?"

"Because it looks like something she would wear, and she's the one who asked me to take you to Purgatory last night," I confessed.

"Do you suppose Apollo will have a matching suit?" She moved in front of the mirror on my closet door to admire herself.

No matter how many years passed, we still got excited over a pretty dress. It was one of the few things Josie and I had in common. We were both shopaholics. Our friendship had been cemented after a brief feud over a pair of custom embroidered jeans shipped in from Olympus. Sometimes, I wondered if we would still be such good friends if Athena hadn't found an extra pair in her stockroom.

"Artemis probably bought an outfit for Apollo. He arrived a little too late to be shopping." I found my gown and held it up for her to see.

"Oh," she sighed in awe. "It's gorgeous."

My mind flashed back to Maalik at Athena's store.

"Maalik's wearing a matching robe," I groaned.

"How do you know that?"

"I ran into him at Athena's. That's where he asked me to be his date."

"It's not like he's a demon or anything. Why do you dislike him so much?" She laid her dress over the back of the couch and scooped up her box of noodles. "Most reapers would be flattered to have the attention of such a high-ranking angel. I would have gone to the ball with him."

"That's just it, though." I sighed and turned to hang my dress up. "He thinks he's so great, that no one can resist him."

"That's probably why he gives you such a hard time. You're the only one who doesn't adore him. You're such an ego bruiser." She grinned and scraped her chopsticks along the bottom of her takeout box.

"I hope Gabriel has a blue robe to wear." I huffed and dropped onto my bed.

"A black one would work, too," Josie mumbled through a mouthful of noodles.

"Can you imagine Gabriel in a black robe?" Anytime he wasn't working, he was in a pair of tattered white pants.

"Well, he can't wear a white one with you in that dress. That would look a little odd." Josie scrunched up her face, and we both laughed.

It was so much easier being her friend when we weren't working. On our ship, I wanted to strangle her half the time.

The other half, I spent avoiding her. I still couldn't believe that I was up for promotion, and she wasn't. I had more soul violations in the past month than she'd had in the past century, which is why something felt off about the whole deal. And it wasn't like I had taken any special classes at the Reaper Academy that qualified me for high-risk work.

Josie took a new class at least once a decade. She was qualified to harvest medium-risk souls in America, Russia, and most European countries. I, on the other hand, could only harvest low-risk souls in America, Canada, England, and France. Pretty much wherever they spoke English or French. I hated school, so I only took the mandatory classes. And since I'd racked up so many soul violations, I'd never had to worry about taking classes for a promotion. Until now.

"Hey, Josie?"

"Yeah?" She sat on the couch and folded her legs up beside her.

"When Horus was hinting to you about the promotion, he didn't happen to mention what classes would be required, did he?"

"Uh, no, not really." Her brow creased, and she picked up a *Daily Reaper Report* off the coffee table. "I'm sure it's a high-risk job. Otherwise, he wouldn't have been so secretive about it all."

"Great." I rolled over and looked up at the ceiling.

"Hey." She waved the paper at me. "Says here a band of nephilim has volunteered to patrol the sea in exchange for deityship rights and permanent residency in Limbo."

"That'll be the day." I rolled my eyes. "I think it's pretty clear by now that the only thing nephilim, reapers, and souls have to look forward to in Limbo is work."

"Maybe." Josie tossed the paper back on the table. "But aren't you forgetting about the soul strike?"

"The souls are still working, aren't they?" I snorted.

"But they have Saturdays off now. It's the first step."

"To what?" I sat up and swung my legs off the bed. "Do you think they'll get paid vacations next? Overtime? The souls that went on strike are long gone, back to the human realm. I'm surprised the Fates haven't taken Saturdays back by now."

"Word of mouth gets around. The other souls have practically turned the strike into a legend."

"Well, aren't you the little soul expert."

Josie blushed. "Sorry, I guess I've been spending too much time around Jenni. I think she's taking some elective class about the history of Limbo. It's all she ever talks about."

"How lame." I laughed and threw a pillow at her.

CHAPTER EIGHT

"Oh these foolish men! They could not create so much as a worm,
but they create gods by the dozens."
—*Michel de Montaigne*

Grim's rooftop sparkled. Gabriel and I had arrived at the ball early so he could impress Peter with his punctuality. We took a slow walk around, enjoying the view.

Thirty round tables sprawled out before the stage. Little vases of violets and orchids lined the silver cloths, along with etched champagne flutes and reservation cards. Somehow, I wasn't surprised to find my and Gabriel's names at the same table as Maalik, but my frustrations disappeared as I took in all the luxury of the rooftop.

Giant pots of lilies lined the dance floor, and a net of ivy and sparkling lights domed above. Crystal-crusted stones formed a thick ledge around the roof, and every few feet, a lantern had been anchored, emitting a soft glow over the ball setting.

Beyond the wall, the city lights glistened and reflected off the Sea of Eternity. Together, Gabriel and I sighed. Every other day of the year could be grimy and frustrating and a pain in the ass. All it took was this one night to make all the others worth it.

A cool breeze circled over the roof and freed a curl from the crystal bands holding my hair up. The bands had been a gift from Saul. He'd given them to me the year my apprenticeship ended, and ever since his death, I wore them to the ball in his memory.

Gabriel had managed to find a blue robe. It was a shade lighter than my dress, but it looked good on him. Ellen gave us a strange look as we signed the guest book together. Josie was coming with Apollo, so I didn't feel too out of place with my date.

Grim arrived just as we finished circling the rooftop. He wore a more formal version of the black robes reapers wore to work. It was just for show. Everyone knew he hadn't gone out to collect a soul in almost eight hundred years. After the third generation of reapers had come along, he retired to his office above the city and focused more on the dealings of the council.

"Good evening, Lana. Gabriel." Grim nodded at my date with a frown. "I'm glad you're here early. Lana, I want you at the council dinner after the ceremony."

My jaw dropped. He had said I was up for a promotion, but I didn't realize it was going to be that big of a promotion. Only council members were invited to the dinner after the ball, or so I thought. I imagined some of the more important gods were there, as well, but I'd never heard of a reaper attending—aside from Grim. Especially not an eighth-generation reaper like myself.

"Uh, ummm, uh." I was suddenly a gibbering idiot.

"I'll make sure to remind her later." Gabriel jumped to my rescue.

"Good." Grim walked away to greet another couple.

"From the looks of it, you weren't expecting that invitation." Gabriel squeezed my hand. His eyes grew worried as he waited for me to gather my senses. "Some promotion." He laughed nervously.

"I think I'm going to be sick." I breathed and closed my eyes.

"Whoa there, Lana!" Gabriel wrapped an arm around my waist and pulled out a chair for me to fall into. "This is a good thing, right? I mean, who gets invited to the council dinner if they're in trouble?" He rubbed my shoulders.

"I'm dizzy." I gulped down another breath.

In that moment, I hated Grim for ruining my perfect evening. I didn't have any idea why I was being invited to the dinner. And I still hadn't figured out who had suggested my promotion. Everything was moving too fast, and before I even had a chance to digest it. Indigestion of the brain, that's what I was suffering from.

Josie was going to slaughter me. After her reaction to my promotion, I could just see how well this would go over. She was my friend, but being a hundred years older gave her the right to be bitter if I advanced before she did. And the fact that she followed the rules so much better than I did wasn't going to help the situation any.

"Don't tell Josie until after the ball," I pleaded with Gabriel.

"Of course."

"In fact, don't tell anyone. There's going to be a new club tomorrow. The I-hate-Lana club. Just you wait and see. Every reaper from generations one through seven will have a membership. Probably the eighth generation, too. I'm done for." I buried my face in my hands.

"Calm down. Just breathe. It's going to be all right, kid."

"I'm three hundred years old. Don't call me kid," I mumbled through my fingers.

"Sorry, darling." He resorted to his John Wayne voice. Even if it was annoying, it made me smile, and he knew it. That's why I loved him and put up with him crashing on my couch all the time.

"There we go," he chirped at my grin.

"Lana!" Josie and Apollo signed the guest book and hurried over to join us.

Apollo wore a cream dress shirt and suede pants that matched Josie's gown. I was sure Artemis had picked it out now. Most of the older gods still preferred the fashions of their youth, but the few who modernized their look did so with style.

A string of leaf-shaped emeralds hung around Josie's neck. When she caught me staring, she touched them fondly and blushed. "Are you feeling okay, Lana?"

"Yeah." I smiled. It wouldn't do any good telling Gabriel to keep quiet if I gave myself away.

A group of cherubs set up a classical band just off the dance floor. One started on a flute, and a harp quickly joined in.

"Come on." Gabriel grabbed my hand and tugged me under the ivy canopy to dance. Apollo and Josie followed. I tried to forget about the dinner invitation and enjoy myself, but every time I spotted Grim frowning at me from across the roof, misery struck all over again.

"Smile, Lana," Gabriel muttered through clenched teeth. "Josie will corner me and make me tell her what's wrong with you if you don't get it together."

"Sorry." I sighed and rested my head on his shoulder.

The roof filled up fast as the guests arrived. Reaper couples swirled around us on the dance floor. They made up at least a quarter of the guests. Every reaper attended the Oracle Ball. It was our unofficial and collective birthday party. The anniversary of our birth into slavery. Sort of the opposite of Independence Day.

By human standards, we weren't slaves. The flaws of slavery were identified in Eternity long before they were dealt with in the human realm. By having us titled as lower-class citizens with limited rights, and tossing us a little coin, Grim could keep a tight leash on us. Payment is a sneaky motivator, convincing reapers to work harder and allowing Grim to keep our numbers low. Barely a hundred reapers tended to the departed.

"Excuse me." A Cleopatra wannabe pushed past Gabriel and me, pulling Horus along by the hand as he scattered short apologizes for his rude and clumsy date. He was halfway through a sorry when he recognized me.

"Lana, right?" His mouth twisted into an uncomfortable smile as his date's sashaying came to a jerking halt. After giving him an unsuccessful tug, she coiled herself around his arm like a python and glared at us.

"Horus, you promised me a dance," she pouted. She obviously fancied herself a temptress, but nagging hussy would have been more accurate. A band of red silk snaked over her breasts and crisscrossed her stomach before disappearing into a trampy excuse for a skirt.

"We have all night," Horus sighed. "What's the rush?" He reached up and loosened his tie with an annoyed frown. The suit was new. Horus's look rarely strayed from the traditional. His mother, Isis, had fought with him for centuries over his headdress. She had finally convinced him to leave it at home about a decade ago.

"Who are your little friends?" the imposter Cleopatra asked, stroking Horus's arm.

"Uh, this is Gabriel, and Lana, isn't it?"

"That's right." I wove my arm around Gabriel's. "Who's your date, Horus?"

"This is Wosyet," he answered with a strained smile.

Wosyet puffed her chest out, trying to look more dignified than her dress would allow. "I'm a goddess." The edges of her mouth twitched into a cocky sneer as she bobbed her head, giving me a quick once-over. "Pasty skin, black hair, limited knowledge of the gods. Let me guess, you're a reaper."

"Must you be so rude to everyone?" Horus's jaw clenched as he tried to reclaim the arm she was molesting.

"It's okay." I grinned. "Some deities just have no manners. Or taste."

"I'm sorry," Horus muttered before trailing after Wosyet as she stormed away.

The cherub band picked up the pace. Gabriel twirled me back around to dance, surprising me with a flamboyant dip. He grinned, holding me in the awkward position long enough to draw attention. "She may be a goddess, but can she dance?" He lifted me out of the dip and right into a double spin.

"That's enough," I warned him, tucking a curl back in place and sneaking another glance around the rooftop.

Peter signed the guest book and then helped Jesus escort Mary and her entourage of saints to their table. Lucifer arrived a moment behind them with his daughter Cindy on his arm.

Cindy was Hell's current representative on the council and an excellent business woman. A handful of the fallen trailed behind her in Armani and Gucci, accessorized with clipboards and pagers. Cindy never went anywhere without her camarilla. Beelzebub made a formal show of greeting Lucifer before luring Cindy onto the dance floor.

Out of the corner of my eye, I spotted Maalik's blue robe. He stood next to Grim in front of the stage. Sour expressions stained both of their faces as they argued and looked my way. I frowned back at them. Gabriel followed my gaze and pulled me closer before spinning around to block their view.

"Do you remember your first ball?" A racy grin lit his face.

Three hundred years, and I still remembered it like yesterday. Saul hadn't exactly been thrilled when Grim had announced me as his apprentice. I didn't blame him, after I found out that I was his fourth. I dreaded the idea of having even one. Saul had taken one look at me and shouted, "Gabriel!"

Gabriel had fluttered over and pulled me onto the dance floor. It was the first time I had laid eyes on an angel. His wild blond curls had me hypnotized. Everything hypnotized me in those days.

Gabriel and Saul had been friends long before I came along. The angel knew exactly what to do. Saul just needed him to distract me while he shouted at Grim for going against his wishes. And distract me, he did.

Gabriel watched the two men argue, and I watched him in awe. When he finally looked back at me, he gave me a lopsided smile and said, "You're drooling, Ms. Harvey."

The memory splashed through me. I tried to stifle my laughter until Gabriel's face crinkled and he exploded with me. When I caught my breath, I looked up and smiled.

The music faded away, and Grim cleared his throat at the podium while everyone found their seats. Our table sat along the second row before the stage and filled up quickly with familiar faces.

Gabriel sat to my right, and on the other side of him, I found Ridwan, the Islamic angel who watched the pearly gates on the rare occasions Peter couldn't. I wondered which angel had volunteered to watch the gates during the ball, and what their next check would look like.

Next to Ridwan sat Maalik, who kept giving me short sideways glances. It was a far cry from the excessive flirting he had been smothering me with, but I wasn't complaining.

To my left, Josie and Apollo whispered sweetly to each other. Artemis had tagged along without a date, but sat happily next to Apollo, admiring her matchmaking.

I flinched when my gaze fell on the weathered face of Meng Po. She cackled softly at my surprise. She was a long way from Feng-Du, the ninth level of Chinese hell, where she served her five-flavored tea of forgetfulness to souls at the end of their stay. I'd only seen her at one previous ball, and I hadn't expected to see her again, considering how she'd spit in the punch bowl and left, complaining about the *bird music*. She seemed to be in a better mood tonight, and she had even dressed up, wearing a black silk dress spotted with gray orchids.

Horus and Wosyet joined Lady Meng, while Coreen took her place on the other side of Maalik. We still had one empty chair, probably reserved for an apprentice. Coreen loved having apprentices and took one every century. This would be her ninth.

"Good evening, gods, goddesses, devils, angels, demons, and reapers! Welcome to the one thousand and three hundredth Oracle Ball!" Grim's thunderous voice carried out over the rooftop. Applause broke, and the band chimed in the background to gather everyone's attention again.

"Let us begin the evening by introducing the eleventh generation of reapers and assigning their apprenticeships."

Six timid reapers appeared on stage, two females and four males. They each wore the traditional cowl and had black hair—like all reapers do.

One of the males stepped forward first. He had too full a mouth for his narrow chin, giving him a feminine look that was only amplified by his shaggy hair. He reminded me of the popular boy bands the human girls pined after.

"Kevin Kraus," Grim announced. "At the top of your class, you will be honored with the privilege of working under an excellent second-generation reaper, Coreen Bendura!"

Coreen stood, and more applause sounded as Kevin left the stage to take his seat next to her. His adoring eyes never left his new mentor as Grim announced and appointed the remaining reapers before moving on with the ceremony.

"Now, for the moment you've all been waiting for. The five council representatives at the end of their hundred-year terms will announce our newest members." Grim bowed and took a seat in one of the black marble chairs behind him.

The council consisted of ten members, including Grim. It had begun with only five in the year 659. In 709, five more members were added. Every fifty years, roughly half of the council was replaced with new members. The available positions on the council were intended to represent the faiths with the most followers, but as it goes with most politics, that wasn't always the case.

The council representatives were essentially chosen by the secondary councils they belonged to and would eventually answer to during their term. The Board of Heavenly Hosts reigned over the heavens of the Abrahamic faiths: Christianity, Islam, and Judaism. Their counterpart, the Hell Committee—as I'm sure you can guess—ruled the Abrahamic hells.

The two Abrahamic councils used to function as one, the Abrahamic Elite. But their conflicting interests worried the rest of the gods, so they demanded the council be split up as a precaution. The two still work together on occasion, and even share their votes. For the past term, Heaven has had three members, and Hell, only one. Three is the maximum number of representatives a secondary council is allowed to have on the Afterlife Council.

The Zen Senate has three seats on the council, as well. Two thirds of the senate is made up of deities from the Hindu faith, allowing them two of the positions on the main council. Their other seat is shared by the Buddhists and a handful of the traditional Chinese faiths.

The remaining secondary councils, the Summerland Society and the Sphinx Congress, only have one seat a piece on the council. Summerland Society is the more diverse of the two, consisting of deities from dozens of ancient religions that are seldom practiced anymore. While the Sphinx Congress is the most exclusive secondary council, allowing Egyptian deities only.

Isis, the current representative for the Egyptian faith, came to the podium first. She wore a simple white gown, with her ebony hair pulled up in a cluster of braids. The traditional Egyptian makeup decorated her eyes, and a thick, silver ankh hung from a cord around her neck.

"What a joy it has been, working with the Afterlife Council to ensure peace among our communities. I will miss it greatly, and I hope that the man taking my place will find it as equally enlightening. Please welcome my brother, Seth."

The Egyptian god stood up from the table in front of us and walked on stage. The whole crowd seemed to gasp as he turned around. His eyes burned like hot coals, a fiery red that looked out of place on his aged and graying face. The only thing giving him a respectable air was the freshly pressed black suit he wore with an annoyed sense of dignity.

Isis shook his hand and gave him a soft smile before taking her place next to her husband, Osiris, and their sister, Nephthys, Seth's wife. The fact that they were all brothers and sisters didn't seem to bother them, or stop them from marrying each other. Whatever floats your boat, I guess. As long as it doesn't sink mine.

The Egyptian council position was a joke. The only traces left of the faith were mashed into the compost heap of new age paganism. The Egyptians were the last of the ancient faiths failing to accept their decline and merge their sliver of territory with Summerland before they lost it altogether. Why they were still in the voting ring was beyond me.

"What an honor." Seth bent over the podium to speak into the microphone. "I hope to do many great things for Eternity." It sounded more like a threat. The sinister smile he directed at Grim only confirmed my opinion.

Yama, one of the Hindu council representatives, stood next. He looked perfectly groomed in his red suit, even if it did clash with his green skin. Yami, his wife, sat at one of the closer tables with tears in her eyes, glad that he would be going back to Naraka, the Hindu hell, with her.

"Thank you for the wonderful experience I've had this past century. Please welcome, Meng Po," he said with less enthusiasm than Isis had.

The crowd hesitated in shock before applauding Lady Meng as she made her way on stage. The Hindu deities almost never shared their council seats. Grim's face hardened as the old woman reached the podium. She gave a small bow and took her chair without giving a speech. Everyone at the first row of tables collectively sighed, like they had been anticipating a reenactment of the punch bowl scene on a larger scale.

Munkar and Nakir, the two Islamic angels on the council, flew the short distance to the podium, sprinkling the first row of tables with a feathery shower and earning them a stern look from their prophet.

"Thank you," began Munkar. "It has been a true pleasure working with the council. And it is a true pleasure to introduce the two taking our places, Ridwan and Maalik."

My jaw dropped. Maalik would be living in Limbo for the next hundred years. Guess a vacation wouldn't spare me from him, after all. The angels stood up from our table and walked to the stage. I frowned, wondering how long they had known, and clapped with everyone else. Gabriel grabbed my hand as Maalik took to the podium.

"Thank you. I believe there is much we can do to benefit Eternity," he said. His eyes rolled over the crowd and paused on me for a brief moment before he took his seat with the council.

Vishnu, the second Hindu representative, stood at the podium last. He adjusted the microphone with all four hands and smiled. As old as he was, it amazed me that he still enjoyed showing off his extra limbs so much.

"It's been a magnificent century here in Limbo City. Please welcome to the council my good friend Shiva's wife, Parvati," his excited voice boomed over the crowd.

Grim had been wise to let Vishnu finish the ceremony. Parvati drew everyone's attention. She was as beautiful as the next goddess, but that's not what mesmerized the older deities in the crowd.

Before the war had ended, Parvati's popularity among her human followers had become entwined with that of several other goddesses, merging them all into one deity before the soul matter could be controlled. Depending on what the occasion called for, she would become the suitable goddess. During the war, the appropriate goddess had been the bloodthirsty Kali, wearing a necklace of human skulls. Not the kind of goddess you forget. As Parvati, she was calm, collected, and a softer image to behold, but not so gentle that her peers forgot what she could become.

"Thank you. I am looking forward to serving my people and working with the council," she cooed into the microphone before sitting down next to the Green Man. His green cheeks flushed pink as he gave her a timid smile.

Holly Spirit, Heaven's current representative, and Cindy Morningstar each had another fifty years left on the council. The Green Man, representing the faiths of Summerland, and Kwan Yin, of the Buddhists, were halfway through their terms, as well.

Grim cleared his throat at the podium to address everyone one last time. "A toast." He lifted his champagne flute. "To a superb Afterlife Council, and all the great works they will accomplish in the following century!" Everyone lifted their glasses and cheered.

My night was getting worse and worse. Grim had invited me to the council dinner, and now Maalik would be there, too. In three hundred years, I'd never had such a strange evening. Call me crazy, but something told me it was only going to get stranger.

CHAPTER NINE

*"Of all bad men,
religious bad men are the worst."*
—*C.S. Lewis*

"**M**s. Harvey, Ms. Galla, please follow me." Coreen found us the second Grim finished the ceremony. Kevin Kraus followed her like a good little apprentice.

Josie pecked Apollo on the cheek as she excused herself, and I gave Gabriel a weak smile. We rose from the table and followed the senior reaper. Josie gave me a puzzled look as we entered the elevator off the roof, but I just shrugged.

Grim hadn't said anything about inviting other reapers to the dinner, but I should have guessed Coreen would be coming, too. If there were any honor to be had as a reaper, she would have a part of it. I didn't want to think about what she might have done if she weren't included. Grim probably didn't want to think about it either.

Why Josie and Kevin were with us was a mystery to me. Josie was as good as any reaper, but still an underpaid peon like I was, and not even half a millennium old. And a brand-spanking-new apprentice like Kevin couldn't have any business dining with the council.

Coreen leaned against the elevator wall and frowned as we descended.

"I'm sorry, where are we going?" Josie finally gathered enough nerve to ask.

"You mean you didn't even tell your sailing partner?" Coreen sneered at me.

"Tell me what?" Josie turned to me now.

I stiffened. Hadn't I just lectured her on keeping information from me? Crap. Coreen crossed her arms and quietly waited for me to explain.

"Grim invited me to the council dinner."

"What?" Josie shrieked. "Why didn't you tell me?" Her face twisted in anger, but instead of lecturing me, she turned back to Coreen. "If Grim invited her, why am I here?"

"It was a last-minute decision." The elevator pinged, and the doors slid open, ending our conversation. Coreen strode out with Kevin. Josie and I followed.

The dinner was being held on the seventy-third floor, two below Grim's main office. It didn't take long for me to realize that I had never been on the seventy-third floor before.

Josie's hand found mine and squeezed. I couldn't tell if the expression on her face was more from excitement or fear. Coreen looked straight ahead, as if bored with the scenery. This was my first visit to the seventy-third floor, and probably my last. I was going to take it all in. Josie slowed her pace with me, and together, we twisted every direction we could.

Dark crown molding lined the hall, anchored above fancy blue and black wallpaper with designs complicated enough to bring on a headache. I tried to focus on something else, like the narrow black tables set against the walls, holding candelabra and pieces of decaying, old-world art. The rug running down the center of the hall seemed to go on forever, until we came to a set of double doors.

"Before we go in, let me tell you the only rule your little brains must remember. Do not speak. It's that simple. No matter what is said, remember that rule. Understand?" Coreen glowered at us as if she were a human mother, threatening her children into submission during a holiday dinner.

I resisted the urge to giggle and smiled at her. "Of course."

Her frown deepened. Josie nodded, still in shock, much like I had been when Grim first invited me. Coreen took a deep breath and opened the doors.

I bit my lip to keep from gasping. The back wall was all glass. It was just as beautiful as the view from the rooftop. The other three walls were a deep blue, tastefully coordinating with the wild paper in the hall, without the optical illusion effect.

An obnoxiously oversized table filled most of the room. I'd only seen a larger one during my apprenticeship in the seventeen hundreds when a servant had stabbed an English noble. I didn't get to collect the nobleman's soul. I wasn't even a century old. Saul had that honor. I got to collect the soul of the servant after he was beaten and hung. We had to chain them up in the hold of Saul's ship to keep them from tearing each other to pieces. I missed Saul and wondered what he would think about me dining with the council.

Vases of violets and orchids were arranged down the table runner, in between polished silver goblets set before dove-shaped napkins. Around the table sat twenty heavily engraved chairs topped with plush cushions in softer shades of blue and silver. A larger chair sat at the end of the table, obviously reserved for Grim. Even though he didn't have a vote on the council, he still fancied himself the king of Eternity.

"Well, come on. Let's get seated before the other guests arrive." Coreen led us around the left side of the table to the four chairs next to Grim's. She took the first one and pulled Kevin down to sit beside her. Josie slumped onto the third chair, and I took the fourth just as Grim entered the room, escorting the rest of the council members and guests.

Clearly, Josie and I weren't the only ones surprised by our invitation. We received plenty of curious looks and one very sour expression from Seth. Maalik pretended not to notice us. I shifted uncomfortably in my chair. Everyone else had looked surprised. Maalik knew we would be here. He had to be the one who'd suggested my promotion, and I was desperately struggling to figure out why. It wasn't like I had done him any special favors. Hell, I wasn't even nice to him.

Soon, everyone had found their seats and quieted their polite chatter so Grim could address us.

"I'm sure some of you are curious as to why there are four reapers at our dinner table this year."

Coreen's face reddened. Being nine hundred years old gave her quite an ego. I didn't think Grim explaining her presence in such an apologetic fashion sat well with her.

"And I'm sure you are all aware of our problem out in the Sea of Eternity." Grim sighed.

I could guess who he was talking about. If I had Caim's address, I would have sent him my dry-cleaning bill. It took five washings to get all the demon guts off my leather pants.

"I've been working with the Egyptian gods," Grim continued, "and we have discovered a way to ensure this problem gets the attention it deserves. I have put together a team of diverse reapers. They will be searching through the next few weeks' inventory of souls to find one we hope can help solve our problem. Horus has been quite a help. He and Wosyet will be organizing the search. I'm pleased to begin our dinner with this good news."

I saw Josie blush out of the corner of my eye. Horus had taken the seat on my other side, and I felt like I would suffocate at any moment from all the tension.

Most of Horus's tension didn't have to do with Josie, but rather the look his uncle was giving him from across the table. Clearly, Seth was still bitter about the ancient fight he had lost to his nephew. The fight had cost Horus an eye, and even though Thoth restored it, the physical and emotional scars were still overwhelmingly apparent.

Seth's jaw tightened as he caught my stare. He opened his mouth to speak, but Grim beat him to it.

"Seth, would you like to be the first to share your goals for the council?" he asked.

"I would prefer to share my ambitions with the council exclusively. When I accepted this position, I was under the impression that it meant something. I believed that as the nine *chosen* leaders, it was our duty to discuss and solve Eternity's problems, not everyone's, and certainly not a handful of your creations," he spat and shot a poisonous look at Coreen.

"And so it is. It just so happens that this problem was settled and agreed upon by the council before you were appointed. There will be a great deal of conferences in the future where you will have the opportunity to share your ambitions exclusively. I simply invited the chosen team of reapers as a courtesy, to make sure all the new members were aware of our current operations."

Grim quickly turned his attentions away from Seth. "Would you like to share your thoughts, Parvati?"

"Certainly," the goddess said and gave me a gentle smile, letting me know I wasn't a threat to her. "I am interested in increasing the price per soul of a certain sect of followers. They are very special to us, and we would like an extra guarantee that they will arrive comfortably. The recent problems over the Sea of Eternity have us…concerned."

Her husband, Shiva, nodded in agreement, provoking soft hisses from the snake beads around his neck. His third eye wandered around the room, taking in each individual with an eerie skepticism.

"I'm sure that can be arranged. Let's schedule a meeting next week, and we can go over the details before presenting them at the first official conference."

"Perfect," Parvati cooed.

The clinking of trays sounded as dinner arrived. A dozen nephilim maids fluttered in, carrying silver platters and bottles of wine. They set the dishes before us and filled our goblets. Several baskets of braided bread were placed between the flowers on the table, and then the winged servers were gone.

The meal was almost too pretty to eat. A bowl of dark broth sat on one side of the plate, and on the other side, thin strips of grilled lamb fanned out under a mound of wild rice and potatoes adorned with a sprig of rosemary.

"I have honorable ambitions for council." Meng Po's raspy voice demanded attention. I was just glad her English had improved. She took a sip of her wine and cleared her throat, casting a disgusted look at the goblet before continuing. "I would like to work with Fates to perfect soul purification methods."

"How gracious of you, Lady Meng," Grim mumbled. "I will set up a meeting with them next week, as well. How about you, Ridwan?" he quickly asked before Meng had a chance to elaborate.

Ridwan looked up in surprise. "I'm just here to serve Allah and make sure Eternity runs as smoothly as possible."

"Yes, aren't we all, aren't we all." Grim picked up a fork and started in on his meal.

Everyone followed his lead, pretending not to notice that he hadn't given Maalik the opportunity to speak. I got the feeling that Grim had heard enough from him for one night.

The meal tasted as good as it looked, but I kept finding myself distracted. Parvati and Shiva used all of their hands to eat with. Parvati held her broth with her lower left hand and stirred with her upper left while breaking a piece bread in half with her right hands. When I forced myself to stop staring, I noticed Maalik had decided it was safe to look at me again, and now watched me with intense concern.

The remaining conversations over dinner were mild as far as I could tell. Politics is just a nasty fungus in my book. Why should I care? It wasn't as if I'd ever have to know any of this crap. I had enough on my mind anyway, like the new search team I had just become aware I was part of. What kind of soul was going to stop Caim? And how had I become one of the four chosen reapers to find that soul?

When the nephilim reappeared to take away our empty plates, Coreen stood. "I would like to thank the council for our invitation. As humble servants of Eternity, we are honored to dine with you and pleased to assist in any way possible. We will take our leave early and let you finish your more private business dealings," she announced, struggling to keep her gaze from falling on Seth, who seemed appalled that she was even speaking.

"Of course. Enjoy the rest of the ball, and thank you for coming," Grim said with a nod.

Hearing the cue, I stood with Josie and Kevin and followed Coreen back through the double doors. She hurried us down the hall and into the elevator, where she finally sighed and relaxed against the steel walls.

"Tomorrow morning, report to the conference room off Grim's main office. Don't be late," she instructed us.

"You're not going to tell us anything until then?" Josie blurted. The shock had worn off, but panic still managed to wedge its foot in the door.

"Don't get your panties in a twist," Coreen snapped. "We're just working as a team so there are no interferences. It will be just like any other job. We're picking up a soul."

"Right. We're picking up a soul. A soul that Grim seems to think will be able to control Caim." I laughed.

"Grim said nothing about controlling Caim. Don't draw such obscure conclusions based on what your tiny little brain thinks it can comprehend."

The elevator doors opened, and she stormed out.

"Well, isn't this nice." Josie sighed. "We've both been promoted." She straightened her corset and smoothed her hands down her skirt.

"Grim can lie down in a grave if he thinks I'm going to work with that woman."

"Lana, let's just enjoy the rest of the evening. We can worry about all this tomorrow." Her pained expression melted away as Apollo came to greet us.

"Gabriel told me you were dining with the council. How was it?" he asked.

Josie wrapped her arms around his waist and tugged him toward the dance floor where Gabriel was doing the Rumba with a Hindu goddess. Her four roaming hands had him more than distracted, but the grin told me he didn't mind.

The rooftop just didn't seem as inviting as it had before. There was too much on my mind to enjoy the rest of the ball. I sighed and pressed the elevator button. No one would notice if I slipped out early. Gabriel had crashed on my couch enough times. I knew he could find his way to my apartment blind if he had to. I just wanted a hot bath, maybe some wine, and the sure voice of John Wayne.

"Going down?" Maalik gave me a sheepish smile. He stood alone in the elevator, so I assumed the dinner wasn't quite over.

"Are you following me?" I groaned.

"Uh, well, sort of. I guess." He tilted his head to one side and blushed. "Come on. I'll walk you home. I don't feel much like a party right now either."

I sucked in a breath of air, ready to bark something nasty at him, but nothing came to mind. My held breath slipped out in surrender. "Fine."

I stepped into the elevator, and the doors closed behind me. Strange didn't even begin to cover the night I was having.

CHAPTER TEN

*"There is a reward for kindness
to every living animal or human."*
—Muhammad

"**W**hy do you dislike me so much?"

Maalik finally asked the dreaded question as we stepped out onto the empty sidewalks of Limbo. I crossed my arms and shivered. The lanterns had kept the rooftop warm, but now I was freezing. Maalik reached into his sleeve, pulled out a shawl, and draped it over my shoulders.

"Thanks," I grumbled.

"So, are you going to answer my question?"

He kept his eyes glued to me as we walked toward my apartment. Four blocks to go. I wondered how much more uncomfortable he could make me before we got there.

"I don't dislike you."

"You had me fooled," he laughed.

"Why do you like me?" I stopped at the curb and turned to face him.

"I don't know. I guess because you're always going against Grim's orders, and you try so hard to save any soul that has even the tiniest shred of goodness. I admire that." He smiled, and we crossed the street together.

"You were the one who convinced Grim to promote me, weren't you?" If he was going ask a bunch of nosy questions, so was I.

"I was," he answered without pause, making me stop again.

"Why?"

"For the same reason I like you so much. You see in souls what most reapers can't."

"Oh."

That couldn't be all there was to it, but I let it go. If he wanted to keep the details from me like Grim, I'd let him. At least his weapon of choice was flattery and not blatant rudeness.

"So, if you don't dislike me, does that mean you'll let me buy you a coffee?"

"I don't know if Gabriel would approve." I still wasn't ready to trust him.

"Please, I know you two aren't a couple. You're a smart girl. Do you really think I wouldn't do my homework before pursuing you?"

"Your homework?" I stopped again. He had to be the most disgustingly confident angel I knew. "Is that how you pick up women? You do a background check and play detective so you can corner them and force them into dating you?"

"I would never force you to do anything." His brow twisted in frustration as he struggled to find his next words. "Forgive me. I've only been in Limbo City for a few days. I've approached you like I have everything else in my life, with research. You are more than welcome to research me before accepting my coffee invitation."

"I'm sorry." I sighed, hating how sincere he sounded. I was so awful to him. I couldn't understand why he was still trying. "There's a coffee shop a block past my apartment. If you still want to go."

"Are you sure?" He frowned.

"Yes." I forced a smile.

He smiled back and looped his arm under mine to escort me over the next crosswalk. Wasn't this just cute? Here we were, in our matching ball attire, going out for coffee.

The Phantom Café was open twenty-four hours. It had been open for over sixty years now. One of the souls who worked at the factory had owned a café in the human realm. His girlfriend was one of the nephilim, and he'd helped her establish the new business in Limbo.

Maggie was one of the wealthiest and most ambitious nephilim I had ever met. Even after her soul boyfriend went back to the human realm, Maggie kept the café open. She was one of the few nephilim who owned a legitimate business in Limbo. Most of her kind just wandered around like hobos, and if they couldn't find a part-time job, they usually ended up getting into some sort of trouble.

When we arrived, there were two soul couples inside, along with one nephilim waitress. Her small wings twitched at the sight of us.

Nephilim either loved or hated full-blooded angels. Some were jealous of the respect and rights angels received, but others admired them and were thrilled to be so closely related. It didn't take long to figure out how our waitress felt.

"Hello, I'm Daisy. I'll be your waitress this evening. Here are some menus. I'll be back in a moment to take your orders." She gave Maalik a shy smile and batted her lashes.

"Thank you," he replied, picking up a menu. His brow scrunched up as he examined all the choices.

I flipped through my menu and found something that sounded tasty. Zombie Chocolate Latte, so good you just might come back from the dead. It was probably a big hit with the soul customers. Our waitress reappeared earlier than expected.

"Have you decided yet?" She clicked her pen.

"The Zombie Chocolate Latte," I answered.

Maalik frowned at the menu, then closed it and handed it back to Daisy. "I'll have the same."

Daisy hurried away to prepare our beverages. I was surprised that Maalik ordered the same as I had, especially after he'd looked over the menu so carefully. Then I remembered he was Arabian.

"You couldn't read the menu, could you?"

"I could read some of it." He looked down at his hands and blushed.

"You know, they have menus in different languages. We could ask for one, and you could pick out something else," I offered.

"No, that's okay. What you ordered sounded good anyway."

"You could read some of it. Does that mean you're learning English?"

"In my spare time. I'll be here a hundred years, so I guess I'd better learn how to get by. Too bad I didn't get the gift of reading along with the gift of tongues," he laughed.

"I guess so." I propped an elbow on the table and rested my chin in my palm. Maalik played with the hem of his sleeve and smiled nervously at me.

"Are you excited about working with the council?" he asked.

"Ha! It won't last long. Coreen is a nightmare. She'll find some way to convince Grim to kick me off her little team, and that's fine by me."

"She won't kick you off." He stated it like a fact, and then glanced away from the questioning look I gave him. "This is a nice place here. I like it."

I wasn't going to let him change the subject that easily.

"And how do you know she won't kick me off her team?"

"Because only Grim has that authority, and I know he won't." He sighed, probably wishing he had kept his mouth shut.

"Here we go." Daisy set our drinks on the table. "Can I get you anything else?"

"No, thank you." Maalik smiled and picked up his drink. A flash of uncertainty crossed his eyes, but he tilted the mug up anyway and took a swallow. "Wow! What is this called again?"

"Zombie Chocolate Latte." I laughed and took a sip of my own. "This is your first time in a café, isn't it?"

"Uh, yeah." He blushed again. I was starting to like how easily I could make him do that.

"Why did you invite me out for coffee if you've never had any before?"

"I watched a few American movies when I first got here. I was actually planning on asking you to go see one with me when we ran into each other at Athena's Boutique. The movies made me think coffee was a better idea, though."

"Well, what do you think of your first coffee?"

"It's divine," he breathed. "I think I'll have another. What about you?"

"No, thanks. I still have half of mine left." I couldn't stop smiling at him. It felt strange now that I had found him so intimidating before.

We drank our coffees and made the typical small talk about soul levels in the sea and major human deaths in the past century. I was enjoying myself entirely too much. I couldn't remember the last time I had gone out on a real date.

I guess dating lost most of its appeal after I turned a hundred. I mean, what was the point? Reapers didn't have the human fantasy of a big house with a herd of youngsters. Reapers couldn't even have children. It was part of the agreement when Grim convinced the council to let him create us. That alone stirred up enough chaos.

The treaty specifically stated that the excess soul matter would not be used to create any more deities. Reapers weren't deities, though. At least, that was Grim's winning argument. We were just servants, his payment for running Eternity.

Technically, souls were the lowest class citizens in Limbo, even though they constituted the majority of Eternity's population. Not to mention, Eternity wouldn't exist without them. But they ruled the human realm, and most of their belief structures rendered them helpless in the spirit world. Their lack of control in Eternity forced the gods to take action. Most souls believed the gods were in charge of the afterlife anyway, so there was little resistance when they'd started changing the rules.

Souls who signed contracts with the Fates were the only souls allowed to reside in Limbo City. They were given a temporary visa and enough coin to live on. Picking their future parents was the final bonus when their contracts expired. That's what ultimately swayed them to sign in the first place.

Nephilim and reapers weren't treated much better. We were considered second class citizens. While the half-breed angels dubbed Limbo their unofficial home because of its neutral position, reapers were anchored to the city by duty—not that we had a say in the matter. We could work for Grim, or be terminated. By giving us a bit of coin and a few basic rights, Grim fooled most of us into believing that we were citizens instead of slaves, but a few of us still knew better.

"Well, I'd better get you home. You have a big day ahead of you tomorrow." Maalik handed Daisy a shiny coin when she brought our bill. There were twelve marks left on it. Our bill was only eight.

"Keep the change," he said.

Daisy fluttered her wings and smiled. "Thank you. Please come again."

Maalik stood and held out his hand for me. I rolled my eyes and placed my palm on his. We left the café and walked back toward my apartment.

"**W**ell, this is it," I said.

The silver plaque on the door read Coexist Complex. What it really meant was cheap rent, if you were willing to put up with everyone Eternity had to offer. On my floor alone resided a demon, two nephilim, a Greek deity couple, and three other reapers.

Limbo had an apartment complex just for reapers, Reapers Tower, but only the better paid and older generations lived there.

"Do you want me to walk you to your door?" Maalik asked. He had been so anxious to take me out for coffee, and now he looked nervous.

"No, maybe next time."

"You mean I can take you out for coffee again?"

"Why don't you come over Thursday? I'll make you dinner, and we can watch a movie."

"That sounds nice," he said and lifted my hand to brush an innocent kiss over my knuckles.

I smiled and ducked inside the building. I almost felt guilty. He seemed so innocent, even if he were a thousand years older than me. Age didn't mean too much in Eternity, especially since most of those who lived in Eternity couldn't remember exactly how old they were in the first place.

I entered my apartment to find Gabriel snoring on my couch and breathed a sigh of relief. Not inviting Maalik up had been a good move, after all. This was going to be fun to explain in the morning.

CHAPTER ELEVEN

*"I know God will not give me anything I can't handle.
I just wish that He didn't trust me so much."*
—Mother Teresa

"**R**un that by me one more time," Gabriel grumbled over his cup of coffee. His crumpled dress robe lay over the back of his chair. He had slept in it, but now wore his usual cotton pants and stared at me like I had just mutated into a league of demons.

"Maalik and I got some coffee, and he walked me home," I muttered as I wiped the table down for the third time.

"You brought him here? While I was sleeping on the couch?" He made it sound as if we had snuck in and stood over him to plot his demise.

"Noooo. He walked me to the front door. He didn't even come upstairs."

"So, did you blow our cover, or does he think he's one up on me now, sneaking around with my girl behind my back? The prick."

"He already knew we weren't a couple. He did his homework." I laughed at Maalik's choice of words.

"Great, now Peter will have something else to torture me about."

"I don't think you have to worry about Maalik saying anything to Peter. He's really not so bad, once you get to know him."

"Yeah, I hear dying in your sleep isn't so bad either," he said and dumped another spoonful of sugar in his coffee.

"Five minutes!" Josie bolted through the door. "You've got five minutes to finish getting ready, or I'm leaving without you." She had managed to enjoy the ball, but now she was back in reaper mode. Full blown Josie reaper mode.

"I'm ready," I groaned.

I hadn't slept well, so I was up on time for a change. After Maalik had walked me home, my mind was sucked back into a pit of despair. I did not want to work with Coreen. The woman was unbearable. There were only so many times a person could call you a pea-brain before you just snapped and slapped the shit out of them. I wagered it would take two days. Three tops.

"Wow." Josie gave me a surprised smile. "You're really taking this promotion seriously, aren't you?"

"No, she was just up all night with Maalik," Gabriel snapped before I had a chance to answer.

Josie's jaw dropped.

"How would you know what time I got home? You were already passed out drunk on my couch when I got here!"

"I thought you didn't like Maalik." Josie grinned at me. "Did you change your mind since he's on the council now?"

"No! Of course not. He asked to walk me home, and we got some coffee on the way. That's all."

She shrugged. "Whatever you say. Let's get going."

I grabbed my work robe and turned back to Gabriel. He picked up the sugar bowl and scowled at his spoon.

"You wanna meet us at Purgatory tonight and hear all the details of our first day on Coreen's team?" Maybe he would forgive me for the sake of curiosity.

He looked up and frowned. "Sure."

"Great. I'll see you around eight?"

"Yeah."

I turned to follow Josie out the door, but Gabriel caught my arm. "Hey, be careful out there today. This whole assignment doesn't feel right. Even though I'm mad at you for going out with that birdbrain, it doesn't mean I want anything to happen to you." He gave me a small smile.

"I'll be careful." I kissed him on the forehead and left just as Josie's booming voice echoed down the hall.

"Take your time. You get to explain why the elevator took so long to all the people waiting downstairs. If you're going to get up early, don't you think you should make it worthwhile and show up on time?"

She griped the whole ride down, definitely in full-blown reaper mode. I changed my mind. Coreen would be lucky if we made it through a whole day together.

Grim's conference room wasn't nearly as decorated as his office. He kept everything simple and sharp, from the straight-backed chairs to the shelves of legal books lining the walls. A cup of markers spilled across an atlas as I smashed my knee into a table leg. I grimaced. That was going to leave a bruise.

"California?" I looked up at Coreen.

"What exit method are we working with?" Josie asked. She was trying her best to keep me out of trouble.

Coreen's snarl subsided. "He's scheduled for a car accident around eleven. We're going to follow him for two hours before."

"So we have an hour and a half. What kind of prep work do we need to do?" Josie synchronized her watch with the clock in Grim's conference room.

"It's San Francisco, so we should probably go over the maps and the most common routes between his hotel and the venue his band is rehearsing at. We can't pinpoint the actual location of the crash, but we do know it will take place in or near the city."

"Swell." I sighed.

Coreen turned to me. I was waiting for the first pea-brain comment of the day, but it never came. Her jaw clenched and then she cleared her throat before unfolding a map on the conference table.

"You can have the honor, Lana," she sneered and tossed a handful of markers on top of the map. "Josie, Kevin, I've got something else for you two to work on. Follow me."

They walked out of the room, leaving me with the map and markers. A sarcastic *swell* was looking more and more like my word for the day.

I grabbed up a marker and walked around the table to get a better view of San Francisco. Why in Eternity did we need four reapers to pick up one soul? It just didn't make sense. I slumped down on one of the swivel chairs and began deciphering all the routes and major intersections. Nearly an hour later, when I had the map covered in jagged lines and circles, the rest of the team joined me again.

"I hope this promotion includes better pay," I huffed.

Coreen snorted. "We'll discuss that when and if we get the soul."

"What do you mean, *if* we get the soul? There are four of us." I spun the chair around to face her.

I knew there was something more to this job, and it was starting to piss me off that I was responsible for carrying it out without all the details. Josie looked paler than she had before they'd left the room. Not a good sign.

"Please tell me you're not so dim that you didn't notice how much Seth disapproves of our kind." There it was, pea-brain comment number one.

"Yes, I noticed, but what does that have to do with this assignment?" I jammed the cap back on my marker.

"Seth is being closely watched now that he's on the council, but that doesn't mean he's completely cut off from his resources. It's possible that he has someone spying on us so he can take the soul for himself and find out why it's so important."

"Why is it so important?"

"Weren't you listening at dinner? Grim can use the soul to help solve our problem in the Sea of Eternity." Coreen cocked a hip and gave me a bewildered look.

I sighed. "Yeah, and Seth heard that version of the story at dinner, too. I don't think I buy it any more than he does."

Coreen gritted her teeth as she pulled a hand up to grasp her hip. "I don't care if you buy it or not. We have a job to do, and if you don't want to be a part of this team, then you can tell Grim yourself. He's in his office right now."

Maalik had been right. She didn't have the authority to give me the boot.

I grinned. "That's all right. I'll figure it out sooner or later." I kicked my feet up on the table and crossed my arms. If she couldn't fire me, there was no reason to be all prim and proper.

Coreen pressed her lips together, flushing color into her pale cheeks as she tried to contain herself.

"We should really get going," Josie intervened.

"Yes, we should." Coreen ripped her glare away from me and pulled a handful of coins from the pocket of her robe.

Kevin reached for one first, and I remembered that this was his first day on the job. For his sake, I hoped everything went according to plan. You always remember your first job and base the success of every job after around it. Today could either make or break his career.

"There's a record store across the street from the subject's hotel," Coreen said. "We'll meet there. Kevin, take my hand. This is your first coin. I want to make sure you know what you're doing."

Kevin obeyed without hesitation. No wonder she liked having apprentices. Grim always gave her the best ones.

"See you on the other side," she said before rolling her coin and disappearing.

Kevin would be fine. He was the best of his generation. Besides, you didn't get to be Coreen Bendura's apprentice if you scored poorly on your L&L, latitude and longitude exam. We're required to know the global coordinates of every major city and then some before being allowed to use coins for the human realm. Besides reapers, most angels are familiar with coordinates, too. That's why they always showed up where they were supposed to, while rogue demons who managed to get their hands on a coin popped up wherever and possessed whomever they could, little girl or not.

I flipped my coin once, and Josie grabbed my wrist.

"Be careful, Lana," she whispered. "Coreen had me pack an unhealthy number of arrows. She really thinks something bad could happen. She didn't want me to tell you because she wants you focused on retrieving the soul. Kevin and I are just backup. I couldn't let you go out there without telling you first."

"Thanks." I found the cold steel of my scythe strapped across my back suddenly comforting. I smiled at Josie and rolled my coin twice more.

The record store was a dive. A zillion fingerprints covered the dust-caked shelves crammed with secondhand albums. A yellow cat stared at me from its napping spot next to the register, while the clerk was off in his own little world, flipping through a dirty magazine.

Josie scratched the cat's chin, and it rolled its head against her hand with a pleased purr. The clerk didn't look up. He wouldn't have seen anything if he had. Souls are blinded by their human bodies. Animals, however, can see us just fine.

The bell on the door jingled as a young, flannel-clad man hurried in. The clerk stuffed his magazine under the register and stood.

"Hey, Mickey! Heard your show sold out for tonight. Congratulations!"

"Yeah, thanks. I was wondering if you wanted some more of our records to sell. Fans will be crawling the city tonight. Could be good for business," he added.

"Sure, sure, I'll take fifty more. Why not?" The clerk laughed and shoved the magazine farther under the register.

"Great, I'll be right back." Mickey hurried off. The clerk gave a sigh of relief and checked his magazine's hiding spot one more time.

"That's our catch!" Coreen shouted.

"He's coming back in," I reminded her. And she thought I was a pea-brain.

Not a second later, the man was back with a box. I peeked over his shoulder to see inside. The cover of the record was a loud orange with scratchy blue lettering spelling out Sabotage. A picture of the band showed our catch sitting behind a drum set.

"Anything unusual about him?" Coreen was standing a little too close when I turned around.

"Like what?"

"I don't know. Is he different from other souls?"

What had Maalik said? I see in souls what other reapers can't. Is that why I was here? Is that why Coreen felt so threatened by me? Was there really something I was better at than she was?

"Well, he's still alive, so I can't exactly see his soul right now," I answered with an annoyed frown.

She narrowed her eyes at me and stomped out of the store with Kevin trailing behind her like a shadow.

"He's on the move," Josie whispered.

Our catch took the check the clerk handed him and skipped out the door.

Outside, the traffic hissed by surprisingly close to the sidewalk. Our drummer boy jumped in front of a taxi, and the cabbie swore at him in a foreign language as he jerked the car around, barely missing him. I wondered if he actually had to be in a vehicle for his death to be categorized as a crash, and decided to stick closer.

Coreen and Kevin were already waiting beside the Sabotage tour bus when we crossed the street. Our catch climbed inside, and the vehicle roared to life.

Coreen lifted her chin, ready to bark orders at us. "We'll do this in two teams. Kevin and I will go first. We'll wait at the next intersection. When the bus makes it through, you two jump ahead to the intersection after us. We'll do that until the accident happens. Ready?"

"Ready," I answered as the bus pulled away.

Coreen grabbed Kevin's hand. They rolled their coins and disappeared. Josie gave me a worried look. The end of her bow peeked out from under her sleeve. She was ready for anything. Then it dawned on me. She had been promoted because Grim knew she was the only reaper I trusted. Coreen was with us because she was the only reaper Grim trusted. Kevin was simply stuck in this mess by default since he was Coreen's apprentice. I was starting to see how much this assignment actually revolved around me, and I wasn't happy about it.

"Our turn," Josie said, pulling me out of my daze.

The bus had made it past the intersection, and Coreen stared from the corner, waiting for us to move. We rolled our coins and appeared at the next light as the bus screeched to a halt. Coreen and Kevin jumped ahead of us to the next corner.

Up ahead, beyond two more lights, stretched the Bay Bridge over the San Francisco Bay. The band's rehearsal location was in the opposite direction.

I swore under my breath and nudged Josie. "Let's get up there with Coreen and Kevin. I think there's been a change of plans."

Josie nodded, and we rolled our coins again. When we appeared next to Coreen, Josie had her bow in one hand and an arrow in the other.

Coreen glared at the bridge. "They're going in the wrong direction."

"No kidding." I pulled my scythe out from under my robe. If Josie was on edge, I was on edge. I didn't see anything out of the ordinary, but it never hurt to be prepared. "Let's just keep going as we are, stopping a short distance ahead of each other until we get across."

"Of course," Coreen snapped.

I forgot she was the one in charge of barking orders. I'd never worked with a team before, so sue me. The light turned green, and the bus pulled ahead. Coreen fumbled with her coin and vanished. Kevin followed. We passed the next two lights, and sure enough, the bus was heading for the bridge.

The October breeze slapped over the bay water and sent random gusts of bone-chilling wind in my face, summing up the last week of my life. I hadn't helped track down a still-living soul since my apprentice days with Saul. This sort of work normally required a dozen more classes that I had no intention of taking. I was starting to see why.

Coreen and Kevin went out over the water first. They stood alert on the narrow ledge, the rush of passing cars and trucks pulling at their robes. Kevin gripped the beam behind him like a lifeline, rendering his knuckles an even paler shade of white. Something told me this wasn't how he had imagined his first day on the job.

I rolled my coin again, but by the time Josie and I made it onto the bridge, the bus was gone, and so was Kevin.

"Lana! Move!" Josie cried as she loosed an arrow over my head.

I dropped and swung my scythe behind me. A dog-faced demon hissed. It was bigger than the ones I had seen with Caim. Lumpy, amber skin just barely held its form. Black eyes burned at me as it licked over the nub where I had severed one of its limbs. Josie strung two arrows at once and sunk them into the beast's skull. It yelped and then vanished in a cloud of yellow smoke, reeking of sulfur.

"Where's Kevin?" I shouted over the roar of passing cars and screeching brakes. Josie was already running in the direction we had last seen our teammates.

A mangled piece of railing hung off the side of the bridge. Traffic slowed as the curious humans tried to catch a glimpse of the chaos. I glanced over the edge and found the bus. Coreen appeared over the bubbling mess as she swan dived into the San Francisco Bay. I took off after Josie.

"How many were on that bus?"

"I don't know! You saw the album cover. How many people are in his band?" she shouted back at me.

"Five, with a driver, that makes six. We can handle six souls."

"And two more demons?" she quaked.

I gritted my teeth. Two more of the nasty creatures waited ahead, near the skid marks the bus had left on the bridge. The marks were too dark and obvious. The demons had pushed the bus over. How the hell had they known where we were going to be?

"Go help Coreen and Kevin! I'll take care of them." Josie fired another arrow through the nearest demon's eye. Pus exploded from the gaping wound. The beast wailed and clawed at its face before Josie darted it through the skull. Another cloud of murky smoke rose in its place. The second demon was quicker. It rolled away from her and scrambled behind a semi. Josie pounced onto the hood of a car and hurried after it.

The sound of traffic crunched in my ears. Angry horns blared as cars and trucks slowed around the charred bridge and missing chunk of railing. Humans may fear death, but they never pass up an opportunity to gawk at it.

I leaned over the wrecked ledge and caught a glimpse of the bus before it disappeared entirely. Kevin and Coreen's robes lay abandoned on the crumbling bridge. I yanked mine over my head and tossed it next to theirs. It was no good to me in the water. I grasped my scythe in both hands and jumped.

The momentum of the fall pulled me under the icy water, and I found the bus, still bubbling as the remaining air inside tried to escape. I latched on to an open window and pulled myself around to the door.

Inside, Coreen and Kevin cut away the passengers' seatbelts. Coreen jerked around and then relaxed when she saw it was only me. Kevin's mop of curls floated around his face, rendered weightless in the dark water. He struggled with a dagger, trying to free the last man. I slipped the blade of my scythe under the buckle and tore it loose from the seat. He gave me a relieved smile, but only a brief one. Air bubbles leaked from the corners of his mouth, and he pinched his lips shut again. He grabbed two of the men under their arms and heaved them out the door.

There were only five. One of the bandmates must have been driving. Coreen grabbed the next two and left the drummer for me. He was unconscious. The others had a chance of making it out alive, and I hoped they did. We had enough problems. We didn't need four additional souls to tend to.

Mickey, our catch, was slowly drowning in my arms. This wasn't how he was meant to go, but I wasn't about to go to the trouble of saving him just so he could die an hour later. That was as far as destiny would take him. I was just saving him the extra trauma.

His soul glowed as I pulled it free from his body, and his eyes flashed open in surprise. I pulled him close and wrapped an arm around his waist to keep him from turning back and seeing his corporeal form. The shock was too much for some souls. I pulled him out the door and swam toward the ascending bubbles, fleeing for the surface.

"There she is!" Coreen gasped as we emerged. "Grab our robes!"

Josie stood on the edge of the bridge. Her whole body slumped with relief. She threw the pile of robes over her shoulder before digging out her coin. Several men in a small motorboat were pulling the other band members out of the water. Mickey called out to them, but no one responded.

"Let's get out of here," Coreen shouted.

I jammed my free hand into the pocket of my leather pants and rolled my coin, anxious to leave the catastrophe behind.

CHAPTER TWELVE

"A friendly study of the world's religions is a sacred duty."
—Mahatma Gandhi

"Well, you can see his soul now. What do you think?" Coreen rubbed a towel over her head. Her perfectly oiled curls were a chaotic mess. It made me smile.

We were back at Grim's conference table, drying ourselves with a heap of towels, courtesy of Ellen. Our timid catch sat in a chair next to me with terrycloth wrapped around his head like a turban.

"He's a soul like any other. What exactly am I supposed to be looking for here?" I shivered and reached for another towel.

The whole situation was ridiculous. After that disastrous encounter, the least she could do was tell us the truth.

"I don't know…something," she said. "You would think after all that trouble, he wouldn't be just an ordinary soul."

She stood and leaned over the table to get a closer look at Mickey. He moved closer to me, probably because I had been the one to pull him out of the bus. I wondered if he would feel so safe if he knew I'd merely pulled his soul from the wreckage and left his body behind.

"I'm not ordinary," he snapped at Coreen. "My band is on the rise, and our show sold out for tonight!"

"Well, if your band doesn't find another drummer, there won't be a show." Coreen laughed at him.

Shock and disgust creased Kevin's face, like he had just caught his favorite rock star in an alley with an underage hooker. The first hint of defiance wove into his expression as he sympathetically watched our catch.

"What do you want with me?" Mickey shrieked.

"Just your soul." Coreen gave him a vulturous smile.

I rolled my eyes. "Just leave him alone."

Mickey looked at me, a silent plea for clarity. I donned the gentle voice I had heard Josie use on disoriented souls so often. "Mickey, this may be a little hard for you to grasp right now, but you're dead. The rest of your band survived. You drowned. We're reapers. We came and collected your soul."

"Reapers? As in, the Grim Reaper?" He chuckled, not believing me.

"Okay, when is Grim going to be here?" I turned to Coreen. I wasn't as patient as Josie when it came to convincing souls. They got one slow and simple explanation. After that, I let them argue with themselves as I dragged them off to their afterlives.

"Ellen!" Coreen roared.

Grim's secretary stumbled in. "Y-yes?" she squeaked.

Ellen was actually a first-generation reaper, but she had been at the bottom of her class. Instead of trying to improve her soul-reaping skills, Grim had dumped his paperwork off on her, and over time, she became invaluable. She was a horrible reaper, but an excellent secretary. And Coreen enjoyed ordering her around.

"Where's Grim?"

"He just finished a meeting, and he's on his way," Ellen answered just as the boss man stormed through the door.

"Let's take a look at this soul," he said, leaning over the table to examine our catch. "He won't do at all. Take him to Duat. Horus and Wosyet are waiting at the harbor. Take them with you," he ordered.

"Duat?" I asked.

"Yes, Duat," Grim growled. "Is that a problem for you?"

"I just didn't realize that he was a believer of the Egyptian faith."

"I'm not!" Mickey stood up, knocking over his chair. Grim didn't even acknowledge him.

"He's of Egyptian descent. I don't have to explain my reasons to you. Do as you're told. That's why you get paid." He stomped out of the conference room.

Out of the corner of my eye, I could see Coreen smirking. She needed to be slapped. I finished patting myself dry and pulled my robe back over my head. This was the first time Grim had actually asked me to bend the rules. I shouldn't have cared so much. I bent them all the time.

"Shall we?" Coreen waited by the door. She oozed with satisfaction, even in her disheveled state. Josie looked up slowly. She hadn't spoken since Grim had mentioned that Horus would be traveling with us.

"Sure," she sighed. "Let's get this over with."

I rested my hand on Mickey's shoulder. He gave me a startled look but let me lead him out of the conference room.

The harbor was nearly empty. It was still several hours before most reapers would be setting sail for the afterlives. A single ferry unloaded on the dock. Festive ribbons and balloons hung from the boat's railing, and loud dance music blared to announce their arrival. A cluster of excited deities paraded down the ramp, ready to go shopping and sightseeing. The tourists hushed their voices as their guide announced us like zoo animals.

"To your left, you will see a group of reapers preparing to take a soul to its afterlife." He paused to frown at us. "Normally, one reaper can handle several souls at once. This could be a demonstration or lesson for one or more of the six apprentices recently added...." His voice trailed off as the crowd made their way past us and into the city.

Horus and Wosyet waited near our ship. Coreen's ship was in the shop, undergoing some repairs and updates—or so she claimed. I had the feeling she just didn't want the mess of demon guts all over her deck. After our earlier encounter, it was highly possible they would attack again.

"Good afternoon," Horus greeted us.

"Hello, Horus." Coreen strode up the ramp ahead of us as if she owned our ship. It was a disrespectful move, and Josie noticed, too. Wosyet wrapped an arm around Horus and tugged him after her. Kevin waited for Josie and me to escort Mickey ahead of him.

On board, Coreen checked every nook and cranny of the ship to make sure there were no uninvited guests, while Josie and I pulled up the sails, and Kevin freed us from the dock. Wosyet led Horus to one of the deck benches and draped her arms over him. She looked almost as done up as she had been at the ball, with precise makeup and an equally tacky gown. Her eyes never left Josie. She must know about Josie's dates with Horus.

As we drifted off to sea, Josie stayed as far away from Horus as she could manage, constantly finding something constructive to do, even if she had already done it twice. It was exhausting just to watch her.

I pulled her aside. "Just go lay down, or talk to the soul. You're better at consoling them than I'll ever be."

"Is that why you rescue them from their dismal fates so often?" She laughed and cast a nervous glance over her shoulder where Horus was busy untangling himself from Wosyet's embrace.

"I'm gonna go fill my quiver. It's nearly empty, and it doesn't look like the two of them are equipped to ward off any demons."

"I'll go see how Kevin's doing. Mickey's settled in the sailor's quarters, I don't much care for Coreen, and those two, well, they just look too cozy to be bothered with." I grinned.

Josie rolled her eyes and hurried off to our cabin.

I found Kevin on the other side of the ship, hunched over the deck railing and panting like he meant it. His robe lay tangled at his feet, and he began to tug at the collar of his black turtleneck.

"Hey now, this isn't one of those party ferries we saw at the harbor. You can't run around naked on my ship."

"Is it like this every time you sail?" He rubbed his face against his shoulder to wipe away the sweat dripping off his brow.

"No, it'll pass. Don't worry about it. Lots of reapers get seasick on their first ride." I patted his back until his breathing slowed.

"Thanks." He ran a hand through his damp hair, and then spun around with a look of panic. "Do you think you could, maybe, not tell Coreen about this?"

"Sure." I folded my arms. "You're not feeling as lucky as you did last night, are you?"

"Maybe she's just having a bad day, but I don't want to give her a reason to torment me."

"Smart boy," I chuckled.

"Did you ever think maybe she would be nicer to you if you were more respectful?"

"I've been around three hundred years. I've already tried the respect technique."

He laughed and nodded his head.

"There you are." Coreen had found us.

"Speak of the devil," I muttered.

"Go check on the soul," she said to me. "Kevin, I want to give you your first lesson in navigation." She ushered him away, shooting me a suspicious look.

I sighed and took off for the sailor's quarters. A muffled voice leaked through the door as I approached. At first, I thought that Josie had finished filling her quiver and had gone to console Mickey, but as I drew closer, I realized it wasn't her voice at all. I jerked the door open.

Wosyet spun around. "I was just telling Mickey about all the wonders of Aaru, his new home," she cooed innocently.

"Out," I demanded.

"Excuse me?" She lifted her chin.

"Even the greater gods have more respect for what we do and don't tamper with our souls before we deliver them. Out!"

She tossed her braids back and pushed past me. Mickey stood in the corner of the cabin, watching in awe and terror.

"You okay?" I stepped inside and closed the door behind me.

"Define okay," he laughed.

"Well, aside from being dead and all?"

"Sure, sure," he answered with a nervous laugh.

"Look, I'm not all that good at helping new souls through their first day in Eternity, but we're not supposed to allow you to converse with any of the gods until we reach the gates."

"Hey, it's not like I invited her in here." He threw up his hands in defense.

"I know. I was just letting you know why I had to make her leave." I reached for the door.

"Thanks. She was creepy anyway."

I paused and turned around. "How?"

"I dunno. I'm used to fans and all, but not fans from other worlds." He laughed, a sound somewhere between pride and confusion.

"What made you think she was a fan?"

"She was asking all the typical questions that fans do. You know, she wanted to know how long we've been together, and if anyone else in my band died in the crash. It was weird. What is she supposed to be anyway, a goddess or something?"

"One of the lesser ones that don't get mentioned all too often."

What a ditz. I couldn't believe it. Wosyet had probably tagged along in hopes of getting an autograph.

"So, is this place I'm going to some kind of heaven or hell?"

"Duat is the Egyptian underworld, but it's also the gateway to Aaru, the Egyptian heaven." I smiled. No wonder he was having such a hard time. He didn't have a clue where he was going. "Don't worry, you'll like it there."

"Thanks." He leaned his head back against the cabin wall and smiled.

I left the room and went to find Josie. She wasn't on deck, so I assumed she was still in our cabin and headed that direction. Horus stood just outside the doorway, blocking Josie in. She had her quiver of arrows over one shoulder, and the expression on her face told me she was ready to beat him unconscious with it if he didn't move soon.

"She's just a co-worker," he said.

"Good for you. What are you telling me for?" Josie glared at him.

Horus sighed, and his shoulders tensed uneasily. He was wearing a pair of tattered pants that looked like something out of Gabriel's closet, but nothing else, so most of his ripe and rippling frame could be seen pressing through his honey-colored skin. I had to hand it to Josie, for as good as he looked, she was holding her pride together rather well. Her gaze drifted over his shoulder and she spied me.

"Lana, how's the soul?" she asked, cutting Horus off.

"Good, except I caught Wosyet talking to him."

"What?" Horus groaned. "I'm very sorry. I brought her along because she's been helping negotiate with the Fates. I'll go over the rules with her more thoroughly."

"Thank you." I stepped aside, an obvious gesture for him to have at it. He frowned back at Josie and gave me a nod before hurrying off to find his dingy partner.

"Who does she think she is? She has no right messing with our soul," Josie whispered as soon as Horus was out of sight.

"I think she just wanted an autograph."

"I can't believe Horus did such a shoddy job going over the rules with her." Josie shook her head.

I shrugged and then frowned at the horizon. A tiny black ship loomed in the distance, and I had a pretty good idea who it belonged to.

CHAPTER THIRTEEN

*"Must not all things at the last
be swallowed up in death?"*
—Plato

Josie and I had fended off Caim on our own before, but this time, it wasn't going to be so easy. It was a wonder his ship was still afloat with all the demons on board. He was definitely working with more than two legions this time, but we were working with two more reapers and two Egyptian deities.

Wosyet clutched Horus's arm. "Why don't we just take the soul the rest of the way with a coin?"

Okay, scratch that, one Egyptian deity.

"Didn't you teach her anything before letting her tag along?" Josie glared at the goddess. Wosyet ignored her.

"Coins are inactive over the Sea of Eternity," Horus quickly explained. "If they weren't, anyone could just sneak onto a ship and steal a soul. It's in the treaty. I thought you already knew that." He shook his head, finally realizing what a mistake bringing her had been. Her worried expression proved she thought it was a mistake now, too.

"Why don't you go wait in our cabin," I offered.

Josie's jaw tightened, but I wasn't about to invite her to harass our soul again. Wosyet nodded anxiously and hurried away. Halfway to our cabin, she turned around.

"Aren't you coming, Horus?"

"No, I'm going to help."

"Suit yourself," she mumbled before stomping off.

Josie strung three arrows in her bow. Caim's ship was still a good distance away, but I remembered how fast his demons had crossed the sea before. We needed a game plan, and fast.

Coreen rounded the sailor's cabin with Kevin. The crinkled skin around her eyes told me they had seen Caim's ship, as well. "Horus, you can fight long-range, right?" she asked.

"Of course." The makeup around his scarred eye faded away as his pupil was consumed by a golden light. He lifted his gaze to the sky.

A falcon cried out. The bird was an unnatural size, almost a third as large as our ship, with feathers the size of palm tree fronds. He jerked his head to one side, and I could see my reflection in his bowling ball of an eye. I gripped the railing behind me, hoping I didn't resemble any creatures he had been snacking on lately.

"Lana, Kevin, and I will watch the deck." Coreen stripped off her robe. "Josie and Horus, stand behind us so you can focus on attacking his ship. The more damage he receives, the sooner he'll retreat." She picked through a handful of what looked like coins.

"I thought those didn't work out here. What are you doing?" I moved up beside her.

"These aren't coins." She grinned. "They're concentrated mirrors, designed to stun demons. Shield your eyes. I'm going to toss them overboard so our guests are partially blind before they arrive."

I threw my hand over my face just in time. When I looked again, a fierce glow peeked out from under the railing. Caim was close enough now that I could see his shock. It must have looked as though our ship was on fire.

"Let's do this!" Coreen shouted.

I decided her determination and courage had earned her another shred of my respect as I faced Caim's ship.

It was like a Carnival cruise for demons. A few dog-faces glowered from the deck, but they were the least of my worries. Dozens of webbed wings flapped in the breeze, carrying the crumpled bodies of skeletal cats the size of horses. My knees were trembling, and the creatures hadn't even crossed half the distance yet.

Josie's lips curled back to expose her clenched teeth. The muscles in her back flexed under the strain of the three arrows she aimed overhead. A pained sigh escaped her as she released them.

Caim's shrieks echoed over the sea. Two of the arrows were lodged in his left wing, but the third had pierced his shoulder. Another wave of demons spilled from his ship and rushed toward us.

My knees began to tremble as the first wave neared. We were so outnumbered. Horus's falcon swooped down and caught four of the hellcats in his beak. The giant bird petrified me, but at least he was on our side. That was the only thing keeping my hopes from plummeting into oblivion.

Josie pulled two more arrows from her quiver. She had stripped down to a green tank top and jeans. Sweat glistened on her forehead and shoulders.

Horus peeled off his pants and let them fall to the deck floor. A small, leather loin cloth kept him from being entirely exposed, but just barely. Strips of leather criss-crossed over his thighs, holding a pair of rustic daggers. He took them and widened his stance, preparing for the army of demons.

"Stay back! Let the mirrors do their part first!" Coreen screamed at Kevin as he inched toward the railing. What the hell was wrong with him? Was he blind? He hesitated, but then obeyed Coreen and took a few steps back.

Horus moved up beside me, leaving Josie in the middle as she frantically loosed arrows, two at a time, over the sea. A band of demons had formed a wall around Caim, but they were slowly shying away under Josie's fire.

Horus's falcon dipped one more time to thin out the first wave, and then the demons were on us.

The terror of the first hellcat crashing onto our deck was only mildly reduced by its lack of grace. Coreen had been wise to use the reflecting mirrors. The beast's eyes glazed over as it thrashed about. Kevin ran forward first, lashing out with his scythe. His actions were anxious, although his face held an eerie calm as he sliced off the creature's front limbs.

Its agonizing shrieks vibrated through my skull, threatening to shatter my will. My own cries were a foreign sound as the trembling in my knees faded, and I bolted ahead, throwing my scythe with all my strength to tear the beast's head off. I would kill a thousand hellcats as long as I never had to hear that sound again.

Blood, thick as tar, ran from the creature's neck, oozing over the deck and between the boards. I cringed, thinking of how long it was going to take to clean and repair the ship later.

"Incoming!" Coreen howled over the roar of wings as more hellcats arrived.

Horus's falcon dove down and plucked up two of them in his beak, snapping them into pieces small enough to swallow. The massacre sprayed us with a scarlet rain. The next cat to arrive slipped in the blood of its fallen comrades and slid dangerously close to Josie.

Horus leapt onto the creature's back and shoved a dagger in its eye. Blood oozed out around his hand and sprayed across his face. The beast's cries roared out, deafening as the last had been, before Horus jerked the blade back and split the cat's skull in half, spilling steaming brains over the deck floor.

Josie's eyes watered, but she continued firing at Caim. His protective circle of demons lay in heaps around him, riddled with arrows. Her backup quiver was almost empty, and the lines around her eyes grew deeper with each shot she fired.

Another hellcat clawed its way on deck, snapping off a chunk of railing as it climbed on board. It snarled and flung the splintered railing my way. I dodged, landing in a puddle of demon goo. Another pair of leather pants, ruined. The boat shifted, and my knees gave out just in time. The hellcat leapt over me, its talons inches from my face, that was now splattered with scalding blood.

The cat rolled into the railing on the other side of the deck, uprooting half the hand-carved spindles, then turned and prepared to rush me again. My scythe was slippery with blood, and my head was spinning in so many circles I could hardly remember how to use the weapon in the first place.

The beast hissed, pulling back the veiny skin around its mouth to show me the rotting arsenal of teeth waiting inside. It lowered its head and charged. Adrenaline ignited in my blood, sending an electrical pulse that ripped through my body and left my fingertips numb and aching. I swung my scythe wildly and closed my eyes, trying to conjure up a picture of Gabriel or Saul or even Maalik. If I were going to die, the last image in my mind was not going to be of some mangy hellcat.

My wrists jerked, and a strangled gurgle hissed past my cheek, carrying the nauseating aroma of sewage. I cracked my eyes open. The blade had pressed through the monster's throat and connected with its spine. Its eyes went empty as it fell into my lap and bled out over the deck.

Everything ached and burned. I hardly realized I was holding my breath until my vision began to blur. I gasped and rolled the dead cat off my legs. Leaning on my scythe, I stood and joined the others.

"Horus! Set your falcon on Caim already!" Coreen shouted from the other side of the ship. One of the demons had nicked her just above the brow, and her own brighter blood was running down her face and into her eyes. Horus wiped the blood off his forehead and nodded. The black of his eye disappeared once again, lost to the light.

The falcon responded and dove for Caim's ship, while another hellcat crashed through the deck railing.

"Here kitty, kitty," Kevin taunted the beast.

His face still held that creepy calm, but his eyes were wilder now. He had torn off his turtleneck, and gobs of sticky demon guts were splattered across his chest and matted in his hair. The hellcat snarled and dug its front claws into deck floor, splintering the blood-coated boards. Kevin took a quick sidestep and thrust his scythe into the creature's middle. It twisted around and hissed at him, ready to attack, but the sound of a distant horn drew its attention away.

One of Caim's demons perched atop his highest mast and blew the horn again, signaling their retreat. Horus's falcon circled overhead, preparing to snatch up the little beast, but the light of Horus's eye found him first and called him off.

The hellcat on our ship looked back at Kevin, enraged that it had been robbed of the chance to devour him, and then it spotted Coreen. She kneeled on the deck, trying to use the sleeve of her turtleneck to dab the blood out of her eye. The cat hurled itself onto her, sinking its claws into her side, before taking flight.

Coreen's screams replaced the sounds of battle. I froze, unable to think or move. Josie reached into her quiver, but it was empty. A strangled sob escaped her before she dropped her bow and clasped both hands over her mouth.

A fleeing hellcat came to help Coreen's captor celebrate their catch. It latched on to her dangling legs, tearing through her slacks and provoking more shrieks. Josie turned away and buried her face in Horus's shoulder. He wrapped a bloodied arm around her and stared ahead, defeated and hopeless. The sound of ripping flesh and snapping bones was horrid, but seeing Coreen's insides explode from her as the demons pulled her apart was almost too much. I had to fight to control my breathing as the creatures swooped down and fetched up body parts like candy from a piñata.

"I should have killed it," Kevin whispered. The blood-thirsty haze had vanished from his eyes. "Why didn't I just kill it?"

"We have a job to do." I tried to keep my voice from trembling as badly as the rest of my body was. Someone had to keep it together, and someone had to help me clean up the ship before the demon blood burned enough holes in it to sink us.

"It's over, it's over," Horus whispered in Josie's ear, rocking her and stroking back her short hair as she sobbed against his neck. The falcon perched itself on the ship, wrapping its talons around the deck railing, or what was left of it anyway. Horus's eye returned to normal, and the giant bird ascended in a beam of light, back above the clouds.

"Why didn't I just kill it?" Kevin was still mumbling to himself, swimming in his guilt and coming down from his first blood-high. He wrapped his arms around himself and shivered. Things weren't starting out well for him. Grim would assign him a new apprenticeship when we got back, but in the meantime, he was going to listen to me.

"Kevin, there's a stack of buckets and a few mops in a closet next to my and Josie's cabin. Go get them," I ordered.

He headed off without responding, still mumbling to himself and shaking his head.

"How far are we from Duat?" Horus asked over Josie's shoulder.

"I don't know, maybe half an hour."

"Let's just worry about the bigger puddles for now. I have a niece that can take care of the rest when we get there."

"You sure she won't mind?"

"Kabauet is the goddess of cold water."

"Thanks." I tried to smile, but the fresh image of Coreen's insides kept crossing my mind, making it a little difficult.

Josie finally pulled away from Horus and faced me. "She was almost a thousand years old. That could have just as easily been one of us," she hiccupped.

I didn't think she was so pleased about the promotion anymore. I was still in shock. That was the only explanation

I had for not sobbing hysterically or mumbling mantras of guilt like my fellow reapers.

CHAPTER FOURTEEN

"This only is denied to God:
the power to undo the past."
—*Agathon*

Although Aaru was a realm in itself, Duat, the Egyptian underworld, was the only way to get to Aaru. That was where the Weighing of the Hearts ceremony took place. Even though it was an old tradition, and there were ways of determining a soul's destination without the ceremony now, the Egyptian gods still insisted that it take place for the few souls who passed through their gates.

"Well, son of a golden cock!" Anubis, Horus's half-brother and the Egyptian god of embalming, greeted us as we docked at Duat's harbor.

Horus blushed, even as he laughed at the old joke. According to the myth, Horus had been conceived after Isis resurrected Osiris from the dead. Seth had become jealous of his brother and murdered him. He cut him into pieces and scattered them. Seth didn't seem to get along well with anyone. Oddly enough, when Isis went looking for the pieces of her husband to resurrect him, she couldn't find his penis. Supposedly, it had been eaten by a fish. So, she made him a new one out of gold. Son of a golden cock, indeed.

"Where's Dad?" Horus asked.

"With Mom. She's been away from home for a hundred years. They have a lot of catching up to do."

Isis wasn't Anubis's real mother, but she had raised him as her own. Even though he now knew Nephthys, Isis's sister, was his mother, he still called Isis "Mom." Maybe the fact that Nephthys had tricked Osiris into sleeping with her helped his decision. The sisters had since reconciled, but Anubis wasn't as forgiving as Isis. The peace treaty kept most deities in line, but bitter grudges were still lurking under the surface.

"We have a new soul. Don't they want to witness the ceremony?"

"I'm way ahead of you, little brother. I sent Kebauet to announce your arrival."

"Good. I was hoping she would be around. I have a favor to ask of her." Horus looked back at our ship.

Anubis followed his gaze and turned sullen. "What happened?"

"We were attacked by Caim and his demons."

"Where's Coreen?"

"Gone." The Egyptian god hung his head in shame. As powerful as he was, I imagined he was being tormented by guilt far worse than the rest of us.

"I see." Anubis cleared his throat and turned to me. "Leave your ship here. I will have it cleaned and repaired before returning it to your harbor tomorrow. For your troubles, I will also cover the coin for your return to Limbo. I am very sorry for your loss," he added.

"Are we there yet?" Wosyet poked her head out of the captain's cabin and sighed with relief. "Well, that was one experience I don't plan to have again. I can't believe coins are inactive over the sea. If someone had told me that before, I would have never agreed to put myself in harm's way."

"Don't worry," Horus snorted. "I wasn't planning on taking you back to Limbo with me."

"Oh, I don't mind going to Limbo to speak with the Fates. I just don't think the boat ride is necessary."

"If we hadn't been on the boat, Coreen probably wouldn't be the only one missing."

"They're only reapers. Grim can make more." She sighed and stormed down the ramp to where Anubis waited. "Perhaps I'm better suited to help you weigh the soul," she cooed and brushed against him.

"Perhaps you're better suited to lick the feet of Osiris and beg for forgiveness for your rudeness toward our guests." He glared down at her.

"You're about as charming as your brother," she sneered before hurrying away.

Anubis shook his head and turned to Horus. "I don't understand what the Fates see in her. Are you sure they won't deal with you directly?"

"I don't know," Horus said. "We'll find out tomorrow."

"Let me know if you plan on taking another soul across the sea. I know it's expensive to travel by coin, but if you have to go by boat, I want to be there to help next time."

"I will. Thank you." Horus gave his brother a weak smile.

"Here." Josie picked up my robe and draped it over my shoulder. She already had hers on. The hood was damp from where she had rinsed the blood out of her hair. She looked like she was feeling better. I still looked like hell, but it was on purpose. I wanted Grim to see exactly what his ignorance had cost. I wasn't sure if he cared, but I was going to make him care, one way or another.

CHAPTER FIFTEEN

"If God did not exist
it would be necessary to invent him."
—Voltaire

I could hear Maalik shouting through Grim's office door as I stepped off the elevator. Ellen jumped up from the front desk and threw herself in front of me with one of her practiced smiles that made her look like a ventriloquist's puppet.

"Sorry, honey, Grim's in a meeting right now," she whispered as she glanced nervously toward his door. I could still hear what Maalik was saying.

"You've put the fate of Eternity on her shoulders, and you refuse her this one request? You use her to hold your position of power. You treat her like a slave and mistrust her after all these years of service!"

I clenched my jaw and glared at the door. "I like you, Ellen. Move."

She lifted her chin and frowned at me. For a minute, it looked like she was going to hold her ground, but then she noticed the blood drying in my hair. She bit her bottom lip and edged out of my way.

I threw Grim's door open and stormed in. He was leaned over his desk, his face red and twisted as his mouth opened, ready to shout something back at Maalik. Then he saw me, and his eyes widened in surprise. Maalik snapped his head around, and most of the anger in his expression evaporated.

"You can take this promotion and shove it up your ass until you find the time to explain to me just what in Eternity is going on," I roared over the room.

I didn't care that Grim was my boss anymore. I didn't care that he could probably convince the council to vote me out of existence. I wasn't going to touch one more soul until he explained everything.

"Well, if that isn't enough proof, I don't know what is." Maalik swallowed and pulled his eyes away from me to look back at Grim. The old reaper glared from me to Maalik and then straightened his tie before sitting down.

"Fine. You take her," he snapped. "Oh, and Maalik, if this creates any problems, I will hold you entirely responsible. No one has ever been voted off the council, but don't let that fool you. It can be done."

"With you running Eternity, I don't fool myself into believing anything." Maalik folded his arms and nodded to me. I followed him out of the office and into the elevator.

Ellen sulked behind her desk, her eyes red and glazed over, as if she could start crying any moment. I hoped she wouldn't be in too much trouble with Grim.

When the elevator door closed behind us, I turned to face Maalik. "So, are you going to tell me what's really going on around here?"

His shoulders tightened, and he frowned, but he wouldn't look at me. "No, but I'll take you to someone who will." His hand gripped mine, and I jerked. An icy coin pressed against my palm. I opened my mouth, but he stopped me. "Khadija," he whispered.

A sharp wind pushed at my face, and I closed my eyes against it. When I opened them again, we stood in front of a stone house surrounded by woods. I wasn't sure where we were, and that terrified me more than anything. The only person I had ever trusted enough to take me anywhere with a coin had been Saul.

"She's waiting for you. I'll be right here when you're finished." Maalik finally looked at me. His eyes were soft with worry, but I couldn't tell what from.

Was he reconsidering dating me? Was I less attractive because of the sudden drop in my life expectancy? Or was it just the demon guts tangled in my hair?

I wanted to ask him a thousand questions, but a nervous urgency pulled my gaze back to the house. I let go of his hand and walked up to the door. It opened before I had a chance to knock. I looked back to Maalik for reassurance, and he nodded. I stepped inside.

While it had looked like an English cottage on the outside, inside was a much different story. Brightly colored silks hung from the ceiling. A few were pulled up and pinned to the walls, forming an entrance into a labyrinth of silky material. I moved through the maze with a familiar ease until I found her.

She was a soul, and an old one at that. It wasn't necessarily the way she looked, but the way she felt. Her eyes smiled warmly, like she had been expecting me, and I was right on time. Her eyes were all I could see from the cover of her scarf. Under the milky haze that all souls have, I could still tell she had an olive complexion.

She waved her hands, and I felt myself sway with their motion until I found myself seated on a cushion before her. The power she held over me set alarms off in my head, but I could do nothing to break free from her invisible leash.

"I know Grim can seem like a tyrant at times, but he really does mean well. He was very worried about us meeting. I'm sure you noticed," she laughed. Her voice was slow and inviting with an exotic accent, but the completeness of her power kept me rigid in my seat.

"Very few know of my existence here. Do you know the importance of my position?"

"No." I could only whisper, for fear my pulse would explode out of my throat.

"Of course not." She tilted her head to one side. "I did rather well creating you, and I know you will be the one who sets me free."

She laughed again at my confused expression. It was a bubbly, sweet sound that beckoned me to laugh with her, but all I could do was tremble.

"Grim has told you nothing? Then we have much to talk about. I am the one responsible for who Grim has become. I am the one who holds the beliefs of humanity so he can use them to his advantage. I am the one who made you," she finished poetically, her eyes sparkling.

Things were slowly falling into place and making more sense. I began to wonder how I had never questioned any of this before, and then I remembered that I had been created to serve, not ask questions. She was Grim's dirty little secret. The skeleton in his closet. She was who Maalik had been talking about back in Grim's office.

"How?" I whispered.

"When a faith is created, those who create it are not believers. How can they be, when they simply did what they had to, to ensure peace and harmony among their people? When those first believers open their hearts and truly give themselves to a faith, that is when gods are born. I am one of those first believers.

"When Grim found me, he could see for himself. That's why he kept me here, instead of taking me on to Firdaws Pardis in Jannah, the Islamic paradise. He showed me the great suffering of Eternity during the war, and he knew with all the compassion I carried that I would not refuse to help end it." Bitterness slipped into her voice, but then she sighed, and her tone went neutral again.

"The war did end, and I have stayed here in Limbo for a very long time, helping Grim contain the excess soul matter, but even a soul can grow weary and old if it stays too long in one place. I told Grim he needed to find another, but his pride blinds him. He doesn't want anyone else to know how he rules Eternity. It would make him vulnerable.

"I know my limitations. This will be the last year I can help him. If he doesn't find another soul to take my place, Eternity will be burdened by war again. Even now, I should not be here. I am not as strong as I once was. I can feel soul matter slipping away from me, and it will not be long before Eternity is faced with a new presence that is uninvited. It cannot be helped, and I pray it will not bring war."

"Is that what he has us doing? Looking for your replacement?" I was disgusted. Why wasn't Grim out looking for the soul himself? It was to ensure his reign of power. "Why me? Why Josie and Kevin and Coreen?"

"Not them, just you," she sighed. "The others were a distraction. There are some who do not approve of Grim creating reapers with the soul matter. They think it is too close to breaching the treaty. The only thing that keeps them from declaring war is the fact that the reapers are controlled as a working class and not respected as gods. If they knew that I made you unique, they would not be pleased.

"Grim is the only other who can feel the importance of a soul. I didn't tell him about you until very recently. I'm sure that's why he's so upset. He doesn't feel so special anymore, but it had to be done. He's too engrossed in the council dealings now. If he left to search for another soul, his absence would be noticed by all. I needed someone I could trust to find my successor. I trust you, Lana."

I could see how tired she was, just speaking to me, and wondered how she could possibly have the energy to hold all of Eternity together.

"You must be very careful," she whispered. "There are those who would wish you dead, even on the council. They would see you as a threat to their power. I don't doubt that Caim had help finding you."

"Coreen," I whispered. It wasn't that I had cared for her really, but rather that she had died because of me. Nausea punched me in the stomach.

Khadija's eyes softened. "Do not blame yourself for her death. She knew what you know now."

"She knew?"

"She and Grim were closer than they let on. She knew everything he knew."

And I thought I had felt bad before. Grim's lover had died on my ship, trying to protect me. How could I continue looking for the right soul, knowing everyone around me was in danger?

"Grim thought if he assigned several reapers to the task of finding the next soul that those who opposed him would not suspect any of the reapers were different or specially designed, but they are still aware that the soul he searches for is crucial to his reign. I have suggested that he declare to the council he has already found the needed soul. It will distract them so that you can search for the soul without fear of attack. You must hurry, Lana. We haven't much time, and I see much in your future that worries me. This will not be your greatest challenge, and if you are strong, it will not be your last."

"Who are you?" The question was too tempting not to ask.

"I am called the Princess of Quarish and the Pure One. My husband was the great prophet, and I, the first Muslim. You may call me Khadija." She nodded, dismissing me, and the force holding me in my seat vanished.

I stood and walked back through the silk maze. What else was there to say to her? Thanks for holding Eternity together. Thanks for making me special so I can be responsible for the deaths of all those around me. Thanks, but I'd rather be an underpaid peon. See you next time, that is, if I don't die first. Yeah, silence was my best bet.

As I was leaving, another thought dawned on me. She was my creator, not Grim. I'm not sure why, but something tightened in my chest. Where Grim had been my boss, she was my goddess. Part of me wanted to turn around and go back to ask where reapers went when they died, but I didn't. Maybe I was just afraid of her answer. Maybe I just didn't want to hear the truth I already knew.

Reapers were one of the few races without a real afterlife to call our own. We have no souls, so an afterlife wouldn't be of much use anyway. Yet, pride struck me all the same. We didn't have to invent our creator like the souls did. How ironic that we should be left without an afterlife, without souls, and without the privilege of even knowing our creator.

Maalik looked up anxiously as I emerged from Khadija's house. Panic clouded his expression. The tightness in my chest grew worse as I narrowed my gaze on him.

"How long have you known about her?"

"A month," he sighed. "Muhammad sent me. He thinks she is simply here to quietly assist and supervise Grim. It's been well over a thousand years. So I'm sure you can imagine his concern. That's why I was elected to the council. Khadija was his first wife, you know. Coreen was the only other who knew what Grim had done with her, until recently."

"How long have you known about me?"

"A week. You should really be thanking Khadija for your promotion. Grim wasn't happy when I explained to him how she had gifted you, but I had to make him understand the seriousness of her retirement."

"You were never really interested in me, were you? You were just keeping an eye on me for her."

It seemed petty to change the subject to something that could never measure up to the importance of what I had just learned, but our relationship, if you could call it that, felt like something I was more capable of understanding and discussing at the time.

"She never asked that of me." He sighed and reached out to grasp my shoulders. "But if she had, I would have been grateful for the excuse to be near you."

"I don't know what to think of all this right now." I wrapped my arms around myself and shivered.

"Let me take you home to get some rest." He made a face at the pulpy demon chunks still clinging to me, but then pulled me into his arms and rested his chin on my head anyway. "And a shower," he added.

Taking my hand, he pressed the coin between our palms once more, and whispered, "Morte."

The air thrashed around us, and then we were back in the elevator at Grim's office. The doors slid open just as the strange wind died off. We were on the main level.

Maalik's hand never left mine as he led me out of the building and toward my apartment. I blushed, almost embarrassed that I was letting him lead me around like a child. At the same time, though, it was comforting. From his worried face, I could tell he wasn't holding onto me possessively but protectively. The tightness in my chest eased away.

"I have a gift for you." He grinned, trying to hide his worry when he caught my stare. "It's at your apartment."

"How did you get in?"

"Gabriel was on his way out." A thread of bother was hidden in his tone.

"What is it?"

"You'll see when we get there." He laughed as he tugged me around the next corner. Like I didn't have enough questions buzzing through my head. At least this one was more pleasant to ponder on, or so I thought.

CHAPTER SIXTEEN

"Man is a dog's idea
of what God should be."
—Holbrook Jackson

"Well, this isn't exactly what I had in mind."

Two enormous black dogs were curled up on my couch, smashing the cushions beneath them flat. One of them lifted its head and bellowed out a welcome call as we entered my apartment. Maalik walked over and scratched the beast behind the ear.

"Aren't they perfect?" he asked cheerfully.

"Exactly what movies did you watch when you first got here?"

"What's wrong?" He frowned and looked back at the giant *gifts* he had bought for me. "Don't you like them?"

"Normally, when a guy gets his girlfriend a dog as a gift, it's a puppy. Normally, it's just one puppy. And normally, they make sure they are allowed to have them in their apartment first."

"I've already taken care of that."

"What?" I all but squeaked.

"I spoke to the complex manager, and there won't be a problem."

"Maalik, I don't want to seem ungrateful, but I don't want two giant dogs. This apartment is hardly big enough for me, and where are they supposed to, um, relieve themselves?"

"Well, first of all, they're not dogs, they're hellhounds. And I've already made sure they're housebroken. They can let themselves out to use the side lawn."

"Hellhounds? Isn't it illegal to have hellhounds in Limbo? Did you even read our laws before coming over here?"

"Yes, I read your laws. You have to have a special license for them, and I've already acquired that for you."

The nearest hound whimpered and rolled its sloppy tongue up the back of Maalik's hand.

"What's this really about?" I frowned and folded my arms.

Maalik looked down in defeat. I wasn't about to accept a gift this strange without a good reason, and he knew it.

"Coreen was supposed to protect you. Now, she can't. I need to know you're safe. Please accept the hellhounds. I'll even help take care of them," he pleaded with me.

I sighed and went to stand beside him. The hound farthest from us lifted its head to follow my movements, while the closer one beat its tail on the couch and nudged its wet nose under my hand. I reached out to the second hound, but it just gave me a sniff and turned away, as if it weren't any more pleased about the situation than I was.

"What are their names?" I decided I had done enough fighting for one day. Maalik's face lit up with relief.

"They're not named yet. I just bought them from Hades today. Technically, they're still puppies. I guess I got one thing right," he laughed.

"You mean they'll get bigger than this?" I raised an eyebrow.

"Not by much. Why don't you go ahead and name them."

I thought about it for a minute. I'd never had a pet before. It seemed like a huge responsibility to give something a name that it would have for the rest of its life, especially if it that something was immortal. It made me wonder if it had been Grim or Khadija who had named me.

"Are they male or female?"

"One of each."

"Perfect. Saul and Coreen," I announced.

The second dog tilted its head when it heard Coreen's name. It had to be the female. The name seemed even more fitting, seeing her attitude. Maybe I could just pretend that reapers were reincarnated into hellhounds. It sounded better than the alternative anyway.

"Saul and Coreen," Maalik repeated. "Good. I have more business to take care of this evening, but I'll be waiting for you when you get back tomorrow. Be careful." He pulled me around to face him and gave me a stern look. "I mean it."

I pulled away from him and smiled. "Hey, this is my job. Get used to it. It's not like I have a choice. It's the price we pay."

He gave me a forced grin and planted a kiss on my forehead. Just when I thought I had some clue about him, I realized I didn't. What happened to the big talking angel who dangerously flirted with me every chance he got? And who was this sweet, timid guy buying me puppies?

Maalik brushed a blood crusted curl out of my face and then turned to leave.

"What do they eat?" I asked as he reached the door.

"There's a bag of food in your coat closet. Cerberus Chow. Just follow the directions on the bag," he quickly answered and ducked out the door.

I smiled and scratched Saul under the chin. Maybe this wouldn't be so bad, after all.

I opened my closet to find a four-hundred-pound bag of dog food. The top was already torn open, and two dishes the size of punch bowls rested on the shelf above my crumpled-up jackets and scarves. The bag read: feed two to three gallons each morning and evening. It wasn't going to last long. Cerberus, Hades' legendary hellhound, graced the front of the bag, looking fierce and mighty.

Saul bounced over to where I stood and nudged me in the back of the knee with his muzzle.

"Okay! Okay," I laughed, taking down the dishes.

I filled them with the instructed two-gallon minimum and placed them beside the refrigerator where I noticed a note stuck to the freezer door. Gabriel's sloppy handwriting let me know something had come up and he had to cancel our date for Purgatory. I laughed to myself, knowing he had written *date* just to piss off Maalik.

Saul crunched away at his dinner and had his dish almost clean before Coreen sauntered over to join him. I dumped another gallon of food into his dish and sat cross-legged on my kitchen table to get a better look at my new companions.

They were almost identical, except for Coreen being slightly leaner. But with her attitude, it wasn't going to be too difficult to tell them apart. Saul finished licking out his dish and turned to find me. He seemed comfortable and aware that he would be staying with me in the tiny apartment. I couldn't say the same for Coreen just yet, but who knew.

Saul spotted me on top of the table and in an effortless movement leapt up to join me. The table squeaked under our combined weight as he made himself comfortable and dropped his huge head in my lap. Coreen snorted at us and made her way back to the couch, just what I would expect from her if she were a reincarnation of the real Coreen. I'd give her some time.

CHAPTER SEVENTEEN

*"Most of us spend the first six days of the week
sowing wild oats, then we go to church on Sunday
and pray for a crop failure."*
—Fred Allen

"Lana?" Josie's confused voice echoed through my head, pulling me out of a hazy dream filled with giant cats and dogs tangled up in silk curtains. Saul's giant tongue lapped up the side of my face, smashing the strange dream into my even stranger reality.

"Oh, yuck!" I rolled away from him.

"Lana!" Josie shrieked.

A low growl that shook the walls followed, and I remembered Coreen on the couch.

"Coming!" I shouted and leapt out of bed, throwing the covers over Saul, who had insisted on sleeping next to me. He untangled himself and bound after me into the kitchen.

Coreen had Josie backed up against my kitchen table. Drool spilled from her jaws as she snapped and snarled at who she thought was an intruder. Maybe she didn't like me, but at least she knew how to do her job.

"Down girl!" I shouted, feeling silly that I didn't know what else to say. Coreen's growling ceased almost immediately. She straightened her posture and pranced back to the couch with a satisfied sniff.

"When did you decide to get a dog? Dogs?" Josie asked, seeing Saul behind me.

"I didn't. Maalik did," I yawned and ran a hand through my curls, still damp with slobber, before glancing at the clock above my kitchen sink. It was five in the morning.

"What are you doing here so early?"

"I wanted to talk," she began and sucked in a ragged breath of air. "I couldn't sleep. I've been up all night."

"Oh."

"So, Maalik got you two dogs?" Her stiff posture loosened as she unclenched her fists.

"Actually, they're hellhounds. Want some coffee?"

"Sure."

Josie was already dressed for work, but we didn't have to be there for another two hours. I wasn't about to change out of my comfy pajamas just yet.

"Don't you have to have a license for hellhounds?"

"Already taken care of," I answered over my shoulder as I scooped some coffee grounds into a filter.

"He must really like you, huh?"

"I guess. We'll see how they work out today."

I turned on the coffeemaker and joined her at my dinky kitchen table. After three hundred years, you would think I would have nicer furniture. I decided to put that at the top of my next shopping list, if I lived long enough to go shopping again.

"Kevin stayed the night at my place. He's still asleep. I'll go back up and wake him later." Josie pulled her knees up to her chest and hooked the heels of her boots on the edge of the chair. Her robe fanned out around her like a skirt. How she made it look so good, I'd never know. The same thing on me looked like a garbage bag trying to pass for a poncho.

"Yesterday was something else," I said.

"Something else?" Her brow creased. "I'm not sure Grim has enough coin to make this promotion worth risking our lives. We don't have souls. It's not like we get to go off to some afterlife if we die."

"Right. All we have to look forward to is a monument in the middle of some crummy park." I sighed, remembering Saul's memorial service.

Grim had a statue made of my deceased mentor, wearing his cowboy hat and all. He had been so thrilled when he collected his first rancher. The soul had given him the hat as a souvenir. I couldn't remember ever seeing Saul without it afterward. He was the reason for my collection of old western movies. I wished he had lived long enough to watch one with me.

"Why do you suppose Grim picked us instead of some of the more experienced reapers?" Josie folded her arms over the table.

I opened my mouth and then closed it. I was almost positive I wasn't supposed to share what I knew. Grim had threatened to vote Maalik off the council, something that had never been done before, and Grim didn't make empty threats. Maalik trusted me. Khadija trusted me. And Josie trusted me, too. It wasn't that I didn't trust her. But the second I thought about telling her the truth, my palms started sweating.

"Are you all right?" Josie tucked a tuft of hair behind her ear and slid her legs back under the table.

"Yeah." I pulled my hands into my lap.

"What's wrong?"

"Nothing."

The coffeemaker sputtered out the last of its brew, and Josie stood. She dug through my cupboard and found a pair of mugs with colorful, apocalyptic scenes hand-painted on them. Gabriel had given them to me a few years back as an apology gift for puking on my couch, a piece of furniture that needed to be replaced even more than the table.

"Maybe you could ask Horus what's going on." Josie filled her cup to the brim but left enough room for sugar and cream in mine.

"I don't think Horus knows anything," I said, taking the mug from her. "He probably traded his services in exchange for extra souls. That last one shouldn't have gone to Duat, but you saw how quickly Grim ordered us to take it there."

I took a sip of my coffee and then sloshed some down my top as Saul rammed into my leg. He had somehow managed to flip his food dish on top of his head and stumbled toward my voice until he found me.

"Shit!" I yanked the scalding top away from my skin. "Hold on, Saul." I set my mug down and pulled the dish off his head. His tail thumped on the floor as I opened the coat closet to get his food. Coreen sat by the fridge, waiting for her breakfast, too.

"Saul?" Josie smiled at me. "You're kidding. What about the other one?"

I smiled and placed the food dishes on the floor.

"No," she laughed. "You didn't!"

"Yup, that's Coreen. I like to think that they've been reincarnated as hellhounds. It makes me feel better anyway."

"Whatever works, I guess." She smiled, looking better than she had when she first arrived.

I grabbed a dishtowel and pressed it to my coffee-stained top. "So, are you going to be okay working with Horus again?"

"I don't even know what to think of him right now, and Apollo's back at Mount Olympus already. You know, Kevin's young, and a wreck at the moment, but I think it'd be easier to just date him," she laughed.

"I wonder who Grim will appoint him to, now that Coreen's... gone." Dead just didn't sound right. We were supposed to be immortal, but like most immortals, if you didn't have a religious following, *i.e.* a fan base, there were plenty of loopholes to fall to your death through.

"I don't know." Josie shifted uncomfortably. "I should go wake him up." She finished her coffee and stood. "I'll be back in an hour."

"I'll be ready," I sighed.

She nodded and slipped out of my apartment.

I pulled my coffee-soaked tank top over my head and went to get dressed while Saul and Coreen finished their breakfast.

My bloodied outfit from the day before was still balled up in the corner of my bathroom floor. I decided to wear something less expensive this time, opting for a pair of worn jeans and a black tank top. If I were going to fight hordes of demons, I was going to be comfortable while doing it. I slipped my work robe over everything before fixing my hair. Once again, I chose convenience over style and pulled my curls back in a ponytail.

Josie wouldn't be back for another forty minutes, so I passed the time by cleaning and sharpening my scythe. I needed to invest in a new weapon, one better suited for warding off demons, but the scythe would have to do for now.

Saul and Coreen were waiting obediently by the front door when Josie returned with Kevin. He looked refreshed, and not at all like the lost little boy I had seen the day before. Coreen jumped up to give him a quick sniff and then took her place next to Saul.

"Hellhounds. Nice." Kevin smiled.

The hounds followed me out of the apartment. I knew they were only puppies, but having them close gave me a new sense of security, and I liked it. We all managed to crowd into the elevator, along with one frightened nephilim who Saul took the liberty of sniffing out.

"G-good doggie," the nephilim quaked. His wings twitched as he wedged himself into the corner of the elevator.

I didn't bother apologizing or assuring him that Saul meant no harm. If I started doing that, I would be doing it all day. No, thank you. Saul finally decided everything was okay and sat back down. Five floors later, the doors pinged open, and the startled half-breed hurried ahead of us.

We strolled outside and headed toward Grim's office. The hounds didn't bother too many people on the way, only those close enough to be potential threats. It was entertaining to watch them. I wondered what Grim would think of Maalik's gifts.

"**O**h, dear," Ellen muttered as we entered the office. "Lana, Grim's waiting for you in his office. Josie, Kevin, and the dogs can wait in the conference room."

"They're hellhounds, and I don't think they're going to let me out of their sight, sorry." I sighed, annoyed that I had ended up apologizing for them, after all.

"Oh, well, okay then. Go on in."

I opened Grim's door, and Saul and Coreen followed me inside.

"What now?" Grim groaned.

"Meet Saul and Coreen, the team's newest members." I plopped down in one of his uncomfortable chairs and kicked my boots up on his desk so he could get a good view of the guts caked in their treads. So it was rude, but so was leaving me in the dark and expecting me to do his dirty work.

Grim ground his teeth. "This is Maalik's idea of a joke I'm sure."

"Seeing as the job you've assigned me to puts me in constant contact with the nastiest of demons, I think they're a perfect addition."

"Stupid girl," he spat.

A low growl came from Saul. Grim glared at the hound and then looked back at me. "Don't you think I would much rather be out there myself looking for the right soul? Every move I make is being watched. Do you have any idea what could happen if I left Limbo City with Seth here? I was forced to put him on the council. He would be waging war against us right now if I hadn't. Being trapped here is the only thing holding him back, yet he still conspires against me.

"My secret, that you unfortunately had to learn of yesterday, is how I maintain peace in Eternity. By keeping that crucial information to myself and few others, I have ensured that all the gods abide by the treaty regulations and maintain their designated boundaries."

"If my position is so important, why wasn't I one of those privileged enough to know the truth?" I pulled my feet off his desk and leaned forward, eager to hear his answer.

"You're three hundred years old," he snorted. "A child! A loose cannon. Khadija should have consulted me before gifting you."

"If you had listened to her in the first place, she wouldn't have."

"You think you have all the answers, do you? Do you think it gets easier each time I am forced to reveal this information, knowing that if placed in the wrong hands it could mean death for millions?" His voice broke, and he reached up to rub both hands over his face and through his hair.

I remembered what Khadija had said about him and Coreen. Guilt slithered in uninvited. "Do you think I desire slaughter any more than you do?" I sighed.

"You weren't here to see the war. You couldn't possibly know what it was like."

"Maybe not, but I do know how loss feels, and I'm sure the war was full of that." I tried to relax in the stiff chair. "Look, Grim, I'm not any more excited about me having this job than you are, but Khadija is right. Even I can see that she's growing weak. I have to find another soul to take her place."

"I hope you do." He shook his head and pushed a black folder across his desk.

I flipped it open. Inside, a close-up of an elderly woman stared back at me. A dozen pages of background and family history were paper-clipped behind the photo.

"You want the truth?" Grim sighed. "Horus has agreed to work with the Fates and pick out souls of old Egyptian descent. As long as I send more souls their way, they won't ask any questions about how I'm going to use the one I keep to solve our problem in the Sea of Eternity. They're that desperate. Their followers have dwindled so much that it almost cost them their position on the council. If that had happened, Seth would have most definitely found the army he needed to wage a war. Right now, our best bet is to find the replacement soul within the Egyptian faith."

"If the soul we're seeking is just Khadija's replacement, how do you plan to fix the problem of Caim running loose in the sea?"

"Here's another truth for you. Caim isn't the problem. Don't misunderstand," he added. "He's a big part of it, but the real problem is an island. It was discovered two weeks ago by Coreen. Caim has been using it to set up camp and hide his legions. The island is a byproduct of soul matter that Khadija is too weak to hold. That's why I understand, even more than you, how important it is that she retires."

"What will be done with the island?"

"Let me worry about that." He folded his arms and pressed his lips together into a frustrated line, clearly regretting telling me as much as he already had.

I crossed my legs and rested the folder against my knee. "This soul we're going after today, if it's not the right one, will we be delivering it by coin or ship? I really don't like the thought of losing another reaper."

"Nor do I, but Anubis is aiding Horus today, and I'm curious to find out if Caim's attacks are random or directed specifically at your team."

I nodded and glanced back at the folder.

"Missouri?" I read aloud. "This one looks like it might be easier than the last." Then I took another look. "Heart attack? I hate those. They always seem to see you before they die and reach out to plead for help. It's unnerving." I frowned as I read over the rest of the details.

Grim stood and walked around his desk. "They were never my favorite either. Let's join the others in the conference room. I have some news to share with all of you."

Josie and Kevin had made themselves comfortable while they waited. Empty creamer cups and sugar packets were piled around their coffee mugs. Josie had her legs stretched over the seat next to her and was so engrossed in friendly conversation that she hardly noticed us enter the room. I remembered what she had said about dating Kevin and wondered if she hadn't been joking, after all. Her gaze fell on Grim, and she sat up straighter, letting her smile fade away into a neutral expression.

I leaned against the wall behind me, still stiff from the uncomfortable office chair. It was entirely possible that Grim had picked it out of an S&M catalog.

"I have a quick announcement, and then I'll let Lana go over the details for today's catch," Grim said. "Kevin, your new apprenticeship will be under Lana."

I jerked away from the wall. "What?"

"Kevin and I discussed this yesterday, and we both agreed on the matter. This could be a great learning experience for him, and I hear he did rather well yesterday. Not many apprentices would have made it through a battle of that nature on their first assignment."

"So you demote him from a second-generation mentor to an eighth?" I argued.

Kevin gave me a desperate look and stood. "I don't care if you're an eighth-generation. I can learn more from you than anyone else, and you had your apprenticeship under Saul, the same as Coreen," he added.

"I've never had an apprentice, and I haven't even taken the required class to be eligible for one. I'm sure there's someone more qualified." I turned to Grim, but his stony expression was all too familiar.

"I've made my decision, and after this assignment is over, you can take the appropriate mentoring course at the academy. I'll even cover the tuition." He gave me a pleased sneer and walked out of the room.

I closed my eyes and counted to ten. When I looked up, Josie and Kevin glanced at each other cautiously. The jerks. They had already known. I slapped the black folder down on the table and pulled out a chair, wondering if I was going to be even half as good at this as Coreen had been.

"We're going to Missouri," I said before either of them could start in about Kevin's new placement. I'd deal with that later. "Old lady. Heart attack. Around nine-thirty. At her home or nearby."

I tore open the envelope stapled to the folder and dumped three coins into my palm. Josie and Kevin both took one and glanced at the paperwork to find the exact coordinates.

"Sedalia?" Josie smiled. "I've been there before. This should be easy. It's a small town."

"Let's just get this over with."

CHAPTER EIGHTEEN

*"God enters by a private door
into every individual."*
—Ralph Waldo Emerson

Joy Henderson lived by herself in a big two-story house across from Liberty Park. It was mid-autumn, so she was outside, bent over flowerbeds of bright blooms and sculpted hedges. A few hummingbirds buzzed around a feeder while a small herd of cats lazily watched from the lawn.

There were some things I'd never understand about humans. Like why old ladies decided to feed all the neighborhood felines once their spouses died.

"Let's keep an eye on her from the park for now," I suggested.

Josie secured her quiver over her shoulder. "I'll take a look around and see if there are any demons lurking about. I don't know how they found us last time, but I wouldn't be surprised if they show up here, too." She nocked an arrow on her bow before taking off around the block.

Saul tilted his head back and gave the air above a sniff. The hair along his back sprang up into a shaggy mohawk as he let out a warning growl and turned to rush deeper into the park.

"Keep an eye on our catch," I ordered Kevin before running after Saul.

Coreen looked back at the woman and whimpered before following me into the park. When we finally caught up to Saul, he was standing under a tree, sniffing the ground. I scanned the branches for what had caught his attention, but there was nothing to see. Behind the tree stretched an old bridge, leading to an island where two little boys sat fishing. A wooden cross dangled from one's neck. They were safe.

Saul nudged my thigh with his nose, a piece of crumpled paper clenched between his teeth. I unfolded it and found that it was an envelope. There were several more littering the ground. I gathered them up and quickly read who they were addressed to. None of the names were the same, but all the addresses were on Third Street, the street running between Mrs. Henderson's house and the park. Not sure what it meant, I turned around and headed back toward Kevin.

"Demons?" he asked as I approached.

"I don't think so."

Saul periodically tilted his nose up, trying to grasp a smell that might prove more useful, while Coreen's eyes never left our catch.

"Nothing," Josie reported as she joined us.

Our catch hadn't moved from her garden. I grabbed Josie's wrist and flipped it around to look at her watch. Nine-twenty. Ten minutes until the fatal heart attack. Everything was going smoothly, and then the mailman rounded the corner.

Saul let out a soft growl. The man paused, only for a second, and then continued down the sidewalk. Had he heard Saul? A human shouldn't have heard a hellhound. And then I noticed that he wasn't stopping at any of the other houses. Something was off. He turned and made his way up Mrs. Henderson's sidewalk.

"Good morning," he called out to her.

"Oh, good morning to you," she answered and went back to her flowers.

"I just love this weather. Don't you?"

Mrs. Henderson turned around again and smiled, seeming surprised that he was stopping in the middle of his route to engage in conversation with her. She wasn't the only one. Coreen anxiously looked from me to our catch. Something was wrong. Something was very wrong.

"The mail," I whispered. "Oh, shit."

"What?" Josie turned to me.

"The mailman is possessed. Shoot him. Now."

"What?" she asked again, baffled.

"Shoot him!" I shrieked as Mrs. Henderson slumped over her flowers and threw a hand to her chest. The mailman jumped at the sound of my voice and then sprang on our catch, pushing a knee into her stomach as he wrapped his hands around her throat.

Two of Josie's arrows darted through the air. At first, it looked like they had pierced the man's body, but then a yellow vapor blew off his back, taking the arrows with it.

A painful wail sounded as the vapor materialized into a more demonic version of one of the wicked witches flying monkeys. It took flight, frantically flapping its webbed wings until Josie pierced one last arrow through its chest. It screeched, clawing at the air above, and then vanished in a burst of flames.

The startled mailman sat up and puked over the bushes, one of the milder symptoms of a dry exorcism, one without the aid of religious ceremony. Mrs. Henderson sucked in her last breath as he turned around.

"Someone help!" he cried out. Then he leaned down and began CPR on the poor woman.

I gagged and turned away. This was going to be nice explaining to her on the other side. Her last kiss was vomit-flavored, from a charming, yet schizophrenic mailman, who'd tried to strangle her and then save her.

"Come on, Kevin. This is your second day on the job, and you haven't gotten to pull a soul out on your own yet," I said.

We walked across the street and stood over the pitiful scene. One of the neighbors had heard the mailman's plea for help, and sirens were growing closer. As soon as Kevin touched Mrs. Henderson's hand, she all but sprang out of her body, desperate to get away from her rescuer.

"Where are your manners, young man?" she shrieked. Then she noticed her body, still limp on the lawn. "Oh! Sweet Jesus! I can't die now. I have a casserole in the oven!"

"It's okay, ma'am," Kevin assured her as he pulled her away from the house.

The paramedics had finally arrived and moved the mailman aside. A young man in uniform bent over her body and then reeled back at the smell of vomit on her breath.

"Get the mask! Quick!" he shouted in between violent gags.

Kevin, the soul, and I joined Josie and my hounds across the street. I half expected more demons, but was nonetheless thrilled when they didn't arrive.

"Mission accomplished." Kevin beamed.

"Well done." Josie smiled and gave him a high five. Mrs. Henderson gave a bug-eyed gasp.

"Let's get out of here." I tightened my scythe over my shoulder and found my coin.

Once again, Grim briefly graced us with his presence to inform us of what I already knew. This was not the soul we were looking for. But I did manage to stop him before he stormed out of the conference room.

"So what do our next paychecks look like?"

"Excuse me?" Grim turned around and stood in the doorway, staring at me as if I had just asked about the price of souls in China.

"Promotions usually include larger paychecks, and we've encountered a significantly larger number of demons than our fellow reapers. Don't tell me what we're doing isn't worth more than the crummy commissions we've been earning for the past century." I folded my arms and glared at him.

"Of course not! I've just been too distracted to go over the minor details. I think we can manage a thirty percent raise. How does that sound?"

"Thirty percent?" I laughed. "That's how much this soul means to you?"

"Forty, then," he grumbled, giving me a threatening glare. "That's more than fair."

"I guess it will have to do." Josie joined the conversation.

Yes, power in numbers. Kevin was still too new to care much about his income yet. He hadn't even received his first check.

"Is it safe to assume that when we find this soul, we'll receive bonuses?" Kevin folded his arms over the conference table. I'd underestimated his team spirit.

Grim tried his best to keep a neutral face, but his cheeks flushed, giving him away. He glared at me. I could guess what he was thinking. Two days, and I was already becoming a negative influence on a potentially brilliant reaper. Maybe he would change his mind about Kevin's future training, after all. I smiled.

"Of course," Grim said, and then he lowered his voice. "Now do your damned jobs and take this soul to Duat. Horus and Anubis are waiting downstairs for you."

He turned to leave again, but Mrs. Henderson latched on to his arm. The little old lady had been so still and quiet that we had almost forgotten she was there.

"Duat? What's Duat? There's no Duat in the Bible! Where are you people taking me? Oh! Sweet Mary! Mother of Jesus, help me!" Mrs. Henderson fell to her knees and squeezed Grim's hand between her own as she began sobbing the Lord's Prayer.

"Someone get her off me," Grim growled.

Saul whimpered at my feet, bothered by the wailing. Kevin moved to help first. I think pulling the soul from her body made him feel somehow responsible for her.

A crazed dove fluttered through the doorway past Grim and attempted a landing on the conference table, but instead stumbled over itself and rolled off the far end with a pained coo. Holly Spirit stood and dusted loose feathers off the sleeves of her robe. Her face flushed.

"I got a 911 page from Mary. What seems to be the problem?"

"This is all part of the amendment Isis ordered last month. If I remember correctly, you signed it," Grim answered.

"I did, but I didn't realize good Christian souls were going to be terrorized in the process." She folded her arms and frowned at Grim.

Holly didn't take crap from anyone. Several years after the feminist movement launched in the human realm, she'd led her own feminist movement in Heaven. Eventually, she even won over her father, who nominated her for a position on the council. The running joke was that he only did it to get her out of Heaven for a while so he could breathe.

"Who are you? And what do you think you're doing bargaining with my soul?" Mrs. Henderson loosened her grip on Grim and twisted around to examine Holly.

"I'm Holly Spirit. I'm here to help you."

"You mean the Holy Spirit?" The woman looked confused.

"No, I mean Holly. Your scriptures are flawed, but not so badly that my father has found the time to correct them," she huffed. "Christ, I am getting so tired of explaining this to people."

"How can you call yourself the Holy Spirit and then take the Lord's name in vain?"

"It's Holly, got it? And Christ is my brother. I'll use his name however I want."

"No, no, this is all wrong." Mrs. Henderson curled herself into a ball on the floor and began sobbing to herself.

Holly rolled her eyes. "Grim, I don't think Isis had this in mind when she ordered that amendment. Have Meng Po mix a tea for her or something. I don't want to be getting emergency pages from Mary and Jesus every time you traumatize a soul. My schedule is busy enough."

"That's a great idea," Grim agreed. "Ellen! Get Meng up here now."

"On it," Ellen answered from the next room.

"Thank you," Holly sighed. In a blink, she turned back into a dove and fluttered out of the room. Coreen watched anxiously. I decided I would have to get her some chew toys. Maybe she would warm up to me then.

Kevin stayed close to Mrs. Henderson, trying to comfort her as we waited for Lady Meng. After twenty minutes, she finally arrived.

"Ah, look like you find more than one use for me, young reaper," she cackled at Grim.

"I'm just trying to make sure you earn your position on the council," he countered.

Meng smiled, multiplying the wrinkles on her face until she looked like an expired potato. "I am pleased to." She gave a bow.

A little Chinese girl peeked into the room. She held a tray of teacups that rattled in her tiny hands.

"Come," Meng said.

The girl entered the room and kneeled, lifting the tray up to her master, only to find herself eye to eye with Saul. She trembled, rattling the tray, until Meng stilled her with a sharp smack from the fan dangling off her wrist.

Meng examined the tray carefully before lifting the lid off a wooden box and scooping a variety of herbs into a cup. Then she filled the cup with steaming water.

"Sit her up," she ordered Kevin.

He took Mrs. Henderson by the shoulders and lifted her. She didn't seem as afraid of Meng as she had been of Holly. Although Meng came from the Chinese hell, it was hard to find her withered frame intimidating, if you were a fresh soul anyway. Everyone else knew what she was capable of.

Mrs. Henderson took the cup from her and sipped its contents in between shuddering sobs. At first, nothing happened, and I began to wonder if old lady Meng was really as good as everyone made her out to be. But then, Mrs. Henderson sat up straight and dropped the tea, scattering soggy herbs over the carpet. Her hair shifted from gray to dark brown, then black as her curls uncoiled themselves and grew past her shoulders. Her features lengthened, and her skin darkened. In a matter of seconds, Mrs. Henderson had transformed into a young Egyptian man.

"How you feel now?" Meng asked.

"I am ready to meet Anubis," he answered bravely.

"So you shall." Meng nodded to her servant girl, who quickly gathered the abandoned teacup and hurried out of the room. Lady Meng followed her out.

"Well, you should get going." Grim turned to me. "Horus and Anubis are probably wondering what's taking so long."

Kevin didn't seem as compelled to touch the soul now that it was a man. This wasn't something you learned about at the Reaper Academy. Peeling away past lives was reserved for very few deities. Reapers weren't typically present for such activities. I knew it was a first for me anyway.

"Follow me," I said.

Josie and Kevin helped the soul to his feet and followed me out of the conference room with the hounds trailing behind. We filed into the elevator.

"Did you see that child soul?" Josie asked as the doors closed.

"How could I miss her?" I had never seen a child soul in Limbo before. The Fates had strict rules on what kind of souls were allowed to work in the factory. *No children* was near the top of the list, along with *no martyrs,* after the strike incident.

Josie squeezed my arm. "Jenni retrieved her last week. She said Grim took her before she could deliver her to her afterlife. He said he had other plans."

"So Jenni finally got her license for China?"

"Yeah, but don't you think it's a little odd that Grim would allow Meng to take a child soul as a servant? The Fates are probably having a fit."

"Something tells me Grim would give Meng just about anything she asked for. She's not on the council because he likes her. There's something he must want from her."

"That woman's vile." Josie shook her head.

When the elevator doors opened, Horus and Anubis were waiting for us.

"Let's get this show on the sea," Anubis laughed, tossing a robe to our soul.

Walking to the harbor would be simple enough. Our catch would almost look like another Egyptian deity. Only those who looked closely would be able to see the ashy haze that marked him as a soul. The problem was, we all knew too well that Seth would have plenty of eyes watching.

CHAPTER NINETEEN

"Religion is the fashionable
substitute for belief."
—Oscar Wilde

"You see anyone overly interested back there?" Horus gripped the deck railing and glared back at the city, a mere sliver of land fading behind a thick fog in the distance.

"No, but that doesn't mean we should let our guard down." I squeezed the handle of my scythe.

Josie had hurried off to our cabin to fill a second and third quiver. After finding herself empty-handed when Coreen was taken, she was determined not to let it happen again. That and she was still avoiding Horus.

Kevin made sure our soul was comfortable, while Anubis kept watch up front.

"Great job on the ship, by the way." I ran my hand over the new railing. There wasn't a trace of blood on the deck floor, and the damaged woodwork had been repaired so well, not a single flaw could be found.

"It was the least we could do," Horus said.

"So, Wosyet decide to stay in Duat?"

"No. The Fates won't talk to me. The only thing they despise more than dealing with other deities, is dealing with men in general. Grim made sure of that. Sure, they support him, but not out of admiration. What do you think would happen to their factory if Grim had the council sign an amendment to allow another soul insertion business? They're already upset about Meng trying to alter their purification methods, not to mention the child soul Grim gave to her without their approval."

"I see."

"Wosyet decided to stay in Limbo this time. No one will miss her in Duat," he laughed. "I'm sure Josie is glad for her absence."

"Well, we have no use for her out here." I cleared my throat and folded my arms over the railing.

Horus bit his lower lip and took a step closer to me. "I hate that there is all this tension between Josie and me."

"I know." I looked away from him. This was not a conversation I wanted to have.

"I know there aren't any laws restricting us from having a public relationship, but it's still frowned on by many."

"Like Seth?"

"It's not that I care what he thinks. I just don't want anything bad to happen to Josie because of me. You understand, don't you?"

"I think I do." I smiled softly. I felt the same way about having her on the team.

"Maybe you could talk to her?"

"Yeah, I don't think so." I laughed. "I don't go nosing around in Josie's business, and she doesn't nose around in mine. I plan on keeping it that way."

"I understand." He sighed and rested his arms on the railing next to me. "If only I could get her to hold still long enough to talk to her."

Josie emerged from our cabin with three quivers packed full of arrows. She had her bow and another larger one tucked under her arm. She looked up, and her eyes paused on the few inches of railing between our arms. I started to move back and stopped myself. Josie knew better than to suspect anything between Horus and me.

"Where's Kevin?" she asked.

"With the soul. His first one-on-one," I laughed. "He should be finished by now."

"Good. I want to give him his first lesson in archery. I know he's your apprentice and all, but I figured since you aren't too thrilled about having him, I would help you out and teach him a few things." She shrugged, forgetting that her arms were full, and dropped the bows.

"That's not a bad idea. We can always use another long-range," I said.

"Yeah. Good, then." She snatched up the bows and nodded politely at Horus before hurrying away to find Kevin.

Horus let out a slow sigh. "She likes him."

"I don't know." I shrugged.

"That wasn't a question."

"Whatever you say." I frowned and glanced over his shoulder. A pair of black birds were following us. Except, these birds had faces and breasts.

"Harpies."

"What?" Horus followed my gaze. Light shot out of his eye, and the falcon I had seen the day before dove out of the clouds.

Coreen and Saul appeared at my feet. They growled at the bird. Two black jackals followed Anubis as he joined us. They were his animal to call, the way the falcon was Horus's. Their snouts were narrower, and their bodies leaner than the hounds, but their bite was twice as bad.

Even though Grim and Anubis were old friends, the council still refused to grant the god extended privileges in Limbo City. If they allowed him the right to call his animal on neutral ground, they would have to allow it for all the gods. It was a recipe for chaos. Yeah, I know I bend the rules, but some just aren't worth the risk.

"I saw your light," Anubis shouted to his brother.

"It's all right. Keep watch up front." Horus's eyes never moved from the Harpies.

Anubis turned and rushed back to the front deck. The Harpies split apart when they saw the falcon. They distanced themselves, hoping to stall us from attacking.

Horus signaled his falcon, and it darted for the closest hag. The Harpy slowed her flight, while her partner sped up, causing the falcon to dive at the other. They switched again. Horus frowned, and the light in his eye flashed twice, signaling the bird. This time, it stayed on course.

When the first Harpy neared, she drew a sword. It was no match for the falcon, but she pressed onward, piercing through his wing as he snapped through her middle. She fell to the sea with a shriek, and the falcon swooped around, abandoning a good meal to stop the second Harpy.

Her features sharpened as she closed in on our ship. Sticky, black eyes glared out of her shallow face, while spit as dark and thick as tar leaked from her mouth and dripped down her chin. She was an assassin of Caim's. I had no doubt that he'd sent the hags to scope out our ship and see if any more deities were lying in wait. But why was he targeting our ship? We had defeated him twice now. If he were hunting for souls, he should have been going after ships he thought he could take, and ones carrying more souls than we were.

I just didn't want to believe that he knew about the soul Grim had us looking for. He couldn't know unless someone directly associated with the council had been making contact with him. How could a demon in exile know what, when, and where?

The falcon covered the distance with a powerful thrust of wings, snapping through the Harpy's legs and jerking her flight to a halt, like a pigeon being sucked in by a jet engine. A strangled cry slipped from her before the bird reached up with his talons and tore off her winged arms. He flipped her torso over his head and swallowed it whole before ascending back above the clouds.

"We should keep watch on all sides of the ship. There might be more." Horus's eye faded back to its normal coffee-brown.

I went to find Josie and Kevin. They would have to stand watch, too. I found them at the head of the ship with

Anubis. Josie grabbed Kevin's elbows and maneuvered him into the correct position with the bow. He squinted down the length of his arm at the arrow resting above.

"Did Horus take care of the Harpies?" Josie asked.

"Yeah, but maybe you two should practice on the north side of the ship. I think it's obvious now that Caim could attack from any angle."

"Sure, no problem." Josie grabbed up the quivers and led Kevin around the deck. Anubis's jackals had vanished like the falcon, but he still maintained a steady watch over the sea.

"So, were those the dogs that everyone swears by?" I asked.

Ancient Egyptians would take oaths and swear by the dog in honor of Anubis. They would even bury their deceased canines in special tombs dedicated to him.

"I suppose," he smiled, still gazing over the sea. "Would you swear by your hounds?"

"I don't know them that well yet, but they've been trusty so far."

"I don't think Caim will attack again. By now, I'm sure he knows I'm here. When his Harpies don't return, he'll retreat, saving his legions for the final battle."

"Let's keep an eye out, just in case."

"Horus has got that one covered," he laughed.

We made it to the gates of Duat without any more surprises. Osiris and Isis were waiting for us. They eagerly accepted the soul and escorted him away like a favored grandchild. Horus turned to the rest of us and smiled.

"You have no other business to attend to, I assume. Why don't you stay and observe the ceremony? It doesn't happen often these days, and it really is a treat to see." He eyed Josie hopefully.

"I insist," Anubis added, trying to help his brother out.

"Sounds like fun." I nodded in agreement.

Josie glared at me, but I knew better. Who wouldn't be excited about an opportunity to visit the Hall of Two Truths and witness the Weighing of the Hearts ceremony? It was like witnessing a planetary alignment and happened just about as often.

"Follow me." Horus led us through the gates and inside the temple of Osiris.

It was a modest place, resembling the deteriorated tombs of Egypt with fading hieroglyphics spanning the walls. It wasn't until we reached the entrance to the main hall that we saw any signs of remodeling.

A small office hid in the corner, just outside the Hall of Two Truths. Horus ushered us inside, where the goddess Ammit sat behind a desk, painting her nails.

"Oh! Hi." She blushed and stuffed the bottle of polish in a drawer.

"Aren't you going to the ceremony?" Horus asked.

"Yeah, though I hardly know why. That soul doesn't look nervous at all. I doubt I'll be needed. I'm just waiting for someone to come and watch the phones."

Ammit was the demon-goddess who devoured the hearts of the unworthy, dooming them to a lengthy sentence in Duat's more colorful regions. Since the number of souls who passed through Duat had decreased so drastically, she had been given the position of secretary in the temple office. Still, on the rare occasion a soul did come through, she was required to be present for the ceremony.

"You have some extra robes in here somewhere, don't you?" Horus glanced over the cluttered shelves behind her desk.

"Yeah, check the closet. Is this your first time?" She turned to smile at us.

"Yes," I answered. Josie and Kevin nodded.

"How exciting! Not many reapers come to visit."

"That's because they never have any souls to deliver here," Horus laughed.

He rummaged through a closet and found three white robes for us to wear over our black ones. Had our skin been darker, we might have gone unnoticed among the Egyptian deities. But along with raven hair, all reapers are created as pale as death. Well, as pale as Grim anyway.

"There you are!" Thoth entered the office in his ceremonial headdress of overflowing ibis feathers, crowding us all into each other's personal space. "I saw Osiris escort another soul into the hall so I knew you had to be around here somewhere," he said to Horus, and then gave the rest of us a puzzled look. "Oh! The reapers are staying for the ceremony?"

"Yes," Horus answered.

"Wonderful! Ma'at will be pleased to meet all of you. You have brought back to us one of her most beloved pharaohs. I hope you enjoy the ceremony."

"Thank you. I'm sure we will," I smiled.

Ma'at was Thoth's wife and the goddess of truth. Truth was always nice to have, especially if you had the job of settling disputes between gods, like Thoth did.

"We'd better get in there before they start." Horus led us out of the office and through the golden doorway of the Hall of Two Truths.

Inside, what looked like jury boxes were lined up against walls displaying fresh hieroglyphics. The walls were drywall, but they had been carefully painted to resemble the block inside the original pyramids.

Osiris, the merciful judge of the dead, waited on a platform at the end of the hall. Mummy wrappings loosely circled his legs. I grinned, wondering if he was having a hard time keeping them on now that Isis was home. Isis stood to his left and Nephthys to his right. They both wore the traditional feathers, hanging from their sleeves like wings. Isis spotted us and gave a small gasp, shocked and embarrassed by our presence, like she'd been caught naked in her front yard.

So many human souls had lost faith, that no matter how well Grim had Khadija contain the soul matter, the human influence still washed over. And the subliminal message was this: Ceremony is dead. Isis could feel the teenage kid being teased because he was an altar boy, and the Islam girl in an American school where every other girl was considered normal except her in her mysterious hijab. Isis couldn't stop a disease that was staining faith as a whole with degradation and shame.

She pressed her fingers to her lips and closed her eyes. When she opened them again, she looked away and pretended as though she hadn't seen us at all.

On another platform, in the center of the hall, waited a large scale. A crowd of deities was seated in the front rows of the boxes to serve as divine assessors, while lesser deities and those not of Egyptian descent stood behind them to observe. Instead of sitting with his people, Horus remained standing with us.

Osiris raised his hands for silence as Anubis entered with the soul and escorted him to the scales. Next came Thoth, Ma'at, and Ammit with her fearsome crocodile headdress that snapped and hissed, provoking gasps of terror from the audience. Judgment Day and a circus, all in one show.

"First," began Osiris, "we shall receive the negative confessions."

The soul bowed before him and began reciting. With each confession, he denied committing a specific sin, and after doing so, he began to fade, taking on a transparent glow. His heart remained solid in his chest, and when he had finished his confessions, Anubis reached into him and withdrew the pulsing organ.

"Now we shall hear the testimony of the goddesses," Osiris announced.

A handful of women approached his throne, and one at a time they spoke of the man's good deeds throughout his life, while Thoth recorded their words on a scribal palette. The deeds sounded out of place, but only because they were a few thousand years old. When the goddesses were finished, they went back to their seats.

Anubis placed the soul's heart in one of the scale pans, while Ma'at rested the single ostrich feather of her headdress on the opposite tray. Ammit kneeled beneath the heart, her headdress snapping hungrily.

The first signs of doubt crossed the soul's face as he anxiously waited for the scales to balance. When they finally did, everyone cheered and applauded. Even Ammit dropped her loathing façade to congratulate the soul.

"Onward we move," bellowed Osiris, "to Aaru, the Field of Rushes!"

Horus turned to us with a smile. There were some pleasures that even thousands of years could not diminish. It made me feel better about growing old in Eternity. Even Josie was smiling.

"Thank you," Horus whispered to me.

"Thank you." I smiled at him, but his expression went solemn.

"Your appearance here, delivering a soul and staying for the ceremony, will strengthen my peoples' loyalty to me and make it difficult for Seth to build his army from Duat rebels."

I hadn't thought of it that way. Any pride I would have felt suffocated under my fear of Seth. I did not want to be on his radar. If he saw me as a threat, it wouldn't only jeopardize my life but also my assignment, and all those helping me. This was a smart move for Horus, but possibly a very stupid one for me. Seth had spies everywhere, and from the few dark glances I received on the way out, I knew not even the Hall of Two Truths was safe.

"I tried to tell you," Josie whispered over my shoulder loud enough for Horus to hear. "He doesn't do anything unless it benefits him somehow."

The skin around Horus's eyes tightened, but he pretended like he hadn't heard her. "Allow me to escort you back to your ship."

"I think we'll manage." Josie shoved past him.

I sighed and raised an eyebrow at Horus. "I don't mind being used. I'm a reaper, that's what I'm good for, apparently. But at least have the fucking courtesy to tell me *what* I'm being used for. I may not have churches or shrines or sacrifices made in my name, but I do have a sense of decency. Do you, Horus?"

"I'm sorry, Lana. I thought if I told you before the ceremony that you wouldn't stay." He dropped his chin and clasped his hands behind his back.

I folded my arms. "You know something? It's not even the idea of losing my life that I'm the most upset about. If you like Josie so damned much, why are you so willing to risk her life?"

"It's not that I'm willing to risk her life. I'm just less willing to risk war." He held out his hands powerlessly, the broken and forgotten god that he was.

CHAPTER TWENTY

*"Let your religion be less of a theory
and more of a love affair."*
—*G.K. Chesterton*

Saul and Coreen rushed down the hall and pushed past me as I opened my apartment door. It only took one day for them to figure out the only safe place to be with me was at home.

Coreen yipped, and I reached for my scythe before flipping on the light in the kitchen.

"Out here a man settles his own problems," John Wayne called from the television, just as I spotted a trail of white feathers leading from the refrigerator into the living room.

"Gabriel?"

"Hey," Maalik and Gabriel both answered. The two of them sat on the sofa, digging through a stack of movies.

"Just giving Maalik a rundown of your favorite flicks," Gabriel laughed. They were still in their work robes.

Coreen barked again. She saw the couch as her territory and wanted them to move. She looked at me and whimpered like a spoiled child. When she realized they weren't going to leave, she snorted and sulked over to join Saul on my bed.

"How long have you guys been here?" The clock above my sink showed that it was nearing midnight.

"Eight maybe?" Maalik answered and looked at Gabriel.

"Yeah, that sounds about right."

"Oh." I smiled.

They had become buddies in four hours over my western collection. And, apparently, Cheetos. Orange crumbs littered the coffee table, and greasy fingerprints graced the edges of a few DVD cases.

"How did everything go at work?" Maalik stood and helped me pull off my robe. I hung it and my scythe on the back of the bathroom door. The coat closet didn't have enough room, now that there was a four-hundred-pound bag of dog food in there.

"Okay, I guess. We had two mild attacks, but no injuries."

"Two attacks?" Gabriel stood. "That makes five in less than a week. That's more than most senior reapers encounter in an entire century. I don't like this, Lana. Maybe I can have Peter grant me temporary leave until things settle down. I can help."

"That's not a bad idea," Maalik agreed with him. That was a first. "I'm not able to leave Limbo City while serving on the council, but I would feel better if one of the heavenly host accompanied you."

"It's not up to me. Ask Grim." I sighed and slumped down in a kitchen chair.

"I will, first thing tomorrow morning." Maalik dusted an orange crumb off his sleeve. "What time is it?"

"Almost midnight."

"How'd it get so late?" He looked at the kitchen clock in disbelief.

"Time flies when you're having fun." I smiled at Gabriel.

"How are the hounds working out?" Maalik quickly changed the subject.

"Good." I smiled at Coreen and Saul, snuggled up together on my bed. They were so tired, they had forgotten about dinner. So had I. My stomach growled.

"Have you eaten yet?" Gabriel asked.

"No."

"Think your hounds would mind me taking you out for dinner?"

"I thought you'd be more worried about Maalik," I laughed.

"I think Maalik and I are on the same page now." Gabriel grinned, and Maalik blushed.

"I'd better get going. I have a lot to do in the morning. If I can work it out with Grim, Gabriel should be able to join your team before you leave for the next soul." Maalik gave me a peck on the cheek and nodded at Gabriel.

"See you in the morning," he said and left the apartment.

I looked back to Gabriel. "Wow. I'm impressed."

"Don't go all Jesus on me. It just happened. I didn't plan on liking your new boyfriend. In fact, I had a whole bag of tricks I was ready to test out on him."

"What happened?" I dug a leather jacket out of my bedroom closet and pulled it on.

"When he showed up, and you weren't here, I could tell he was really worried about you. I guessed if you meant that much to him, he wouldn't be so bad to have around, with your new job and all." Gabriel opened the apartment door for me.

"Where are we going to eat?"

"Purgatory."

I stopped in the middle of the hallway and stared at him.

Gabriel shrugged. "What? They have good food. Besides, I want you to meet someone."

"Who?" I asked as we continued down the hall.

"Well, you'll meet her when we get there, pilgrim." He wagged his eyebrows at me.

"Her?" I stopped again.

"What? You think you're the only one who knows how to meet people?" He grinned and fluttered his wings in mock offense.

"No. I'm just surprised. Where did you meet her? Wait, let me guess—"

"Lana, you're starting to sound like Peter," he grumbled.

"That's what I thought. Purgatory."

"Be nice."

It was cool outside. Nighttime in Limbo was always cool. During the day, it was warmer. Our weather was pretty consistent. That's how Grim liked it. Occasionally, he would mix it up and pay Zibel, a storm god who worked at Bank of Eternity, to make it snow or rain.

The souls liked snow in December. It didn't matter how many gods or goddesses they met, Christmas had become immortalized with the ever-erect Christmas tree as its holy symbol. Santa would prevail, even if he were only a collage of random deities.

Gabriel and I quietly walked the few blocks to Purgatory Lounge. When we got there, two motorcycles were parked outside, along with a rusty Ford pickup.

"Looks like Xaphen's here," I nodded toward the truck. Xaphen was the owner of Purgatory Lounge.

"Oh! Yeah, I guess so." Gabriel froze.

"What's wrong?"

"Nothing! Nothing." His eyes were still glued to the truck as he took the last few steps toward the bar.

"After you." He grabbed the door. I gave him a puzzled look and stepped inside.

"Lana! I haven't seen you in ages," Xaphen greeted me from behind the bar. Little flames flickered around his crown. He was a fire demon and one of the original fallen angels. He had been the one to come up with the idea of setting fire to Heaven before all those serving Lucifer were cast out during the war. After tending the flames of the abyss for a few thousand years, Xaphen decided it was time to retire. He relocated to Limbo to fulfill his lifelong dream of opening a tavern.

"Hey there, Xaph." I tugged off my jacket and hopped onto one of the barstools. "I was wondering what happened to you."

"Well, I try not to come in on busy nights anymore. The hair's a little hazardous around all this alcohol, ya know?" He set down the glass he had been polishing and dug a pack of cigarettes out of his shirt pocket.

"Gabriel says you have good food here." I smiled and looked behind me. Gabriel was gone. "He was just here."

"He's probably in the john." Xaphen shrugged and pressed the tip of his cigarette against his forehead. He took a deep breath and the flames along his brow roared to life. At least he didn't have to worry about losing lighters. "We've got hot wings and baby back ribs on special tonight."

"That sounds good. How about an order of each and a pitcher. I'm making Gabriel pay."

"Atta girl," he laughed and strutted through a doorway behind the counter.

I stole another glance around the bar. There were a couple of nephilim playing pool, and one soul pumping quarters into the jukebox, determined to play Elvis songs into the wee hours of the morning.

When I turned back around, Gabriel stood beside me.

"What the hell!" I jumped. "Were you outside?"

"Yeah, why don't we eat somewhere else?" He grabbed my arm and pulled me to my feet.

"I just ordered. What's wrong with you?" I swatted his arm away and glared at him.

"I'll explain later. We've just—"

"Gabe!" Amy, Xaphen's daughter, appeared out of nowhere and threw her arms around Gabriel's neck. His face flushed in panic.

One of the bikes out front had to be hers. Sparkling flames danced up the seams of her leather pants. Her matching jacket rode up her back as she squeezed Gabriel, exposing a tattoo on her lower back that read *Aestus*, Latin for passionate fire. Just above the firm and shiny curve of her bottom, a slender tail, red as sin, sliced through her leather pants and flicked its pointy tip.

"Hi, Lana," Amy greeted me as she released Gabriel and swept her copper curls over her shoulder. "How's the soul business treating you?"

"I'm staying busy," I groaned.

"You two have met?" Gabriel raised an eyebrow.

"Once or twice," Amy laughed.

"Wait a minute." I turned to Gabriel. "This is who you brought me here to meet?"

He blushed and ran a hand through his curls. "Well, yes, but—"

"Gabriel, you got a death wish or something?"

Peter was going to have a fit. Amy wasn't just any demon. She was one of the presidents of Hell. She commanded thirty-six legions and had no interest in retiring like her father. Her fierce ambition had even caught the notice of Cindy Morningstar. Amy had been Cindy's right hand lady on the Hell Committee during her campaign for the council position.

"So, Gabriel." Xaphen reappeared behind the bar and placed the hot wings and ribs on the counter.

The flustered angel turned to face him with twitching wings. "Yes, sir?" he squeaked.

"I hear you're dating my daughter." He looked about as thrilled as I imagined Peter would be.

"Yes, sir," Gabriel answered.

Xaphen's glare migrated to Amy. "It was bad enough when you brought home your human familiars, but an angel? An archangel? What would your mother say? What will your legions say?"

"I don't care what they say. After construction on my chateau is completed, I'll have enough work to keep my legions busy until Judgment Day." Amy cocked a hip and folded her arms.

"Chateau?" I asked, changing the subject for Gabriel's sake. Amy brightened at my interest.

"The Inferno Chateau. It's going to be fabulous! I bought this quaint little piece of land about a year ago, and construction on my castle should be finished any day now. This retreat will be the highlight of Hell. Fire Lake view. Volcanic hiking trails. You'll have to come and stay for a weekend."

"Hmmm." I nodded and tried to smile. Quaint and Hell just didn't add up for me. But maybe Maalik would be interested in a weekend getaway.

"Sound like fun, Gabriel?" Xaphen chuckled.

"I'd give it try." Gabriel gave Amy one of his adorably goofy smiles. She beamed and threw her arms around him again. Xaphen rolled his eyes and began filling a pitcher with beer. It wasn't against the law for an angel and a demon to date, but it could have an effect on your career, not to mention your health, if you weren't careful.

"I hear you've been having some problems with demons lately." Amy pulled up a barstool next to me. I frowned at Gabriel as he snatched one of my hot wings.

"Hey, she might be able to help." He shrugged.

"Yeah, we've had some problems." I turned back to Amy.

"Let me guess, Caim?" She snorted and poured herself a beer.

"How'd you know?" I shot Gabriel another unpleasant look.

"I swear, I never mentioned his name." He pointed his hot wing at me.

"I have to return to Hell tonight because he's got some-one on the inside trying to recruit my legions. If he thinks my real estate venture means my men are up for grabs, he's got another thing coming." Amy smirked.

"So he's trying to build an army?" I pushed the basket of hot wings toward her. Talking shop always spoiled my appetite. I had really hoped going to dinner with Gabriel would take my mind off work for a while, but there are some things a girl just can't run away from.

"He won't be building an army with my demons. Here." She flipped over a cardboard coaster and scribbled something on the back. "This is the address of an old friend of mine. He's nephilim, but he knows all there is to know about demons."

"Nephilim?" I frowned.

She rolled her eyes and gave me an embarrassed grin. "He paid me to sneak him into Hell so he could find his father."

"Did he?"

"Well, yes, but it didn't go the way he had hoped. His father wasn't exactly thrilled to meet him. The poor kid barely escaped. He hasn't left Limbo City since. Tell him I sent you and you should get a discount."

"What's he selling?"

"The answer to all your problems, and hopefully mine, too. If my legions see what you do to the next demons you come across, maybe they'll think twice before joining Caim's ranks." She handed me the coaster.

I was being used, once again. So far, this promotion sucked. At least Amy was being upfront with me. And this time, I could actually gain something from it.

"You really think demons are going to find me threatening?" I scoffed.

"I'm scared already." She winked at me.

CHAPTER TWENTY-ONE

*"If only God would give me some clear sign! Like making
a large deposit in my name in a Swiss bank."*
—Woody Allen

"I see you've figured out a way to pull strings within the council," Grim sneered at me from behind his desk.

I wasn't sure if my discomfort had more to do with his mood or his poor choice in furniture. If I kept finding myself in his office, I was going to have to make a trip to the chiropractor.

"What are you talking about?" I sighed and crossed my legs, hoping that would ease the ache growing in my lower back.

"Maalik tells me if I don't allow your feathered drinking buddy to join your team, he'll write it up to be voted on by the council. I already have Holly riding my ass about the psychological effects on souls. If we don't find the right one soon, she'll be drawing up papers for the council, too. Then we'll never find the soul, and Eternity will be hurled right back into the chaos I saved it from."

"You mean that Khadija saved it from?"

Grim's face tightened, and he narrowed his gaze on me. "Mention her name again, and I'll show you a chaos she can't save you from. This isn't a game, Ms. Harvey. If you screw this up, we all go down."

"Look, adding Gabriel wasn't even my idea. But if you do add him to the team, I'm sure Holly will back off. Most Christians love Gabriel. He would take care of the psychological issues with souls, don't you think?"

"He damn well better."

"Where are we going today?" I scanned over the mountain of paperwork on Grim's desk for a black folder.

"You're going shopping." He cleared his throat.

"Excuse me?"

"Oh, you heard me," he spat. His cheeks flared as he pushed an envelope across the desk. "I'm going to tell the council that you found the soul. It's the only way we're going to find out who's behind these attacks. Take today off and go spend some money with your team. Tell everyone it's from your bonus check. Word will get around, but you'd better be here bright and early tomorrow morning because the job still needs to be done."

I opened the envelope and peeked inside.

"Holy shit," I whispered.

"That's what I feel like," Grim groaned. "Bring me the receipts. I'm using them as a write-off."

What do you know? Even Death paid taxes. I stood to leave the office.

"Oh, and Lana?" Grim pressed his fingertips together and glared at me.

"Yes?"

"I expect to see you at Coreen's memorial service this afternoon."

"Of course." I gave him a quick nod and ducked out of the room.

Ellen was away from her desk. I closed my eyes and leaned my head back against Grim's office door with a sigh.

The memorial service started at four. I could push it out of my mind long enough to enjoy shopping. Couldn't I? The council would be there, and I was pretty sure the I-hate-Lana club would be in attendance, too. Maybe I could use my bonus check to buy a disguise.

"What?" Josie gave me a bewildered look. Before she had started working with me, her life had been full of order and predictability. My surprises—and there had been quite a few lately—enraged and confused her most days, but not this time.

"Shopping? Are you serious?" She laughed.

"Dead." I held the check up for her and Kevin to see.

"Wow." Kevin leaned in closer. "We have to spend all of it?"

"Yeah. Grim wants receipts."

"Well, we'd better get going." Josie stood and then frowned down at her work robe. "Maybe we should change first."

"After we stop by the bank. It'll be more convincing if we look like we've just finished the job." I tucked the check in the front pocket of my robe.

Bank of Eternity stood like a fortress in the center of Limbo City. Enchanted beams of steel arched over the entrance so that no one could simply jump inside with the flip of a coin. Inside waited a labyrinth of marble hallways lined with metal and charm detectors. You couldn't so much as catch a glimpse of the teller booths without being searched at least half a dozen times. A stray paperclip in the pocket of my jeans set off the alarms, and we had to go through the whole process again. By the time we made it to the end of the customer line, I was exhausted. And humans think airports are bad.

The lobby was full of chattering. "I need to wire some coin to Hell." "This is a deposit for my Nirvana vacation fund." "Withdrawal for twelve coins, twenty marks each."

We finally made it to the front of the line, and I placed our check on the counter. The teller tilted her head as she examined the slip of paper.

"Sorry, but this is an awfully large number. I'll have to double check it with the account holder." She smiled nervously and disappeared. After what seemed like an eternity, she returned with Cern, the bank president.

There was no competition when Cern decided to open a bank in Limbo, and no one opposed him when he proudly named it Bank of Eternity. He was still in favor among the pagans. They lovingly called him the Horned God or God of the Hunt. But even if the pagans had forgotten him, I doubted anyone in Eternity would stand in his way, or live to tell about it.

Cern stood seven feet tall with a rack of antlers that could make any high pedigree buck cower. Gold rings dripped from his horns, chiming like music with each step he took. His smooth locks and penetrating gaze still tugged the heartstrings of most ladies, freezing them somewhere between smitten and petrified.

"What seems to be the problem," Cern sighed, drooping his antlers forward.

"This check," answered the teller, blushing. "I tried to confirm it with Grim, but he's in a meeting. His secretary says it's a bonus check, but I wanted your approval before handing over that much coin."

"Bonus check?" Cern's eyes rolled over the slip of paper. "I'll say. That's quite a bonus. Well, if Grim's secretary approved it, go ahead. It's not like he doesn't have the funds." He gave us half a smile and hurried back to his office. That would get the word out.

The teller divided the coin into three small bags for us. It didn't look like much, but we were going to have a hard time spending it all in one day. I found myself wondering what sort of purchases would look best on Grim's tax return. High heels? Lingerie? Demon porn? But I also found myself wondering if this were the only bonus check we would receive. It didn't seem fair that we had to spend it all right away. Oh, the price we pay to save Eternity. Well, the price Grim pays, anyway.

After leaving the bank, we headed back to the Coexist Complex to change out of our work robes. When Josie and Kevin showed up at my door, I was surprised to find that Kevin had changed, too.

"He left some clothes behind when he stayed over the other night," Josie answered before I had a chance to ask. She gave me a strained smile, the kind she only uses when she's quietly praying for me to keep my big mouth shut.

"I'm almost done. Just gotta fix my hair. Come on in." I hurried back to the bathroom to finish taming my mess of curls. After five more minutes of waging war with the curling iron, I gave up and twisted everything back with a handful of bobby pins.

Saul and Coreen snuggled together on my bed. After their first day on the job with me, Coreen decided she needed a little more comfort than the couch had to offer. I could give them the day off since we were only going shopping.

"Where to first?" Josie asked as I pulled on my boots, the same pair she had rendered holy. She raised an eyebrow. "Shoe store?"

"I have a better idea." I dug the coaster Amy had given me out of my jacket.

Warren, Amy's nephilim friend, lived along the west coast of Limbo, as far away from the harbor as he could get. I guess it made him feel safer. Most demons traveled to Limbo City by boat. Any coin they managed to get their hands on, they saved for the human realm.

We circled Warren's block four times before spotting the crumbling steps that led to his basement apartment, hidden behind an avalanche of garbage. The patio, if you could call it that, looked like a ransacked garage sale. A herd of mice unraveled a soggy, wool sweater, while a mangy cat kept watch from a lopsided shelf overflowing with cracked flowerpots and limbless figurines.

Amy had written down a strict set of knocking instructions. Twice, then once, then three times, pause, then twice more. I knocked and stepped back with Josie and Kevin to wait. A light flickered on behind a tiny, fogged window before a choir of mechanical pops and clicks sounded. The door cracked open.

"Can I help you?"

"Amy sent us," I answered. "We have a demon problem."

"Shhhhhh," he hissed at us.

Josie inched closer to Kevin.

"They will hear you. Come in, come in." Warren opened the door just enough for us to squeeze inside.

The dim lighting did little to hide the catastrophe he called home. A pile of pizza boxes crawling with mold sat in the corner of the kitchen, and shredded flannel shirts covered the floor and sofa. The one he wore looked like it was ready for the garbage, and I wondered if maybe that's where he did his shopping.

"Can I get you something to drink?" He fluttered his wings, shaking off loose feathers, and combed his fingers through his greasy hair.

"No, thank you." I smiled. "We really can't stay long. Can we see your inventory?"

"Right! Right." He bent over and shoved a stack of pizza boxes off what had looked like a coffee table, but was instead a chest. He flipped the latch and opened it. Gold silk lined the inside, embroidered with Latin protection spells. Crystal bottles of holy water were stacked off to one side, imprinted with gothic crosses, while an array of charms and holy symbols dangled from the lid. Strapped to the inside of the lid was a double-headed axe. The oldest Latin spells I had ever seen danced up the iron handle, promising strength and endurance. I reached out to touch it, but Warren was quicker. He slapped my hand away.

"Oh! No, no, no. That's not for sale." He paled and pulled his hand away from mine. "So sorry, but that's not for sale."

I glared at him. "Why not?"

"I, I still need it," he stammered. His left wing twitched.

"For what?" I looked around the apartment again. "This place isn't exactly plagued by demons. And no offense, but it doesn't look like you get out enough to ever run into one. So what gives?"

"There's a demon I have to kill first." He pushed himself up straighter, trying to project bravery, and then looked down at his flannel shirt with a defeated frown. He couldn't even fool himself anymore. "There's a demon that I need to protect myself from."

"And when was the last time this demon attacked you?"

"Many years, but he promised he would come for me. Until that day, I will be prepared. My sources tell me he recently left Hell. So it won't be long now."

Demons generally stayed in Hell. Sure, on the rare occasion a coin found its way into the wrong hands, a rogue demon could terrorize the human realm until a priest performed an exorcism or the council sent someone to retrieve it. And then there were a few demons who retired or got a temporary passport to vacation in Limbo City, but they had to register first.

"What's this demon's name?" My gaze drifted back to the axe.

"Why do you need to know?" He wasn't the most trusting nephilim.

"If he's not registered with the council, you have nothing to worry about. There's a six-month waiting period for any demon requesting a passport for Limbo."

"Six months is nothing to a demon or me," he said.

"No, but it's enough time for me to take care of him for you."

Warren's wing twitched again. "You're a reaper, not an assassin. There are laws against what you suggest."

Josie laughed and picked up a vial of holy water. "And there are laws that require you to have a license to carry this in Limbo. You do have a license, don't you, Warren?" Josie grinned.

"Now wait just one minute. Amy would never give you my address if she thought you meant me harm." Warren stood and backed away from the couch.

"We don't." I frowned at Josie. She put the vial back in the trunk and shrugged.

"You're not the only one who bends the rules, Warren." I gave him a gentle smile. "Sell me the axe. I'll give you enough coin to pay for six month's rent at Holly House."

Holly House was home to Limbo's most Christian and most paranoid citizens. The tenants were a mixture of angels, nephilim, and even a few senior souls from the factory who had saved up for a decade or two. The place was owned by and named after Holly Spirit, but she didn't have time to run it. That job was left to her feathered assistants. They made sure their guests were provided with the utmost security. The council even agreed to let them construct an eight-foot fountain coursing with holy water in the front lobby, provided they framed and posted their license on the gate outside.

"Holly House," Warren sighed. "That would be lovely, but where will I go after six months?"

"Like I said, I bend the rules, too. Give me the demon's name."

He paused and licked his lips. I could almost see the visions of Holly House dancing behind his eyes. He looked around his apartment one more time, disgust leaking through his expression. "His name is Varren. He told my mother it was Warren. She thought she had named me after him. My human grandmother took care of me after my mother died delivering me, but when my wings began to develop, she prayed for the Virgin to come and take me away. And the Virgin did."

"Is that all you can tell me about him?"

"When he was in Hell, he served under Azazel. I hear not even Azazel knows where he is now. I think I'm ready for Holly House."

"Good." I reached for the axe, and he didn't stop me this time.

It was lighter than it looked, probably from one of the Latin spells. The double blade sparkled, even in the dim light. Warren watched me from behind the couch with awe and worry twisting up his eyebrows. Clearly, the weapon had never been used. Part of me couldn't help but hope for another demon attack so I could try it out. Stupid? Yes. But the chances of us running into demons again were high enough, it felt like divination instead.

CHAPTER TWENTY-TWO

*"A religion that gives nothing, costs nothing,
and suffers nothing, is worth nothing."*
—Martin Luther

"**G**rim's gonna be pissed when he finds out you didn't get a receipt from Warren." Josie sat cross-legged on my new faux leather sofa. At least the fake leather smelled nice. After buying the axe, I couldn't afford the real thing. But I did have enough coin left to buy a good pair of boots.

I sat on the edge of my coffee table and laced the charcoal duds up my calves. They were shorter than my last pair, but a whole lot tougher. The heels and toes were reinforced with steel. A cluster of braided leather cords fell over the boot tongues, dangling black barbs around my ankles.

"He'll get over it," I sighed. "You can tell him I bought the axe at the market. That it was too good a deal to pass up, and that the vendor had hooves and couldn't write out a receipt."

Kevin frowned. "Everyone knows hoofed vendors employ sprites to help with that sort of thing. And why does Josie have to tell him?" He sat on the sofa next to Josie, flipping through a pamphlet for the Coexist Complex. The only apartment available happened to be on the same floor as Josie's.

"Because Lana's a terrible liar," she answered for me. "I'll tell him the pixies were away for lunch." She folded her arms over her lap, flashing her new charm bracelet, the only luxury item she had bought with her bonus money. Silver holy symbols looped around the leather band tightly fastened to her wrist. She had used most of her coin to sign up for advanced classes and scolded me more than once for not doing the same. Why bother? Hadn't Grim said he would cover the tuition for my mentoring course? That was enough school for me, thank you.

"We should go to the memorial service early." Kevin sighed and tossed the pamphlet on the coffee table.

"What for?" I scrunched up my face.

"Because Coreen died working with us." He folded his arms. "Maybe you didn't like her, but she still deserves your respect. And she was Saul's first apprentice. You were his last. You should feel compelled more than anyone to attend."

"You're right," I groaned and slumped down on the edge of the coffee table. "But you have to remember, there are dozens of reapers far more experienced than the three of us who weren't picked for Grim's special little assignment. We'll be dealing with more resentment than sympathy today. You'll see. Wear comfortable shoes. You'll wanna get out of there just as fast as I do before it's over." I patted his shoulder and went to dig my nicest robe out of the closet.

Seeing Seth at Coreen's memorial service was like catching Hitler lighting Hanukah candles. Hypocrisy at its finest. Three days ago, he had verbally slapped her and belittled Grim for allowing reapers at the council dinner. Now he stood solemnly at the head of the crowd, patting a hand here and there and nodding in sympathy like the good little snake that he was. His eyes locked on me as I entered the park, breaking the façade of sincerity. His pupils darkened and his brow furrowed, but his mouth twisted into a self-assured smirk. I looked away. I didn't want his attention. The more insignificant he found me, the better.

Coreen's memorial statue stood ten feet from Saul's, done perfectly to scale in a gritty bronze. Grim had the sculptor pose her with one arm erected over her head. Light seeped from between the fingers of her raised hand, symbolizing the keen battle tactic she had used to help us defeat the demons before they took her.

Beyond the new statue, Craig Hogan pushed his way through the growing crowd and toward me. My chest tightened as I sucked in a surprised breath.

There were six reapers in my generation. According to most, Craig was the best of us. He still held the highest score ever seen on an L&L exam. After his apprenticeship, he became the youngest member to join the Lost Souls Unit. They were responsible for collecting CNH souls that mysteriously left their bodies before harvesting.

Craig's squared jaw and buzzed head could terrify any soul into submission, but his tough guy look lost most of its effect once the constellation of gray freckles splattered across his nose and cheeks came into view. When he smiled at me, I almost forgot how much I resented his success.

There was a time when Craig could do no wrong. As long as he smiled the way he did, I was defenseless. We'd dated for a short while during our training. After he'd been assigned his apprenticeship under Coreen, he delivered to me a brief and mechanical speech, explaining how there was no room for me in his ambitious future plans. I'm still convinced he was promised the position on the Lost Souls Unit under the condition that he ditch me.

Luckily, the heartache only lasted half as long as the relationship had, which wasn't long. Two pairs of shoes and a latte later, I was over him. But that didn't mean I felt like doing somersaults whenever I happened to bump into him.

"So, are the rumors true?" He smiled, baring his perfectly straight, white teeth. I used to consider his smile his best asset. Now, knowing how insincere it was, I just wanted to smash his face in and watch him choke on all those pretty teeth. He moved closer, invading my personal space. I fought the urge to step back and held my ground, returning his fake smile with one of my own.

"Hello, Craig."

"I missed you at the ball," he said.

"That's funny. I didn't miss you."

Craig's brow pinched, but his phony smile never faltered. "The word out on the street is that you were invited to the council dinner. Is that true?" He was still predictable as ever, never giving anyone the time of day unless they could somehow be useful to him. Helping him study for the exams was the last bit of help he would be getting from me.

"Craig, I'm here for Coreen's memorial service, not an interview." I turned my back to him and picked up a glass of club soda from the refreshments table.

I could still feel him standing behind me. His desperate annoyance crashed in waves against my back. When he spoke again, his breath hissed along my neck, tickling my ear. "Yes, Coreen," he whispered, tilting his head over my shoulder. "How exactly did she die? You were with her, weren't you?"

My insides shivered, remembering the softness of his voice in a more intimate setting. The jerk thought he still had me.

I turned around slowly, pacing myself so he wouldn't see the disgust in my expression. His eyes rolled over me with some new wonder I hadn't noticed before. He loomed in front of me and crept subtly closer until I snatched an abandoned program off the table and smacked it in the middle of his chest.

"Read for yourself." I smiled and walked away from him and the growing crowd.

The ceremony wouldn't begin for another twenty minutes, and I needed a break already. Now that the word was getting around about my new placement, I doubted Craig would be the last skeleton creeping out of my closet. I pulled the hood of my robe up to keep anyone else from recognizing me and found a quiet place to rest near a fountain on the other side of the park. The quiet didn't last long.

"Congratulations on your promotion." Jenni Fang spotted me as she entered the park.

I looked up and sighed. "Yeah, thanks."

Jenni was Josie's roommate. Rumors about her developing an underground association of reapers had been circulating for a while now, but in the few times I had been around her, she'd never mentioned anything about it. I assumed they were just stories.

She stopped on the sidewalk and glanced toward the crowd, and then back to me, struggling to make a decision of some kind.

I laughed. "If you're looking for gossip, you can count me out."

"I'm not." She frowned and then dashed behind the cover of the fountain before anyone noticed her. She sat down next to me on the concrete ledge and held her hand out to catch the spray coming off the copper angels behind us.

Jenni was a rarity among the reapers. If anyone could pass for human, it was her. Though her almond eyes were solid black, the Asian influence on her features complemented the ghastly flesh that marked her as a reaper. She was born less than a century before the Japanese invasion of Korea, proving the strength of Grim's ties with the Fates. The Fates rarely made prophecies anymore, and if they did, it came with a hefty price. Grim was keeping them in business in more ways than one. It wasn't mere coincidence that he knew the exact number of new reapers needed each century.

Jenni crossed her legs and wiped her hand off on the sleeve of her robe. She hadn't spoken since joining me on the fountain, but that was no surprise. Harvesting mass quantities of souls in a war zone paid off. She found a way to apply every battle tactic she witnessed to her daily life, something Grim hadn't counted on. But it made promotions easier for her to obtain. She was waiting for me to start the conversation so I couldn't accuse her of badgering me. Some might call it polite. I called it trickery, but it worked.

"How's the Mother Goose Unit working out for you?" I decided if I kept the focus on her, I might be safe.

"Awful," she groaned and shot me a bothered frown. "I've harvested too many soldiers. I've taken every class offered, but I still can't seem to find my footing with children. I'm thinking about transferring to the Recovery Unit next year."

The Mother Goose Unit specialized in harvesting child souls. Every now and then, if there was an epidemic in the human realm, a few child souls found their way onto a freelance harvester's docket, but not often. Child souls ranged from infants to fifteen-year-olds. Although the human realm rose the age of adulthood in most countries, Eternity's independence gave the council the option of voting, and they chose to keep the adult age at fifteen. After fifteen, souls don't listen as well, so they have to be moved individually. Child souls can be moved in classes of five to twenty, depending on a reaper's experience and the ages of the children.

The Recovery Unit was the best of the best reapers. If a soul didn't escape its body but was somehow overlooked and buried before harvesting, or if a body ended up at the bottom of a lake, the Recovery Unit was a soul's only hope. A reaper had to make contact with a body to harvest the soul. There were numerous ways to recover a body, and lots of required classes and exams to get a license to do so.

"How many classes do you need?" I hooked the heels of my boots on the fountain edge and folded my arms over my knees.

"Six, but I've already read the textbooks. The only one that looks difficult is the Animator course. They just added it. They're bringing in Professor Zombi from Vodun City, Summerland. There are rumors that he's one of the most likely candidates for the Summerland council spot after the Green Man, but it's really too soon to tell."

"Hmmm." I nodded.

"I hear you'll be returning to the academy next semester." Her cheeks flushed, but she smiled, pleased that she had found a way to shift the focus to me. "You really lucked out, you know. My first apprentice was a handful, but Kevin, now there's a true pupil. Coreen didn't deserve him."

"He deserves better than me." I frowned and pulled at the hem of my robe.

"I don't know," she said, casting me a sideways glance before sliding the hood of her robe up over her long hair. "I always thought you had more to offer than low-risk harvests.

Stop by the apartment sometime. I'll give you my notes for the mentor's course." She stood and gave me a quick nod before taking off toward the crowd.

"Lana?" Josie rounded the fountain on the opposite side just as Jenni left. "They're getting ready to start. Grim looks like he's about to bring on the apocalypse. We'd better get up there." She looped her arm under mine, and we made our way to the seats reserved for us in front of Coreen's memorial.

"What did Jenni want?" Josie didn't sound happy.

"She offered me her school notes for the academy."

"Oh." Her shoulders relaxed.

"Why? What's wrong?" I pulled her arm back, forcing her to slow her pace. Grim saw us coming now, and his temper deflated, leaving red blotches along his brow.

"Nothing. Don't worry about it." She sighed, and we took our seats next to Kevin.

The sky shifted into a misty gray as the ceremony began. Almost two thirds of the reaper population were present, but they looked more grumpy than sad. Cutting work early today just meant more work for everyone tomorrow. A handful of Coreen's closer associates huddled together in the row ahead of us. Maalik sat with Ridwan and a few other angels in the row across from us. He gave me a soft smile and then turned his attentions to Grim as he began the memorial service.

"Thank you for joining us today." Grim stood behind a concrete pulpit in a sharp, black suit. I had half expected him to don his formal robe again, but maybe it reminded him too much of his own vulnerability. Who knows, maybe it was still at the dry cleaners.

"We are here today to honor and remember an elite reaper who is no longer with us." His eyes watered, and he stopped to clear his throat. "Coreen was a dear friend of mine, as was her mentor before her."

A soft grunt passed over my shoulder and froze my heart for a beat. I held my breath and tried to swallow the bile racing up my throat. I couldn't see him, but I knew he was there, and in the seat behind me no less.

"Friend? Please. She slept her way to the top," Seth whispered to whoever sat next to him.

I pretended like I hadn't heard, and squeezed my hands into fists to keep them from shaking.

"And I wouldn't be surprised if her mentor had, too," he added with a snicker. He had a lot of nerve. I ground my teeth together and blinked back a tear of rage. Saul had been a good reaper and a good mentor. He didn't deserve a slug like Seth soiling his memory. But starting a brawl in the middle of Coreen's memorial service was beyond stupid. I wasn't about to go there.

I pressed my lips together and closed my eyes. I tried to forget Seth and focus on Grim's speech, but my mind kept echoing Gabriel's John Wayne impersonation, "I won't be wronged, I won't be insulted, and I won't be laid a hand on."

A good portion of the gods like to think they're better than reapers, but the truth is, we're all made the same. Whether the soul matter manifests into something sponta-neously or is manipulated by a powerful force, it's still soul matter. None of us can escape the human influence. We still have the human desires for love and family, even though we're expected to do without them and peacefully serve our so-called superiors.

We are the backbone of this world. Reapers, who are denied everything from positions of power to the ability to start a family. Eternity has never run so proficiently. Souls have never flowed in such orderly and vast numbers. Because of the work we do, Eternity has peacefully thrived for over a thousand years. And how do they thank us? No paid vacation, no retirement plan, no position on the council, and no respect.

"Congratulations on finding that soul." I suppressed a yelp as Seth's hand squeezed my shoulder.

"Thank you," I answered without turning around.

"I'm sure Grim will be promoting you to one of the specialty units now that your assignment is finished." He was fishing in the wrong pond, but I think he already knew that.

"Grim has enough on his mind right now. He'll assign me to a unit when he knows I'm ready." I shrugged, hoping to shake his hand away, but he only gripped tighter.

"If only all reapers knew their place as well as you do." He let his hand drop away and stood to leave.

Grim stuttered in the middle of his speech. When I looked up, his eyes cut into me with a grueling panic. I would not, *would not* be getting in the middle of all his political garbage. It was my job to find the replacement soul. That's all. I was already making myself a target for Seth, thanks to Horus. I had a demon to assassinate for Warren, and I still needed to find a replacement soul for Khadija. If the pleading look on Grim's face meant what I thought it did, I already knew the answer. Hell, no. But it could wait until morning.

CHAPTER TWENTY-THREE

"Men never do evil so completely and cheerfully
as when they do it with religious conviction."
—*Blaise Pascal*

"**H**ell, no."

"Excuse me?" Grim squeezed his hands into fists until his knuckles turned so white, they looked like they might pop off.

I stood behind one of his uncomfortable guest chairs, sparing my back from the decorative torture device, and glared at my boss while my guts hardened into a throbbing ball. If I had been any other reaper, he would have terminated me on the spot.

"You heard me. I'm in over my head as it is. So is Khadija. She trusts me to find the replacement, and I won't be wasting time going after a phony soul so you can trap Seth. In case you've forgotten, I'm only a reaper."

"I own you. You'll do what I tell you to do." Grim slammed his fists down hard on his desk, sending an avalanche of paperwork over the edge.

"I'm the only one who can find the replacement. How do you expect me to do that if you get me killed first?" I rolled my tongue against the inside of my cheek. My mouth had gone dry like my body was trying to override my brain to stop me from blurting out anything else fatally stupid.

"What do you suggest we do? How else can we stop Seth without risking the soul?" he snorted and pushed his chair around to glower out the window at the dusty morning clouds.

Samhain, better known in the human realm as Halloween, was only days away. Zibel, part-time teller at Bank of Eternity, part-time Limbo weather consultant, must have been bumped a few extra coin from one of the goddesses. Or else he was just practicing for the big night. A sticky fog hung over Limbo City, thick enough to mistake dawn for dusk.

I closed my eyes and shuddered, feeling the gloom seep through the window and sink into the heart of me. "Let's look at what we know, Grim. There's obviously someone working from the inside. Who all had access to our pickup locations?"

"Well." Grim sighed and rolled back around to his desk. "Besides you and the team, there's me, Horus, and the Fates."

"No one else on the team knows the truth about the soul. Horus is too desperate for the souls you bought him with, and last time I checked, the Fates' factory was doing just fine."

"Where's that leave us?"

"I know, I know. But the demon attacks are growing consistently more advanced. Caim actually sent Harpies after us the last time. I'm not sure what we would have done if

Horus hadn't been there. Caim may be confined to the sea, but if Seth has an inside contact, sooner or later, he'll get tired of taking the burn for his lackeys. He'll slip up and show up, and then we'll have him. But if Seth knows we're going after a fake, and I'm sure he will, I doubt his contact will risk exposure with another attack. We really don't have time to waste on an elaborate trap anyway."

"Fine, but if the next soul doesn't get us anywhere, we do it my way. I hope you know what you're doing." Grim shook his head and shoved a black folder at me, knocking another stack of files off his desk and into a depressing heap on the floor. "And Gabriel can't come with you."

"Why not?" I snatched up the folder and frowned at him.

Grim folded his arms and huffed, giving me one of his you-should-know-better scowls. "Peter suspended him. Something to do with his recently questionable behavior. He's been consorting with nephilim, demons—"

"Reapers?" I spat at him.

"Booze." Grim laced his fingers together and rubbed a thumb against his chin. "What did you really expect would happen?"

"Last time I checked, it wasn't any of Peter's business who the archangels socialized with."

"That's the Board of Heavenly Hosts problem, not mine. I have enough to worry about. Like that soul." He nodded at the folder in my hands.

I sighed and opened the folder. "Hell, no."

Grim's brow dropped in a menacing line. "Lose the catty attitude. You may think you've got me by the balls because you know my secret, but don't forget, you have a secret, too. And I have more,"—he paused and rolled his eyes up with a grin—"creative ways to handle my problems."

I tore my eyes away from him and snapped the folder shut before it slipped from my moist fingers. Creative, huh? I'd show him creative.

CHAPTER TWENTY-FOUR

*"Life is pleasant. Death is peaceful.
It's the transition that's troublesome."*
—Isaac Asimov

Winston Gale sat cross-legged in his hospital bed, furiously clicking away on a handheld electronic game. His brow crinkled, wrinkling up the pale skin of his shaved head. The IV poking out of his arm jerked violently, threatening to pull free with each attack he administered.

Something unnerved me about collecting child souls. I didn't have to often. Most of them were handled by the Mother Goose Unit, but every now and then, one ended up on my docket. Winston groaned in defeat and discarded his game in the lap of his paper gown. Then he paused and looked me directly in the eye. I froze.

"Do I have time to call my mom and tell her goodbye?" he asked.

I blinked a few times, wondering if I had imagined it. This kid couldn't see me. Could he? But there he sat, staring at me, waiting for an answer.

"You can see me?" I took a step back and looked from Josie to Kevin. Their eyes had gone wide, and their mouths gaped in a cross of confusion and terror. Saul and Coreen tilted their heads in unison, a cute admission of wonder. I would have smiled if I hadn't been so freaked out.

"Yeah." Winston raised an eyebrow, or the skin where an eyebrow would have been if he had any, and looked me up and down. I took another step back while my pulse slapped at my temples. This was not how things worked. And why was he only looking at me?

"Can you see them?" I pointed to Josie and Kevin.

Winston frowned and glanced around the room. "No, just you. So, can I call my mom?"

"Uh, sure, I guess." I pulled at the neck of my robe. They certainly hadn't covered this in my Soul Communications class.

Josie and Kevin turned their attention away from Winston and stared at me. How was I supposed to explain this? Obviously, they knew we were looking for a unique soul. But they didn't know they were working with a unique reaper. I planned to keep it that way. I liked my head where it was, and I was under enough thumbs.

Winston picked up the dinosaur phone beside his bed and cradled it between his shoulder and ear before punching in his mother's number. Dinosaurs seemed to be the theme for the room. A dozen plastic T-rexes stood guard over the blinking heart monitor, while pterodactyls nested in a tangle of IV tubing. A stuffed saber-toothed tiger was curled up at the foot of the bed.

"Hey, Mom!" Winston sounded too cheerful for a dying little boy in the presence of Death. "I just wanted to tell you I love you... no, I feel great today. Never better."

I frowned. Most souls had a hard time accepting their death. Even suicides seemed disoriented at first. Never had I seen a soul acknowledge their own demise with such grace. He had to be the one.

Winston hung up the phone and looked back at me. "Okay. I'm ready."

"Uh." I looked up at the clock above his bed. "We still have an hour to wait."

"What?" Winston laughed. "Why are you here so early?"

"Well, you see," I stammered. I'm so not good with kids.

"You're special," I began.

"That's what the doctors told me when I was six, and they strapped me to all these machines." He frowned at me then. "You're not going to strap my soul to a bunch of machines too, are you?"

"Not exactly." I didn't have any idea what Grim would do with his soul, but I was pretty sure it didn't involve machines, and I was pretty sure he had to agree to take Khadija's place.

"What's your faith?"

"My mother's a Scientologist." He tilted his head at me again. "But if I didn't already know better, I would now."

"Okay." I folded my arms and paced in front of his bed. "You can A, be dumped in a sea full of faithless souls, or B, save Eternity from Chaos by unofficially working for my boss, Grim."

"Save Eternity from Chaos? Well, that's better than the options the doctors gave me. When do I start?"

I sighed. Grim owed me big time. I looked up at the clock again. "In fifty-three minutes."

"I've been in constant pain for three years. I doubt another hour will kill me. Oh, wait," he laughed. "It will." He picked up his game and clicked away with a pleased grin. "You know, I thought you'd be scarier."

"Yeah, and I thought you'd be quieter. Most souls can't see me until they're out of their bodies."

"But I'm special," he mocked in a squeaky voice. It would have been easier putting up with him for another hour if he couldn't see me, but at least he was cooperating.

I straightened my robe and paced across the hospital room to cast a menacing glare out the window at the angry Cleveland traffic below. Josie slipped up beside me and nervously squeezed my elbow, quietly drawing my attention back to her. She gave me a worried frown and peeked over her shoulder to make sure Kevin was out of hearing range.

"What the hell is going on?" she whispered.

"I'm not sure." It wasn't a total lie. Lately, there wasn't much I was sure about. I shrugged and gave her half a smile. "But let's make it work to our advantage."

"Who are you talking to?" Winston reached for his stuffed tiger and hugged it to his chest. He glanced around the room again with a skeptic frown, trying to decide if he should be afraid.

"Since you can see and hear me," I said, returning to his bedside, "there is something you should probably know."

"What?" He clutched the tiger's tail and anxiously pulled on it until the seams stretched and bits of fuzzy rump stuffing sprang out.

"In the next,"—I looked up at the wall clock—"forty-five minutes or so, we will more than likely be attacked by demons."

"Demons?" Winston rested his head on top of the tiger's and bit down on one of the unsuspecting creature's ratty ears.

"Yes, demons." I sighed. "So far, we haven't lost any souls, but they keep trying to take them from us. So be careful, and if anything happens, hide. We'll protect you."

"Okay," he answered meekly, letting the soggy ear fall from his mouth.

This was the first time I was able to plot with a soul before a guaranteed demon attack. I could do better than this. I grinned down at the tiger, a deliciously deceptive scheme forming in my head. "Scratch that, there's been a change of plans, Winston."

CHAPTER TWENTY-FIVE

*"Beware when the great God
lets loose a thinker on this planet."*
—*Ralph Waldo Emerson*

"This is the stupidest idea you've ever had," Josie rasped as my shoulder cracked into her hip for the second time.

You would think hospital closets would be larger, or at least big enough to hold a piece or two of their bulky equipment. This one could make a mop bucket claustrophobic. Thankfully, we would only have to suffer for a few more minutes.

I kneeled down and peeked through the keyhole again to make sure Winston was staying put under the hospital bed. His valiant tiger and company were piled into a believable lump under the sheets that also hid the IVs still attached to his arm.

"This'd better work," I mumbled to myself. The moment of truth was creeping silently closer. Over-anticipation sent a rush order of adrenaline through me, bringing on an acute case of the Chihuahua shakes and a tingling sensation that took over my knees.

"Maybe Grim's announcement worked." Kevin tugged at the neck of his robe, trying to conjure even the slightest breeze to relive the unbearable heat three smashed bodies created in such a tiny space. "Maybe everyone thinks we've already got the soul, and the demons gave up. Maybe—"

"Shhh," I hissed.

Soft and sneaky footsteps echoed down the hall and stopped just outside Winston's door. I peeked through the keyhole again and watched Winston curl himself into a tight ball, pulling completely out of view. Good.

The door clicked open, and a young nurse stepped inside, carrying a lunch tray.

"Well?" Josie asked.

"Shhh." I squeezed her leg. The possessed mailman had heard us just fine. I didn't want to take that kind of risk again.

Nurse might have been an overstatement. This girl looked like she was barely out of high school. A reddish-brown ponytail bobbed between the straps of her protective paper mask, and I felt a pinch of shame that I hadn't bothered asking Winston what he was dying from. Not that I had to worry about catching it.

"Lunch is served." The nurse placed the tray on the bedside table and gently stroked the heap on the bed, noticing right away that the unusually squishy form was not Winston.

"Winston?" She yanked back the blanket and clutched the front of her kitty-cat scrubs with a gasp. "No."

"It's okay, Karen. I'm right here." Winston sprang out from under the bed, IV cords trailing behind him like a dog chain. I closed my eyes. Crap. Guess I should have told him about possession. Too late now.

Karen's eyes welled up as she helped Winston climb back in bed, scolding him for scaring the daylights out of her. "I thought I was going to die, just die!" she wailed through the paper mask.

"I'm sorry." Winston dropped his head with a sensible amount of guilt. "It was just a joke."

"I can't take this closet anymore, and we only have, what, four minutes?" Josie glared down at her watch in the dim light.

"She doesn't look possessed to me," Kevin sighed.

I tilted my head up to look at him. "Did the mailman?"

He shrugged and folded his arms, accidentally ramming an elbow into Josie's back.

"Damn it!" she hissed, tensing her shoulders and casting the blaming grimace at me instead of Kevin. "It's nearly time, Lana. Let's just step out there and see if she can see us or not. Anything's gotta be better than staying in here. Unless you and Kevin have some sort of sick bet going to see who can give me the most bruises today."

I bit my lip and squinted at the wall clock through the keyhole again. Two minutes to go. It didn't get much closer than this. "Fine. Get ready."

The door popped open, and we tumbled out of the closet like a mountain of garbage bags in our black cowls. Josie scrambled to her feet and jerked her bow up, aiming it directly into Nurse Karen's face. She didn't even flinch.

"Are we good?" Kevin asked, holding his scythe above his head like an action figure in mid-swing. I nodded. He and Josie lowered their weapons.

"Have you been playing in the closet, Winston?" Karen walked right past me and pushed the closet door shut. "You really shouldn't be doing that. What if you pulled out an IV or something?"

"I'm sorry. I won't do it again." Winston pressed his lips together and blinked at me, giving his head a quick jerk up at the clock behind him. It was time. Any second now.

I went to stand by the bed and rested my hand on his shoulder, ready to bolt the second his soul was ready. Karen stood on the other side of the bed, dutifully reading the machines and making neat little checks on her clipboard, humming to herself all the while. When she finished, she tugged down her mask and smiled at Winston, resting her own hand on his other shoulder.

I wasn't the only one disturbed by the weirdness of otherworldly symmetry. Winston rolled his shoulders and struggled not to look up at me in front of Karen.

"Lana? Everything okay?" Josie stepped up behind the nurse, leaning around her to see what was going on.

Karen's eyes shot up and froze on mine with a familiar disdain. The room filled with a static tension, fading the electric hum of machines until my own panicked heartbeat was the only sound I could hear. Karen reached into the pocket of her kitty-cat scrubs and in one fluid movement yanked out a syringe and plunged it into Josie's stomach without even turning around.

"Josie!" Kevin dropped to his knees to catch her fall. She slumped into his arms, twitching and wide-eyed. Her mouth gaped open in shock as she reached down, clumsily hunting for the source of her pain with shaking hands.

"Get her out of here!" I screamed at Kevin. He swallowed and cast a nervous glance up at the nurse.

"Now!" I reached under my robe and grasped the handle of my new axe.

Kevin reached into his pocket to find his coin before he and Josie vanished. I wasn't sure what was in the syringe, but Grim would know what to do.

"What's going on?" Winston gave up his ruse and turned to look at me. Not a good idea.

Karen's eyes bulged excitedly, and she finally tore her gaze off of me long enough to look down at her patient.

"You can see her?" she breathed. "Then you're the one. Finally, my job is almost complete. Now, if you could just die." Her fingers slid up his shoulder and wrapped around his neck.

"Think again, bitch." I jerked my axe free, slicing through the back of my robe, and swung at her like a lumberjack. Her free hand reached up and caught the handle right under the blade, spotting my vision with splashes of white agony as my shoulders tried to disconnect from their sockets.

"I'm not one of those demons you're used to swatting away like flies." Karen laughed, high and long with a silky stream of satisfaction.

Winston struggled in her grasp, sprawling his little hands out until he found the buzzer beside his bed. He smashed his fist into the button over and over, signaling a faint alarm in the nurse's station across the hall.

"You little brat," Karen hissed and lifted him out of the bed by the neck. "Why aren't you dead yet?" She flung him across the room and into the far wall, spraying the collage of dinosaur posters with blood as the IVs ripped free from his arms.

With Winston out of the bed, I had a clear shot at the possessed nurse. I took it. My foot connected with her stomach, and she dropped the head of my axe with a soggy grunt and staggered back a step. I lifted the axe again, ignoring the burning sensation running through my shoulders, and rushed another wild swing at her.

Instead of trying to stop the blade again, she recoiled within an inch of losing her head and gave the handle of my axe a quick push in the direction it was already going, sending me spinning like a top. Her knees lodged between my shoulder blades as she slammed me down on the hospital floor and tangled a hand in my hair to jerk my head back. My axe clattered noisily away from me.

"Thought you could fool Seth with your little shopping spree, did you? Well, you didn't fool me," she hissed as she loosened her grip on my hair long enough to crush my face into the cold linoleum. She jerked my head back again and leaned in closer, invoking the intimate sort of terror reserved for serial killers. "Your time's up, little reaper. And I doubt

Grim will be erecting any monuments in your honor." She rocked back on her heels, giddy with victory.

Blood leaked from my lips and sprayed across the floor as I rasped, willing my throat to work despite the twisted angle of my neck. She dropped my head back to the floor, shooting sharp lines across my vision as she stepped around me and kneeled down with one hand still tangled in my hair.

"I tell you what," she sighed. "Seth and I will drink to you tonight. That should be honor enough for a lowly reaper. Don't you think?" She smiled, and the silvery edge of a blade came into view as she lifted my head, exposing my neck.

I managed a strained smirk, giving her a moment's pause. A moment was all I needed.

"I'd tell you to rot in Hell, but I have a feeling you've been doing that for most of your pathetic life," I spat at her.

Her face scrunched up and pulsed with a ghostly light. It was like watching a soul try to fit back into their body. It never quite worked. Foggy features pressed through Karen's skin, giving her a hologram likeness until I finally recognized the glowering goddess Wosyet. She had manipulated a human into invoking her.

"I had hoped you would learn some humility before I ended your worthless existence," she sighed and lifted her dagger.

A sharp howl vibrated through the hospital room just as the handle of my axe rammed into my hip. I rolled my head to find where my salvation had come from. Coreen sprang out from under Winston's hospital bed and pummeled into

Wosyet, sending the startled goddess-in-nurse-skin smashing into the food cart. Mashed potatoes and peas rained down on her as she shrieked with rage. Coreen chomped down on her arm, jerking the holographic Wosyet out of the nurse's body.

Saul pressed his wet snout against my cheek and nudged me with a distressed whimper. I reached for the axe with trembling hands and pushed myself up on my knees. My legs didn't want to work just yet.

Wosyet squealed at Coreen, waving her free arm around chaotically until she remembered her dagger. She plunged the blade into Coreen's neck.

"No!" I fumbled with the axe, straining to lift it over my head, and flung it with all I had. The blade squished through her chest, just inside her shoulder, almost severing her arm and pinning her to the wall. Her dagger clanked to the floor.

"Wosyet," I whispered. So that was how Seth and Caim always knew where to find us. I stood and jerked the axe free, watching her slide to the floor.

"That was a cheap shot," she hissed.

I raised the axe again.

"You can't kill me," she tried to laugh, but ended up choking on the blood running over her lips and into a pool on the hospital floor. "I'm a goddess."

I smiled at her and snorted. "Not anymore." I forced the axe down harder this time. The double blade sliced through her neck, rendering her head airborne. Coreen fell back on her hind legs and with steely jaws, snatched the head by a cluster of fuzzy braids. Her tail thumped the floor like a sledgehammer. The wound Wosyet had made with her dagger was already healing, leaving a single smear of tacky blood down her shaggy spine.

My legs gave out, and I slumped back to my knees, shaking. Sunlight filtered through the window and glistened off the puddle forming around Wosyet's lifeless body. At least the humans wouldn't notice.

Coreen pranced over to me and dropped the head in my lap, giving me an anxious whine and bouncing on her paws like I was stalling a prized game of fetch. I sighed and stared down at Wosyet's twisted face, frozen somewhere between smug and confused.

I pulled a canvas sack from my robe and picked her up by one dangling braid. I wasn't sure what I would do with the head yet, but I'd figure that out later. Her glazed eyes stared out at nothingness as her mouth mechanically opened and closed like she had more to say. I was done listening. I dropped her into the sack and fastened it to the belt under my robe. Coreen gave a frustrated grunt, while Saul lapped the blood off my face. I twisted away from him and tried to stand.

"Am I dead yet?" Winston whispered. He lay slumped against the hospital wall with his tiger clutched in his bloodied arms. His eyes glistened, and he blinked them, trying to stave off tears as his breathing grew more labored.

"Almost." I kneeled down beside him and pressed my hand to his forehead, not sure if he could feel me the way he could see me.

"You're warm." He smiled in surprise. "I thought you'd be colder."

"I thought you'd be quieter," I laughed.

The alarm in the nurse's station died off, and more footsteps echoed down the hall. Winston took one last shuddering breath and his soul slipped out of his body and into my arms. I hugged him, not just because I thought he could use a hug, but because I could.

We stood together, watching the nurses and doctors lift him back on the bed and begin CPR. Someone called for the paddles and Winston turned away, spotting his tiger abandoned on the hospital floor.

"I can't take him, can I?" He frowned.

"Sorry, kiddo." I sighed and glanced down at what was left of Wosyet, sprawled out on the floor. "Let's get out of here."

"Okay." Winston reached for my hand, something a soul had never done before. I took it and smiled.

CHAPTER TWENTY-SIX

*"I have never made but one prayer to God, a very short one:
'O Lord, make my enemies ridiculous.' And God granted it."*
—*Voltaire*

Article VI of the Treaty of Eternity specifically covered the various punishments to be doled out in the unfortunate case that a deity was killed. Amendment four, covering the consequences for reapers, said in more or less words that I should be terminated immediately for what I had done to Wosyet. But hidden in the fine print, it clearly stated that the rule only applied to Eternity, not the human realm. And then there was the even more controversial issue of just cause.

However true that may be, it didn't stop the sweat from trickling down my spine as I waited in Grim's office. I had to tell him Wosyet was there, but I was still trying to decide if I should have dumped her head before bringing Winston in.

Grim had whisked the poor kid away the second we arrived, without so much as a word about Josie's condition. Without Winston around to distract me, I had spent the last half hour fretting over all the worst-case scenarios my pessimistic imagination could launch into the forefront of my mind.

"Lana." Grim sighed and stepped into his office, quietly closing the door behind him. He looked ten years younger, as if he had just taken the bubble bath of all bubble baths. "You did good today," he said.

"Where's Josie? Is she all right?" I turned away from the window and unfolded my arms with a shiver.

"She'll be fine. Kevin took her to see Meng Po. That syringe was full of some sort of laced hellfire. Meng should be able to sort it out." He straightened his tie and sat on the edge of his desk with a carefree smile. "I don't suppose you found anything out about the demon attacks, did you?"

"Well, actually…" I could feel Wosyet's head, still pressed against my hip under the robe. "It wasn't a demon this time. It was Wosyet."

"Nonsense." Grim stood and walked up beside me to stare out at the fog curling into lazy clouds outside his window. "She left for Duat before your team even arrived this morning."

"I'm telling you, she was there." I stepped in front of him, blocking his view of the city.

"And I'm telling you, that's impossible." He turned his back to me and shuffled through a stack of files on his desk, pausing on a manila envelope. "You're mistaken, but it happens. Don't worry, it won't cost you your bonus." He handed the envelope to me and began picking through his mail. "You're dismissed."

"I don't think you're listening, Grim." I slapped the mail out of his hand, and he glowered up at me, his eyebrows twitching with annoyance until I reached under my robe and withdrew the canvas bag. "Wosyet was there." I dropped it in his lap.

"Lana?" His eyebrows sprang up, terror tinting his expression so painfully that I wanted to look away, but I couldn't. Normally, I couldn't care less if Grim took me seriously, but the fate of Eternity would not be falling on my shoulders. Seth had to be stopped. So much for saving my own ass.

"What have you done?" Grim whispered.

"What I had to." My legs went numb as I dropped down into a chair.

"Did Kevin or Josie witness this?" he asked, lifting the lip of the bag to peek inside and confirm my story.

"No. I told Kevin to get Josie out of there before I finished her off." I rubbed my hand over my forehead, wiping the sweat back into my tangled hair.

"All right, then." He blew out a frustrated breath and dropped the bag into a desk drawer before scrunching his brow into a thoughtful line. "We can handle this. Just let me think a minute." He swiped a tissue from an ornate box on his desk and feverishly rubbed it over his hands, trying to expel any trace of Wosyet's remains that may have leapt onto him.

"It happened in the human realm, not Eternity. I should be safe. Shouldn't I?" I whispered, pushing myself onto the edge of the chair.

Grim looked at me with a disgusted glare. "You think you can fit through that tiny loophole? It's not like reapers run around knocking off gods on a regular basis. It would be drawn up and voted on by the council at the very least. You may have Maalik wrapped around your finger, but what about the other eight members of the council? No one wants to believe a reaper is capable of slaying a god. What do you think this could do to the rest of your kin?"

"They're your kin, too," I reminded him with an equally disgusted grimace.

He cleared his throat. "That's why we're taking care of this my way." He leaned over the desk and lowered his voice, casting a nervous glance at the closed office door. "You're not going to tell Kevin and Josie, or anyone for that matter. Say she was a mere demon and that she got away, but not before revealing that Seth was her master. So everyone can just assume that she's on the island with Caim, which will be destroyed this afternoon."

"This afternoon?" I bunched my hands under my sleeves, trying to warm them as a nervous chill engulfed me.

"Yes, this afternoon, as soon as the new soul is in place."

"What will you do about Seth," I asked, wondering if he already knew Wosyet wouldn't be coming back.

"Don't worry. I'll take care of him." He reached for the boxy phone resting on the corner of his desk and then hesitated, casting me one of his famously annoyed frowns. "Do you mind?" He waved his hand, shooing me out of his office.

I stood and turned for the door before remembering the bonus envelope. Snatching it off the desk, I gave Grim one last troubled grimace. Now he had two secrets to hold over my head. Isn't life grand?

CHAPTER TWENTY-SEVEN

*"Respect the gods and the devils
but keep them at a distance."*
—*Confucius*

Limbo City is considered the new frontier by most Eternity citizens. The America of the afterlife. A melting pot of various cultures and races protected by the strictest set of laws this side of the grave.

Of course, there are always a few ancients that perceive the city as a festering trash pile of rejects, a few building blocks short of an empire. They conveniently forget that Limbo is home, not only to the reapers who make their desperate existence possible but also to the Afterlife Council, who have ruled with a cold and ghostly fist for over a millennium. Meng Po is a prime example. Which is why her placement on the council would have been surprising even if she hadn't taken one of the Hindu seats.

I tossed the nephilim cabbie a coin and stepped out of the taxi. He nodded his thanks and peeled out, sending a cloud of dust twirling around my ankles.

Lady Meng might have been thrilled to be on the council, but she certainly wasn't thrilled about city life. Her newly constructed temple rested along the southern coast of

Limbo, surrounded by a forest that had been fed some sort of magical steroids, shooting the trees up tall enough to block out the skyscrapers in the distance.

I hurried down the gravel path, past a pond of fat goldfish and drifting water lilies. It was a far cry from the hell Meng was accustomed to, but the Chinese architecture told me she wasn't about to give up her entire way of life for the duration of her century-long term on the council.

The ceramic tiles of the temple's three roofs sloped and curled outward, grinning at me like demons in wait, while framed gray screens stretched between the corner columns, casting a gloomy aura over the garden.

I stepped onto the porch and lifted my fist to knock, but a sharp clash of cymbals beat me to it. A squealing gargle of laughter interrupted the echoing ring. I followed the sound and spotted a tiny monkey perched under the lip of the first roof hanging over the porch. My mouth dropped open in surprise.

"Can I help you?" a meek voice called from behind me. I turned around to find the child soul Meng had brought with her to Grim's office, peeking through a small crack in the door.

"Uh." I looked back at the giggling monkey-demon. "Isn't your roof supposed to deter those little guys?"

She opened the door a little farther and poked her head out. "It does, but that's just Meeko. He may be annoying, but he's not evil." She made a face at the creature.

"Right." I smiled at her. Child souls didn't seem so scary anymore, not after Winston. "Is Josie here?"

"This way." She walked through the foyer and down a narrow hall with quick, short steps, struggling against the tightness of her blue dress.

Josie's room was in the belly of the temple. Meng detested electricity, along with most inventions of the last thousand years or so, so the only source of light came from a single paper lantern, looming like a nuclear beach ball in the corner of the room. I blinked, willing my eyes to adjust and felt behind me for the doorframe.

"Lana?" Gabriel was the first to come into focus. He stood at the foot of a raised bed in the center of the room, slowly leaking into view. Josie was propped up on the bed, surrounded by dusty pillows and sipping a cup of tea that made her whole face pucker. I sighed and smiled. She was going to be all right.

"So." Kevin sat to the side of Josie's bed. "What did we miss back there at the hospital?"

"What?" I took a step back, wishing I had taken the time to come up with a convincing lie. Grim would kill me if I told them the truth.

"Yeah." Josie set her tea in her lap and suppressed a gag before glaring at me. "Tell me you nailed that demon bitch."

I crossed my arms, hoping my nervousness would look more like guilt instead. "Umm, no, actually. She went out the window, and Winston's soul tried to come out of his body on its own, so I had to get him to safety."

"You've got to be kidding me." Josie closed her eyes and dropped her head back on the pillows with a sigh. "Of all the demons to go free, why that one? You know I have to drink four more cups of this crap before Meng will release me?"

"It not crap." Meng scurried past me and pulled Josie back into a sitting position with a firm jerk. "It good for you. Burn nasty drugs out." She lifted her withered face to give me a snarl. "You city kids and you drugs."

"Hey." I lifted my hands in defense. "She was poisoned. Didn't you guys tell her?" I looked at Kevin.

He rolled his eyes and shrugged. "Enough times that I got bored of arguing with her. She's nuts." He shook his head, bouncing his dark curls around like an enraged Muppet.

"Watch it, boy." Meng pointed Josie's empty teacup at Kevin like a wand. "Or I fix a tea for you."

The child soul appeared at her side, holding the herb tray. Meng filled Josie's cup to the brim with yellowed leaves and dried fruit and then soaked it all with steaming water.

"You watch, Jai Ling. You make last two cups and send them home. My bedtime," Meng told her and hurried out of the room. Jai Ling cradled the tray tightly with a faint but anxious smile and wandered out of sight.

"Tell me something good, Lana." Josie turned away from the tea. I didn't blame her. I could smell it from across the room. It reminded me of Saul's breath. The hellhound Saul, not my deceased mentor. Butt-licking breath, mixed with the sickly aroma of rotting grave flowers.

"Well." I cleared my throat and pulled the bonus envelope out of my pocket. "Grim's feeling awfully generous. Or guilty." I removed three hefty paychecks from the envelope and held them up for Josie and Kevin to see.

"And you're going to use yours to sign up for additional classes. Right?" Josie raised an eyebrow.

I sighed. "Fine, but only one extra class. Grim already has me signed up for one, remember. My certification is on rush-order. Thanks, Kevin." I frowned at my illegitimately acquired pupil.

Josie picked up her tea, pretending not to notice the smell, and grinned. "Good. You can come with me when I go to sign up, and we can pick a class together."

"Sure." I tried to smile and decided it was time to change the subject. "Gabriel?"

Gabriel's wings fluttered as his attention jerked away from the ceiling. He stared at me, looking half dumbfounded as if I had interrupted a pleasant daydream that he wasn't quite ready to let go of.

"I thought Peter suspended you?"

"Yeah." His wings fluttered again as he diverted his gaze away from mine. "But when I heard Josie was hurt, I decided to use some of my vacation time to make sure she was all right."

"Ha!" Josie slurped at her tea, pointing her pinched features at Gabriel. "Yeah, right. You were all over the cover of *Limbo's Laundry* with that slutty succubus. I bet the only reason you're taking a vacation right now is because she is, too." Josie held her tea out in front of her like a dirty diaper. "Don't you have any self-respect?"

"Do you believe everything the tabloids say?" Gabriel stood up taller and put his hands on his hips, fluffing out his wings in defense.

"Are you denying it now?" Josie pinched her nose and took another sip of tea.

"Well, no," Gabriel sighed.

Josie suppressed another gag and turned to me. "Lana, let me sign my check so you and Kevin can go cash it before Bank of Eternity closes."

"Actually, Lana, would you cash mine, too?" Kevin dug around in his robe and blushed up at me. "I just don't want to leave Josie here by herself with that crazy woman."

"Thanks." Josie smiled and took the pen he offered.

"Good idea." I handed them their checks.

A mentor running errands for her apprentice was unheard of. I might have been offended, if I were a real mentor. The following morning would be my last chance to change Grim's mind about Kevin's placement, but the panic had already set in. Even if he did get transferred now, I was still going to be stuck taking some lame class with Josie.

CHAPTER TWENTY-EIGHT

*"Beer is living proof that God loves us
and wants us to be happy."*
—*Benjamin Franklin*

After hitting the bank, I decided to stop by Purgatory Lounge. It was only Wednesday, but my week was so over. My bonus check was just enough to pay tuition for one class and three vacation days. Thursday, Friday, and Saturday were all mine. I planned on informing Grim in the morning, after pleading for Kevin's transfer.

Somehow, I wasn't surprised to find Amy's motorcycle parked outside when I arrived at Purgatory. Josie was such a tabloid whore. Amy wouldn't have come back to Limbo so soon if she weren't on vacation.

Inside, a handful of nephilim were busy shooting leagues around the single pool table. Every few minutes, someone called a time-out so the stray feathers could be cleared away. Two roman deity couples slouched in a corner booth, attempting a sloppy conversation over several empty pitchers and a graveyard of sticky shot glasses.

I found Amy hunched over the bar, muttering to herself as the speared tip of her tail danced angrily around her chair. A magazine was spread out before her. A line of empty beer bottles stood guard, towering over the article she read like quiet soldiers, ready to dispense their last wisp of foam and ruin the rebel paper on their mistress's command.

"Hey, Amy." I pulled up a stool beside her.

"Oh!" She threw her hands over the magazine and then frowned at me. "What am I doing? You've probably already seen this. You're Gabriel's best friend." She handed the magazine to me and tossed her fiery curls back with a sigh.

I scanned the article, pausing on the cozy picture of her and Gabriel having dinner at The Hearth, the fanciest restaurant in Limbo City. They were holding hands over the table. Amy had on some glitzy red evening gown, and Gabriel was in a sharp black robe.

"I didn't know Gabriel even owned a black robe." I laughed and dropped the magazine back on the counter.

"I bought it for him." Amy sighed and drained the last of her beer. "Hey, Dad! Can you bring me a couple more bottles?"

"Double-fisting it now, are we?" Xaphen burst through the kitchen door and heaved a box of liquor onto the counter with a grunt.

"One's for Lana," Amy said, then gave me a funny look. "You will have a drink with me, won't you?"

"That's why I'm here." I smiled and glanced back at the magazine. "You know, that's a really good picture of you."

"Did you read the caption?" she snorted. "We're the Romeo and Juliet of Eternity. Forbidden love at its most extreme. And I look ridiculous with my tail coiled around that chair leg. I was just so nervous." She rolled her eyes and snatched the bottles Xaphen handed her.

"Yeah, but won't all the publicity be good for your new chateau?" I chugged down half my beer, hoping to quickly render myself incapable of complicated dialog before Amy had a chance to go there.

"It damn well better," she answered and tipped back her beer for a long swallow. If we kept drinking at this pace, we'd be falling down in no time.

Amy closed the magazine and stuffed it in the messenger bag hanging off her barstool. "At least I don't have my legions to worry about anymore." She crossed her legs and smiled at me.

I nodded and downed the rest of my beer. "You're welcome, but I think that has more to do with the assignment finally being over. We only ran into one demon today," I said, hoping she wouldn't ask for any details.

I waved my empty bottle at Xaphen. He huffed and jerked a bucket down from a shelf. After loading it with several bottles and a mountain of ice, he set it between Amy and me.

"On the house," he said, giving Amy a stern, fatherly glare that suggested this wasn't her first night of heavy drinking.

"Wow, thanks, Xaph." I giggled, feeling fuzzier than I would have if I had eaten dinner—or lunch for that matter. In times of crisis, food is the first thing I forget. I'm queasy enough without hot wings and lasagna waging war on my intestines.

"So, are you all ready for Friday?" Amy asked as she pulled a bottle from the bucket.

"Halloween? Gabriel will probably drag me off to some lame costume party. Unless, of course, he has plans with you." I blushed and reached for another beer.

I was still getting used to Gabriel having a girlfriend. There was a small pinch of jealousy, but not the romantic kind. Who was going to get tanked and watch John Wayne save the day with me now?

Amy leaned back in her stool and grinned at me. "You mean he really didn't tell you?"

"Tell me what?"

"I asked him to let me tell you, but I didn't think he would be able to keep it to himself," she laughed, looking tickled that Gabriel had honored her request, and stroked her tail fondly. I just wished she would get it over with and let me have it. My shitty surprise quota had already been reached for the week, hence the beer and immediate vacation.

"Do tell," I groaned and rested my forehead on the bar.

Amy raised an eyebrow and tilted her head like a confused puppy. "Council Lady Cindy Morningstar was so pleased that you put such a prompt halt to Caim's demon recruiting that she's offering an all-expense-paid weekend getaway for your team to my new chateau. Gabriel really didn't tell you?" Her gaze drifted off, making her look lost in whatever la-la land Gabriel had been visiting at Meng's earlier.

"The Inferno Chateau? This weekend?" I paused, waiting for a punch line that never came.

Amy swiveled her stool around and crossed her legs. "I know it's a little early in his term, but perhaps Maalik could take the weekend off and join us."

"You're serious?" I laughed and twisted the top off another beer. "Well, hot damn. I guess I'd better start packing."

"Don't forget an evening gown. We'll be dining with the Hell Committee Saturday." Amy giggled and pulled at one of her coppery curls. "At least Ms. Morningstar doesn't mind my taste in men. I do hope Gabriel has a good time." She bit her bottom lip and gave me a worried frown.

"He'll have a blast. We all will." I gave her a reassuring smile and bottomed-up my second beer. "I've got a few things to take care of in the morning. I'd better take off. Thanks for the drinks." I nodded to Xaphen and pulled my jacket off the barstool.

"See you Friday," Amy laughed, pulling the bucket of remaining beer closer before her dad could snatch it off the bar.

Outside, a heavy fog wove around the buildings, illuminated by scattered circles of light cast from the street lanterns and flickering candles melting inside carved pumpkins perched on every other stoop. Halloween had an eerie charm to it in Limbo City. Of course, we didn't have trick-or-treaters, what with the no child souls rule of the Fates. But we did have some pretty kick-ass parties. I'd been going to them for three centuries, though, so missing out this year for a weekend getaway to Hell wasn't a problem.

With all the demon attacks I'd been through recently, you would think Hell would be the last place I'd want to go for vacation. But the demons interfering with my work were rebels, no longer welcome in Hell. Most of them were probably gone by now anyway. If Grim were telling the truth, the island had been destroyed already. I hoped Seth and Caim went down with their legions, but somehow, I doubted it.

I stuffed my hands in the pockets of my leather jacket and headed down Morte Avenue. A cool breeze hushed past me, stirring the fog like cotton candy. I made a left on Ghost Alley and ran smack into a hooded figure.

"Excuse me," I groaned, feeling ridiculous for being spooked until the figure reached out and snatched my wrist with a massive hand, jerking me behind a building.

"What the fuck!" I flailed my arm around, failing to free myself, and lifted a leg to kick my captor in the groin. He grunted and slammed into the brick wall behind him.

"Lana," he sputtered.

I ripped back the hood of his robe and found Horus gasping for breath.

"What's wrong with you?" I stepped back and rubbed my sore wrist, glaring at him with more annoyance than fright now.

"I," he whispered, struggling to catch his breath. "I need to talk to you."

"In an alley at night?" I snorted and folded my arms before taking a step back to glance out at the still empty street.

Horus stood up taller and pulled the hood of his robe up to cover his face again, making him look more like a fellow reaper than a god.

"I know about Wosyet," he whispered.

I took another step back and pulled my jacket around me tighter as I fought to keep my face neutral. This was no time to make assumptions.

"What about her?" I huffed.

"She was at the hospital today. Wasn't she?"

"So you've talked to Grim. Why are you bothering me?"

"I haven't seen Grim since this morning." Horus leaned in closer. I squeezed my hands into fists and widened my stance, ready to bolt if he turned out to be as corrupt as his psycho girlfriend.

He took in my posture with a confused frown and edged back to a comfortable distance. "I went to see Josie. Wosyet's been known to experiment with hellfire and every other drug that crosses the sea. When Anubis told me she never arrived in Duat, I knew she was the one leaking information to Caim for Seth. Just like I knew she would try to get the soul herself this time. Seth doesn't take failure lightly." He sighed and rubbed a hand over his jaw.

"So she was there. That still doesn't explain why you're lurking around in an alley, waiting for me." I folded my arms again and leaned against the opposite wall as a small crowd of souls shuffled down the street, heading home from a costume party. A playboy bunny rode piggyback on a generic Dracula, while salt and pepper shakers wobbled behind them, tripping and giggling like drunk school girls.

Horus waited for them to pass and then set his eyes on me. "No one's seen her since she left this morning, and Seth has disappeared now, too. When Grim finds out, he'll notify the council, and I will take Seth's place."

"Why are you telling me all this?" I sucked in a chilly breath and hugged myself tighter. Horus wouldn't be sharing so much vital information if he didn't have a point to make. I just hoped he made it soon.

Drops of condensation flicked off the edges of his robe as he pulled out a silver disc the size of a dessert plate and a small bag of jingling coin. He handed them to me.

"What's this?" I asked, taking the silver compact and bag of coin with a frown.

"A token of my appreciation and a job offer."

"Job offer?" I made a face and tucked the bag of coin in my pocket. A brass clip on the edge of the compact flicked open to reveal a delicate set of six ivory bracelets. "These aren't for Josie, are they?" I snapped the disc shut and shoved it at him. "I already have a job."

Horus glared down at me and lowered his voice. "I know what you are."

"And now I know what you are, too," I hissed.

The bracelets were old magic. I'd seen them before, but only in pictures of expired academy textbooks. They were for tracking souls, and Grim had only allowed their use for half a century. After it was discovered that the bracelets absorbed enough faith from the soul's previous life to cause interference with its current life, they were outlawed by unanimous council vote.

Horus cleared his throat. "Grim hasn't been just picking out souls of ancient Egyptian descent. He's been picking out the most beloved pharaohs of Ma'at. That last soul was one of my very first descendants. If my son can help Eternity, then so be it. But I won't have him trapped in some prison of Grim's for a millennium or longer."

I dropped the compact and stared at him, too shocked to pretend I didn't know what he was talking about anymore.

He smirked and tilted his head back to squint at me. "You think no one's noticed Khadija's absence but Muhammad? You skip around here, posing as a low-risk harvester, and yet you know of her. Explain that one to me? And while you're at it, explain why Grim promoted you before Josie? You know I suggested her for the task? She's been working her ass off for decades to get a promotion, and a slacker like you gets bumped up instead. How long do you think you can hide from the council? From Seth?"

He bent over, picked the compact up off the pavement, and handed it back to me. "I can help you just as much as you're going to help me."

"What do you want?" I whispered, squeezing the compact to keep my hands from shaking.

"Go to work, like usual, and next time you come across a usable soul, put one of these trackers on it. When my term is up, I *will* leave here with my son. The disc in your hand tracks the souls and charts their current locations and life spans. It will be up to you to bring Grim a replacement again, I'm sure. Next time, your search should be much easier. See, I told you I could help you, too." Horus sighed and shook more dew drops off his sleeves. If the fog got any thicker, they would have to shut down the harbor for Halloween. Grim would have a fit.

"Why didn't you just talk to Grim about this?" I shoved the disk in my pocket, next to the bag of coin that was feeling more and more like a bad idea.

Horus cleared his throat. "You know as well as I do that Grim would have me exiled from Limbo if he found out I knew his secret. Look how long it's taken him to replace Khadija. No, this is something you must do on your own. Don't even tell Josie." He gave me a stern frown. "And I won't tell her any of your secrets either."

I frowned right back at him. Dew dripped from my eyelashes, but I refused to look away. He might be a god, but this staring contest was mine. "And if Grim figures it out?"

"Well, we just won't let that happen, now will we?" He stepped out of the alley and took wide, fierce steps down the street until the fog engulfed him and I was alone again.

He hadn't said I killed Wosyet, just that he knew she was at the hospital. And he hadn't said what I was, just that he knew there was something different about me. Maybe he knew what he was talking about, but then, maybe he didn't.

I dug the compact out of my pocket and opened it again. I was risking my ass either way. What was the difference? But at least with the bracelets, it would be easier to find a replacement if Horus did make good on his threat to take Winston at the end of his term.

Decisions, decisions.

CHAPTER TWENTY-NINE

"Work out your own salvation.
Do not depend on others."
—Buddha

Flora, the Roman goddess of blossoming flowers, owned one of three flower shops in Limbo City. Flora's Power Flowers. I thought it sounded too aerobics class to be tasteful, but you wouldn't catch me saying that to her face. Goddesses had some pretty skewed ideas about revenge.

It took me an hour of digging through shelves full of cheesy figurines and music boxes before finally finding a stuffed animal remotely close to Winston's saber-toothed tiger. Flora's part-time clerk, Buttercup, giggled as she rang me up.

"That's so cute, getting your boyfriend a stuffed animal." She paused and pressed a finger to her pastel cheek. "I don't think I've ever seen a reaper do that before."

I rolled my eyes. "It's a chew toy for my dogs."

"Dogs?" She giggled again. "Shouldn't you be getting more than one, then?"

"No, I'll come back for another one next week." I took the paper gift bag from her and smiled at her puckered brow before ducking out of the dewy shop.

The fog had eased up, letting morning sink in with a bright clarity. It wasn't even seven o'clock yet, but I wanted a chance to talk to Grim before his office exploded with phone calls and angry council members.

"**H**ey, Ellen. Is Grim in his office?" I folded my arms over the high counter of the front desk.

"Is he expecting you?" She gave me a strained smile. Ellen seemed on edge when I was around lately. I didn't blame her. I'd bring her an apology gift when I got back from my vacation.

"Probably not. I'll wait if you want to announce me." I stepped back from her desk so she could intercom Grim.

The bulletin board outside the conference room had been cleared of all the ferry attack articles, and a new headlining story had been tacked in the center. I cocked an eyebrow as I made out a tiny picture of Josie and me at Coreen's memorial service, with Seth sitting behind us. The featured article picture was a close-up of Coreen's statue, titled: *Fellow Reaper Loses Life to Save Eternity*. Figures she would hog all the credit, even beyond the proverbial grave.

"Go on in, sweetie." Ellen gave me one of her puppet smiles and dug a candy bar out of her purse.

I brought the gift bag into Grim's office. He sat behind his desk, reading over documents and periodically jotting down his signature with a feminine flourish.

"What now, Ms. Harvey?" he groaned and glanced up from his paperwork to scowl at my outfit as I sat down. I had left my robe at home and wore a pair of knee-less jeans and a black sweater. Hey, I was on vacation.

"I'm taking a few days off. I wanted to let you know in person. Also, I was wondering if you might consider switching Kevin's apprenticeship to Josie. She's a generation above me, and ten times more qualified to give Kevin the proper training he deserves. Besides, they work well together."

Grim dropped his pen and laced his fingers together to form a cradle for his jaw to rest in. "You would just love that, wouldn't you? Then you could get out of that class I have you signed up for."

"I'm suggesting this for Kevin's sake," I half-lied.

Grim sighed and shook his head. "I've already made my decision, Lana. You're going back to the academy. It'll be good for you." The phone on his desk rang, interrupting the lecture. Grim sighed and snatched up the phone.

"What's that? Are you sure?" His face twisted into an unsettling mass of lines, pulling the corners of his lips down into a loathing frown. "Notify the rest of the council. I'm holding a conference in one hour."

He slammed the phone down, and then ripped it off his desk and heaved it at my head. I ducked and pulled my knees up to my chest, curling into the stiff guest chair. The plastic box smashed into the far wall and squealed its last ring before crushing into a dozen pieces on the floor.

"You just had to kill her, didn't you?" he hissed, keeping his voice low since Ellen had obviously heard the commotion. "Seth's gone," he growled.

"Well, at least the council will be convinced he was involved now." I pushed my legs back down and tried to look less like a cowering dog.

"I already knew he was involved," Grim whispered angrily. "And now we've lost our chance to contain him. At least he doesn't have an island to hide on now."

"So Winston agreed to work for you, then?" I tried to steer the conversation in a less violent direction.

"Winston?" Grim gave me a menacing glare. "You're on a first-name basis with my new soul?"

"Well, we had an interesting encounter. I doubt he'll be forgetting me." I pulled the gift bag into my lap.

Grim smirked and scooped up a stack of files off his desk before standing. "He forgot you five minutes after you arrived. Lady Meng fixed up a nice batch of tea for him and Khadija." He laughed as my shoulders slumped. "Why else do you think I allowed Meng on the council? And in place of a Hindu representative? Everything I do is for good reason, Lana. You'd do well to remember that."

Winston being gone was bad enough, but Grim wiping away Khadija's memory crushed me in a way I'd never been crushed before. I felt like a three-year-old that had just been told someone intentionally ran over the Easter Bunny. It was my turn to have a tantrum. I dug my fingers into the paper gift bag and flung the stuffed animal at Grim. He caught it and chuckled again, giving me an amused sigh, the kind a grandfather would give a pouting child.

"Have a nice vacation. I think you've earned it."

I stood and ripped the gift bag into pieces with a frustrated growl before storming out of his office.

Ellen gave me another fake smile as I stepped into the elevator and punched the button for the main floor. When the doors slid shut, I pressed my forehead against the cool metal and sighed.

Maalik had used a coin to reach Khadija through the elevator. But if Grim had stripped away Winston's lives, there was no telling what his current name was, and no way for me to find him. It was probably best that I didn't. Seth might have disappeared, but he still had plenty of spies. And if I could find Winston, so could they.

I tucked a curl behind my ear and composed myself before the elevator doors pinged open on the ground floor.

Maalik waited in the lobby, wearing one of his formal robes. His curls were sleek and oiled.

"Lana?" He blinked a few times, confused to see me at Grim's office so early. "Grim called a conference. Are you okay? You don't look so good." He reached for me and then stopped to glance around the lobby before stepping into the elevator and pushing a random button.

"Sorry I didn't come by last night. I had to escort Khadija on to Fidaws Pardis. And then Muhammad asked me to stay the night. I can't refuse the prophet." He gave me a sheepish smile and wrapped his arms around me. I didn't return the hug. Not being seen in public with me was probably a good idea, but it didn't hurt my feelings any less than him not showing up the night before to check on me.

My lip was busted, and a real rainbow of a bruise circled my right eye, nothing that couldn't heal in a few days' time. But still, what's a girl to think when her boyfriend's a no-show after an ass-kicking like that?

"What's wrong?" He pulled away, running his hands up my shoulders, and gave me a puzzled frown.

"Seth's gone." He was still too new. My pride was none of his business yet. I shrugged and pressed the button for the ground floor again. Maalik gave me a hurt look as I stepped around him and into the lobby.

"I'm going to Hell Friday," I said, turning around to face him. Paranoia crawled across his face. I sighed and rested a hand on my hip. "I need a vacation, and Amy's Inferno Chateau is having its grand opening. I don't suppose you would want to come with me, would you?"

"Of course I would," he whispered and chewed at his bottom lip. "I'll do my best to be there, but with Seth gone...." He closed his eyes and took a deep breath. "Let me deal with Grim first." He reached for me again, forgetting the bystanders, and pulled me into his arms. I exhaled against his chest and all but purred when his wings brushed up my back.

"I'll come by this afternoon, I promise. Besides, it's Thursday. Don't you owe me dinner?" He smiled down at me and pressed his lips to mine in a warm kiss.

"I do," I breathed, pulling away from him with shaking knees. The sneaky bastard. I couldn't be letting him off the hook with nothing more than a kiss all the time, but maybe just this once.

Cindy Morningstar stepped around us and into the elevator. She wore a black dress suit trimmed with a red collar and cuffs. Two of the fallen, yakking away on cell phones, followed her.

Cindy cleared her throat and smiled at us. "Job well-done, Ms. Harvey. I look forward to dining with you this weekend."

"Thank you, Council Lady." I blushed and ran a hand through my curls.

Cindy turned to Maalik. "Going up?"

"Yes," he answered, giving me another of his sweetly confused smiles. "I'll see you later, Lana."

Maalik crowded into the elevator with the demon princess and her crew, folding his wings back tightly to keep from unintentionally giving one of them a mouthful of feathers.

I waited for the doors to close and turned around to find Horus scurrying into the lobby, trying to straighten his tie with a briefcase twisted in one hand.

"Good morning, Lana." He pressed the up button and stepped into an empty elevator without another word. Did everyone decide I was bad news today or what?

At least Josie would talk to me, even though I couldn't tell her about anything that was bothering me. But maybe we could just go shopping instead.

CHAPTER THIRTY

*"As a well-spent day brings happy sleep,
so life well used brings happy death."*
—*Leonardo da Vinci*

Josie and Jenni's apartment wasn't much bigger than mine, but their exquisite taste and minimalist décor really opened the place up, making it appear three times larger.

A vase holding a single white lily sat in the middle of their clutter-free dining table made of real oak and not some crummy imitation like mine. The living room was home to a full set of matching, olive green furniture. It gave the city dwelling a naturist appeal and went well with the sand-colored walls. A stone fountain, resting on top of the entertainment center, transported me back to Meng Po's garden pond with its bubbly music.

So the place didn't have the lived-in feeling of my apartment, but every time I visited Josie, I left feeling like I had just come from a spa, minus the pedicure, of course. It was refreshing.

"Hey!" Jenni strolled into the kitchen in a silk bathrobe. She sounded happy to see me. Normally, I got a brief nod before she disappeared into her room to study. Studying was what she did best, and most often, right after working and taking extra classes. In three hundred years, I had never seen her out on a date or drinking with friends. In my opinion, her life sucked. But she seemed rather proud of her accomplishments, and she was practically Josie's idol.

"I've got those notes ready for you. I'll go get them." She padded off down the hall, just as Josie emerged from her bedroom, yawning as she tugged on a tee shirt.

"What are you doing here?" she snapped.

"Good morning to you, too," I grumbled. "Would a cup of coffee be too much to ask for?" I sat down at the table and rested my chin over my folded arms with a sigh.

"I guess not." Josie glanced down the hall and gave me a nervous smile. "Just let me, uh, brush my teeth first?"

"Whatever."

She raced down the hall and slammed her bedroom door shut behind her. The panicked whispers that followed let me know she had a visitor. At first, I thought maybe Apollo. But she was being too secretive. Josie knew I approved of the god, even if dating him did break protocol. And it was obviously not Horus. That jerk was tied up in a council conference.

A minute later, Josie stepped back into the kitchen and fired up her high-tech coffeemaker. Her cheeks burned with little red splotches of guilt as she hummed and circled the counter with a dishtowel to wipe down the table.

"Kevin stay the night?" I asked.

Josie gave a little gasp of horror and threw her hand to her chest, trying to look offended.

"I don't care. You know that." I sighed and dangled an arm off the back of my chair. "I just wish Grim would have assigned him to you instead of me."

Josie dropped her theatrics and gave me half a smile before pulling out a chair. "Yeah, but mentors and apprentices aren't allowed to have anything more than a professional relationship."

"Hey, don't think just because you're sleeping with him you won't be helping me train him."

"I know," Josie laughed and glanced down the hall again. "I think Kevin's more worried about it than I am." She giggled and lowered her voice to a girly whisper. "He's hiding in my shower right now, so why don't you go check on your hounds for a few minutes so I can send him home."

"Sure."

Jenni stepped up next to her and set a bundle of overflowing folders and notebooks on the table, giving them a worried but proud pat, like she was leaving a beloved poodle in the hands of an inept dog-sitter.

"Well, that's everything you should need next semester. Use it well, and keep it in order," she demanded, giving me a stern eye.

"Will do." I picked up the pile and cradled it in my arms. Jenni smiled at Josie and gave me one of her familiar nods as I left the apartment.

I almost tripped over Saul when I stepped through my front door. He was sprawled out on the kitchen floor, huffing bored sighs into the food dish nestled between his paws.

"Hey there, pilgrim." I reached down and ruffled his ears. His tail thumped once, and Coreen let out a welcoming yap as I set Jenni's notes on the kitchen table.

My old couch was pressed up against the wall next to my bed. When Coreen tried to bite Kevin while we were moving it, I knew it had to stay. Saul had even compromised and let me have the bed to myself, since the couch was closer now.

I filled their food dishes and checked the clock to see if I had given Josie enough time, before pulling on a jacket and stuffing a few coins in my pocket. I had quite the stash accumulating in a hat box. The thought of depositing Horus's so-called thank you money made me nauseous. But that wasn't going to stop me from spending it for all the grief he was causing me.

"Tell me that's not what you're wearing to sign up for classes," Josie groaned when I stepped back into her apartment. She gave my holy jeans a pained look.

"Sign up for classes?" I slouched down at the table and grabbed the mug of coffee she had set out for me.

"Don't play stupid. We just talked about this yesterday." She took a sip from her mug and finished buttoning up her silver blouse. I could still make out the fresh iron creases in her black pencil skirt. Josie dressed to impress for anything that had anything to do with work. If Grim ever held a generation reunion at a barn, you could count on Josie showing up in high heels and pearls.

"Do we have to sign up today?" I whined. "I just wanted to go shopping."

"We can shop afterward. And yes, we have to sign up today. The deadline for next semester is Saturday, when we'll be vacationing in Hell. So this is our last chance." She raised her eyebrows, waiting for my next excuse.

"When did Gabriel tell you about the Hell vacation?"

"Yesterday, after you left Meng's," she confessed, giving me a sneaky grin.

"You're not going to have a problem with Amy, are you?"

"Gabriel's a big boy. He can date whoever he wants." She pressed her lips together and sighed. "I just worry about him sometimes."

"Yeah. Me, too." I yawned and gazed out the window. The fog was creeping back in, but it was lighter and more transparent than the last batch. Zibel was using Halloween to perfect his rusty skills. An old god, trying to relearn all the tricks he'd forgotten.

"What class am I going to end up taking with you?" I looked back at Josie, too exhausted to argue.

"Well." She smiled and folded her hands. "There's this really great wandering souls course I've wanted to check out. The instructor this semester is Grace Adaline, the only active first-generation reaper left. Wouldn't it be amazing to learn from a colleague of Saul's?"

"Amazing isn't the word I would use. You are talking about school, aren't you? Where you sit in a hard chair for hours upon hours while some know-it-all tries to cram your head with an overload of information, half of which you'll never even use on the job?"

"And half of which may save your snotty little ass someday." She sighed and swallowed down the rest of her coffee before glancing at her watch. "The academy should be open by now. Let's get going."

The Reaper Academy loomed over Council Street on the far side of town, just down from Grim's office. It glared down at me from a gentle hill that marked the end of civilization and the beginning of a small crest of wilderness that ran along Limbo's western coast. Six stories of purely prison-styled architecture did not deserve a backdrop of cheerful evergreens. If only the irony stopped there.

White tents spotted the front lawn, hung with bubble-lettered signs displaying course names and their instructors. Josie grabbed my hand and dragged me through the maze of tables, politely greeting fellow reapers along the way.

We stopped in front of a tent advertising the wandering souls course. Grace Adaline reached out to shake my hand as Josie scribbled our names down on the growing list of students.

"Welcome back to the academy," Grace beamed. "An apprentice of Saul's is always a pleasure in class. And congratulations on your recent success with Grim's new specialty unit."

"Yeah, thanks," I sighed. Specialty unit, ha. More like, last-minute-or-we-all-die unit.

Josie picked up a class syllabus, then snatched a second one and thrust it at me. "Isn't this exciting?"

"I can't even find the words." I stared down at the list of essays we had to write for the semester. The fundamentals of traumatized soul transportation was at the top of the list. I glowered at Josie. "Did you really just sign me up for this?" I smacked the page with the back of my hand and raised an eyebrow.

"Come on, Lana. It'll be fun, and I can proofread your work for you," she pleaded.

"I was thinking more along the lines of copying your work."

"Lana," Josie hissed and glanced over her shoulder. "Are you trying to get us kicked out before the class even begins?"

"It had crossed my mind." I smiled at her aggravated scowl and stuffed the syllabus in my jacket pocket. "Can we go shopping now?"

"Sure."

"I thought I might see you here." Craig Hogan approached our tent and grinned with one of his perfect I'm-a-stud smiles. I folded my arms and glared at Josie as he plucked up a pen and printed his name below mine. Terrific.

"Sorry, Craig, but we have some shopping to do." Josie's hand shot out and grabbed my clenched fist, pulling me back toward the street before I had a chance to scratch my name off the tainted list.

"Yeah, let's take a class together. It'll be fun," I squeaked mockingly at her, throwing my free hand up for dramatic measure. Tonight was calling for a long, therapeutic session with John Wayne.

CHAPTER THIRTY-ONE

*"Call on God,
but row away from the rocks."*
—Indian Proverb

"What's this called again?" Maalik asked as he twisted his fork around the noodles and sauce dripping from his plate.

"Chicken alfredo," I mumbled through a mouthful of garlic bread. It probably wasn't the best food choice if I planned on getting any action later, but it was good comfort food.

"Chicken alfredo," he repeated. "It's great." He stuffed another forkful in his mouth, smearing sauce down his chin.

He had changed out of his work robe and into a pair of jeans and a green sweater I had bought him while shopping with Josie. Athena carried a few angelic items, but the specialty angel outlet, recently opened by a nephilim duo, had a lot more to offer. Sure, it was kind of pricey, but so was having alterations made to a garment so you didn't get your wings pinned in the process of putting it on.

The sweater wasn't quite as exciting or surprising as the hellhounds had been, but we needed something normal to ground our relationship before it took off altogether. Yes, even Death needed a little peace and quiet.

"Are you sure you don't want any wine?" I reached for the bottle of expensive red I had set out just for the occasion and refilled my glass. Comfort food needed comfort drink to go with it.

"I'd better not." Maalik eyed the bottle with a regretful frown. "I'll wait until this weekend when we're on vacation. I'd just hate to show up with alcohol on my breath if Grim decides to call another emergency conference."

"Yeah, that could suck." I picked at a second piece of garlic bread and sighed.

Coreen stretched across the old couch, periodically kicking in her sleep with little whispery barks. The few days of working with me were enough to bring on nightmares for anyone. After being kicked in the gut one too many times, Saul nipped Coreen on the rear and decided the next best place to nap was under the new dining table, curled around my feet.

I'd donated the old table to the Kevin Fund. His apartment was starting to resemble a respectable bachelor pad. Of course, he had made more coin in his first week than most reapers made in their first three months. I had a feeling the I-hate-Kevin club was meeting more frequently than my club.

"Are you ready for some John Wayne?" Maalik asked, wiping his napkin over his face and hands.

"You have no idea," I groaned and pushed my plate away.

"Maybe some good news is in order first." He raised an eyebrow and brought his hands up to rest under his chin, giving me a sneaky smile.

"Good news?" The only thing good about all the news I had received in the past week was the extra coin that came along with it. I was still trying to decide if it had been worth putting my neck on the chopping block and praying that the blade would get stuck. So far, I had been lucky.

I ran my fingers along the glossy surface of my new, mahogany table. It was bigger and sturdier and required advanced mathematics, Josie's skills, *not mine*, to get it through the front door. Who knows, I might even learn to overlook the fact that it had been purchased with Horus's dirty coin.

Maalik cleared his throat. "After Grim's first conference, announcing Seth's disappearance, Horus and Grace Adaline approached me, requesting my signature on a unit placement proposal for you."

"What?" I rubbed my hands over my face and through my hair. And just when I had some glimpse of peace in my future. Khadija had warned me, though. Was it entirely stupid to assume that she might have been joking?

"I thought you might want to know what unit you'll be working with next year." Maalik reached across the table and pulled my hands into his with a tender smile.

"Unit?" I was going to kill Horus. Maybe Grace, too. Units always meant more classes at the academy. Maalik would learn to hate school just as much as I did soon enough. Studying might be a favorite pastime of Jenni's, but for me, it was more like a very long bout of PMS. Things got thrown, people got screamed at, and I became about as pleasant as a migraine. Josie could vouch for that.

"Meg Engles is leaving the Posy Unit and going back to freelance work so she can free up her schedule enough to teach at the academy next semester. And Grace said you signed up for her wandering souls course." Maalik frowned at me. "That's the first prerequisite for the Posy Unit. I thought you'd be happy."

"The class was Josie's idea. I was planning to drop it before it even started." Wishful thinking.

"Why?" Maalik tilted his head. He liked to blame his ambitious work efforts on his desire to serve Allah, but really, who honestly threw their hands together in prayer and said, "This buck's for you, big guy"?

"Let's just not talk about it tonight, please," I said, squeezing his hands and giving him the begging expression Saul had successfully used on me to obtain a chicken breast while I prepared dinner.

"Okay." Maalik nodded. "We'll worry about it after vacation." He grabbed up our plates and carried them off to the kitchen sink.

I tried to push the new bit of information out of my mind, which was about as easy as removing Gabriel from a bar. I should have guessed the Posy Unit. Where else would I come in contact with the most souls for Horus's illegal job offer?

The Posy Unit took care of some pretty messed up shit in the human realm. You might think the afterlife is a screwy place, but just look at the realm of those who created it. Genocide. Mass suicide. Who do you think has to round up all those traumatized souls before they figure out how to escape their bodies?

The Posy Unit got its name during the early years of the Black Plague, when people in Europe began carrying posies of herbs in their pockets, insisting it would save them from the Black Death. Maybe it didn't save their lives, but it did save a soul or two from being overlooked and stuck on the CNH roster, a list of Currently Not Harvestable souls who could end up waiting as long as two and a half centuries before being found.

The smell of rotting herbs quickly granted the reapers working the plague a nickname as unoriginal as they come, the Posy Unit. Of course, it couldn't be anything cool or macho, like the Big D Swat Team or Death Merchants United. The Posy Unit didn't even have a catchy slogan. It wasn't fair.

The Recovery Unit: No Grave Too Deep. The Lost Souls Unit: The Haunting Stops Here. The Mother Goose Unit: Because Little Souls Count Too. And the Posy Unit: Bulk Souls at Discounted Prices. It sounded more like an ad Grim would run if he ever decided to open a Death-mart. Why couldn't it be something like: For all your Genocide and Cult Salvage Needs or For When the Bad Kool-Aid Strikes?

Maalik bent down at the entertainment center to reassess my John Wayne collection, selecting *The Alamo*, his new favorite. I was surprised he hadn't questioned why Horus was pushing higher placement on my behalf. Maybe he was assuming it was because I had delivered more souls to Duat recently. I wasn't sure if I wanted his opinion on my new side job. I wasn't sure if I wanted anyone's opinion just yet. I was screwed no matter how you looked at it. It didn't really matter what altar you were being sacrificed on, it was gonna sting either way.

The opening credits of our movie had just begun when the doorbell rang. I turned around on the sofa and raised an eyebrow at the front door.

"Were you expecting someone else?" Maalik asked.

"No." And my regular visitors usually let themselves in.

Coreen hopped off the couch and raced Saul to the door, pressing her muzzle along the doorframe with a series of obnoxious sniffs. Saul's tail thumped, and he sat back on his haunches, waiting to greet our next guest.

I opened the door a crack and scanned the hall before looking down. Jai Ling, Meng Po's child soul servant, kneeled before me as she set a small black box on the welcome mat. She looked up and sucked in a startled breath as Saul's tongue lapped up her forehead. Hiking up her dress, she gave me a choppy bow and scurried off toward the elevator.

I looked down at the box. The top had been sealed with a star and crescent moon, the symbol of Islam. So why was Jai Ling delivering it?

Harold, one of my nephilim neighbors, nearly tripped over the little Chinese girl as he stepped out of the elevator.

"Bless my feathers!" he huffed. Stepping around her like she was a rabid squirrel and staring down the hall to give me a quizzical frown.

I snatched up the box and slammed my door.

"What's that?" Maalik asked as I joined him on the sofa again.

"Who knows," I sighed, snapping through the waxy seal as I yanked the lid off.

Inside, a copper coin glistened at me, resting on top of a blue, silk scarf and a piece of frilly stationery containing a message I couldn't read.

"It's Arabic," Maalik announced with a proud smile. He held his hand out. "Want me to translate it for you?"

I hesitated, trying to decide if I wanted to go through the trouble of learning a new language, and regretfully handed the note to him. He glanced over the random zigs and zags and blushed.

"It's from Khadija," he whispered. "Dearest Lana, I hope this coin is reaching you in joyous times. Soon, my days will be filled with joy, as well. Do not regret Grim's decision to give me Lady Meng's tea. I will willingly drink it. My successor has requested a visit from you. I know Grim would not approve, but a soul in his position deserves much more than this simple request. Stand to the west of Coreen's memorial statue and use his second name. There you will find him. Keep faith, and never forget how truly special you are. Peace be with you, K."

Maalik looked up at me and frowned. "I don't know, Lana."

I swiped the letter from him and stuffed it back in the box with the scarf and coin. "Maalik, I don't want to think or talk about anything that's happened in the last week. I just want to watch John Wayne kick some ass. Can we please?"

I set the box on the floor and kicked it under the couch with my heel, mentally fitting a Winston visit into my Friday schedule, somewhere between breakfast and going to Hell. I would have to fit in another trip to Flora's Power Flowers, too. Asking Grim to give back the stuffed tiger would look a little suspicious. I didn't need him switching Winston's access location before I even got a chance to see him.

"Sure." Maalik gave me a strained smile and wrapped his arm around my shoulders before hitting the play button again.

CHAPTER THIRTY-TWO

"They say that God is everywhere,
and yet we always think of Him as somewhat of a recluse."
—Emily Dickinson

The park had an ethereal feel to it on Halloween morning. Zibel had definitely perfected the art of fog. A soft swirl of clouds rode a breeze around the fountains and trees and settled in a haunting puddle under Saul and Coreen's bronze statues. A pair of dusty crows stabbed at the ground with their beaks. The morning light stained everything a sallow gray, giving the world a dreamy haze.

I pulled up the hood of my robe and stepped out from behind the shade of a knotty oak. The fact that Khadija's letter had encouraged me to visit Winston didn't make the reality of it feel any less stupid. I surveyed the park one last time to be sure no one had followed me and ducked into the shadow of Coreen's statue.

The note had said to use Winston's second name. I guessed that meant his last name, Gale. If it meant his middle name, a nickname, or a past life name, I was going to end up looking like an asylum escapee, arguing with Coreen's memorial statue.

I pulled out my coin and crossed my fingers. "Gale."

The same strange wind that had accompanied my visit to Khadija descended on the park, momentarily dispersing the haunting fog and kicking up the golden leaves littering the sidewalks.

The statue faded away, and a familiar cottage came into view. I half expected to find Khadija waiting for me. I didn't want to believe she was gone. How could she have drunk Meng's tea? I could understand why Grim would want her to, but why would she want to? There were so many questions I'd never have the chance to ask her now.

I stepped up to the cottage door and reached to knock, nearly falling off the stoop when the door sprang open, revealing a broad-shouldered Egyptian man.

"Uh?" I held the stuffed tiger up in front of me, wishing it were real and a bit larger. Maybe I should have brought Saul and Coreen.

The man gawked at me, looking about as startled as I felt. Then he glanced down at the tiger clutched in my hands. A grin seized his face as he let out a melodious laugh. "Lana, I'm so glad you made it."

"Winston?" I took a step back and gave him a scrutinizing frown. "You're...taller?"

"And darker." He stretched his arms out to admire them. "And stronger," he said, flexing.

"But you still remember me?"

"The hood threw me off. Maybe you should come inside." Winston opened the door and squinted over the front lawn like snipers were moving in on us. Once we were safely inside the main sanctuary, his friendly smile returned, a shadow of his former self. Or future self, if you wanted to get technical.

"Is that for me?" He pointed at the stuffed tiger, still dangling in my grip, and laughed again.

"It was." I blushed and tucked the animal under my arm.

"Well, can I have it?"

"Sure, I guess." I frowned.

He took the tiger and gave it a loving squeeze. "I'll make sure Grim doesn't find it. He'd probably shit a pineapple if he knew you were here."

"He'd do a little more than that, I'm afraid." I sighed and shook my head. "How did you, I mean, you obviously drank Meng's tea, didn't you?"

"Yes." Winston grinned and pulled on the tiger's tail, a habit that had survived the tea along with his memory, apparently.

"I thought the tea was supposed to peel back past lives and make you forget them." I pushed back the hood of my robe and rubbed a hand over the back of my neck.

"It does, unless you're initiated onto the throne of Eternity before drinking it."

"Huh?"

Winston dropped the tiger on a shelf behind him and led me over to a small table set with tea. The silk curtains that had been hanging from the ceiling were gone, leaving the mother of all chandeliers to fill the lonely space.

"When Khadija turned her power over to me, not even Meng's tea was strong enough to shake my past lives."

Winston dropped down on the couch and lifted a teacup. "Would you like something to drink?"

"Thanks, but I don't do tea."

"It's Pepsi." He took a sip and laughed. "I haven't exactly told Grim how much I remember and how much I don't. Honestly, I don't like the guy, but I told you I'd take the job."

"Sorry, I would have explained everything better if we had had more time." I sat down beside him and picked up a teacup to sniff its contents.

"I don't mind the work so much." Winston crossed an ankle over his knee and stretched his arms back along the top of the sofa cushions. He looked happily at home. "Grim could be a little nicer with his requests, though. I mean, come on, I'm the man. Don't I deserve a little respect? Maybe some groveling?"

"You're letting this go to your head awfully fast, aren't you?" I laughed and sipped at my dainty cup of soda.

"I know, I know," Winston sighed. "But hey, I did take care of a demon you're looking for. What was his name, Varren?"

"How do you know about him?" I asked, dumbfounded.

"I know all sorts of things." He wagged his eyebrows at me. "And I read the paper, too." He tossed the *Daily Reaper Report* at me and shrugged. "I never imagined the afterlife would have its own newspaper."

"Why shouldn't we?" I glanced over the headlines and quickly dove into an article detailing the destruction of a secret island where nearly eight thousand demons were drowned in holy water. The demons were listed alphabetically, in reverse. Varren was near the top of the list. At least I didn't have to worry about scheduling him in on top of school and my new job.

"Pretty impressive, don't you think?" Winston leaned over my shoulder. "Of course, the credit must go to Holly Spirit. She donated the Holy Water. Did you know she has it on tap at Holly House?"

"I knew it was in the fountain out front. Wait a minute." I turned to frown at him. "Does Grim know you go out gallivanting around Limbo City?"

"Don't look at me like that. You know I'm being careful."

"I sure hope so. If you go missing, do you know what could happen to Eternity?"

"Duh." The kid Winston was still alive and well. But it was still a little unsettling talking to him in a different body.

"How often does Grim stop in to check on you?" I know, I sounded like a frantic parent, ready to alert the press about a negligent daycare.

"Enough," Winston groaned. "So far, he's come in around six in the morning, right before heading to the office, and then again around eight in the evening. He stays for ten minutes, barking orders the whole time. The jerk doesn't even laugh at my jokes."

"If I laugh at your jokes, will you promise to stay here while I'm gone this weekend?"

"And miss the parade?" He threw his legs up on the tea table, rattling the dishes with a disheartened grunt.

"I'll bring you back a souvenir from Hell," I bribed.

"Hell? That's right. I almost forgot." He grinned. "Get me one of those horned masks so I can go out in disguise."

"And you'll stay put this weekend?" I folded my arms, wondering just how much personal information had been bestowed upon him by his newly acquired powers.

"Yeah, I'll stay put. I'm sure I can find a few scary movies to keep me occupied." He stuck his hand in between the couch cushions and retrieved a remote control. "A satellite receiver was one of my first requests." He grinned and flicked on a theatre-sized widescreen that filled the room with booming surround sound. "Tell me I don't rule," he smirked.

I sighed and gave him a pat on the shoulder before leaving the cottage. Varren was off my list, but it didn't seem to matter much now. Winston was going to be a handful. And I wasn't even getting paid to watch his back. I was suddenly thankful reapers couldn't have children. I just wasn't cut out for this sort of worry.

CHAPTER THIRTY-THREE

"Slow but sure
moves the might of the gods."
—Euripides

"**B**last it all!" I wailed as I dropped the edge of my travel trunk on my big toe. Why had I decided to wear flip flops instead of my new boots?

Gabriel soared up beside me and lifted the trunk by one handle, turning it on its side. "I got it."

"So much for folding everything," I grumbled.

Trumpets sounded as Limbo City's eclectic marching band of souls and nephilim came to the end of Morte Avenue and curled around Market Street. The Olympus Ballet trailed behind them, swishing their sequined costumes, all handmade by Athena, who was regretfully attending Samhain in Summerland. A dozen Draculas on miniature motorbikes zipped around the ballerinas.

I sighed and draped my arms over the ship railing. Everyone was packed and present, except Maalik. Dating a council member was not turning out to be much of a picnic.

Josie and Kevin had shown up in matching tee shirts and quickly disappeared into the captain's quarters after shooing out Saul and Coreen, who were furiously disassembling a stuffed frog I had picked up at Flora's. Even Gabriel and Amy, the Romeo and Juliet of Eternity, were having a blissful time, canoodling around the deck hand in hand.

I looked down at the flowery cocktail dress I had stupidly decided to wear and shivered. It was perfect for Hell's weather...and a perfect excuse for Maalik to snuggle up to me. If he ever showed up.

"What's wrong with those people?" Maalik shouted to me as he flew over the harbor, cradling a canvas bag the shape and size of a typical soldier's pack.

I laughed and popped a hand on my hip. "It's called a parade. Now I know you have those in Hell."

Maalik's eyebrows twitched inward as he landed on the deck. "I didn't get out much in Hell. My work schedule kept me pretty busy."

"I would say so," Gabriel huffed behind me. "I haven't packed one of those things in a long time. You need Lana to take you luggage shopping when you get back."

"What's wrong with my bag?" Maalik frowned at the lumpy sack in his arms.

"Nothing," Gabriel smirked. "If you don't mind ironing everything before you wear it again."

Maalik shrugged.

The parade was finally winding down. Two Hindu deities on stilts blew bubbles over the cheering souls crowded down the sidewalks. Behind the four-armed clowns, a frilly float sporting a huge inflatable skeleton signaled the end of the parade. A gust of wind swept up the skeleton's arms, sending its Styrofoam scythe up in a menacing pose.

I fixed my stare over the gasping souls, hoping I wouldn't find Winston among them. He was stronger than Khadija, but it would have been nice if she had given him a little more of her modesty and simple wisdom, and not just raw power and nosy insight.

"All ready?" Josie rested an arm on the railing beside me and blushed as I made another face at her "Now where did I put that handbasket?" tee shirt.

"Finally," I sighed and leaned around her to watch Gabriel drag Maalik off to the guest cabin, giving him a thorough tour of our ship.

"Cut him a little slack. He is on the council." Josie turned her back on Limbo City as it drifted farther away.

Kevin was determined not to get seasick this time, and he had even volunteered to man the ship all the way to Hell. It felt almost naughty, traveling the sea without any souls or having to do any of the navigating. Maybe being a mentor wouldn't be so bad, after all.

"Do me a favor, would you?" I turned to Josie.

"Sure."

"Don't remind me about school until we get back."

"I won't, if you promise not to cut class this time."

"That was for Saul's memorial."

"And what about the three months after that?" Josie scoffed.

"I was in mourning."

"At Purgatory Lounge?" She nudged my shoulder with hers. "I mean it, Lana. No slacking this time."

"I won't," I sighed. "I can't. You're not going to believe this, but I think I'm up for another promotion."

"Shut up." Josie gave me one of her disbelieving stares and stepped back to throw her hands up in a frustrated eruption. "Please tell me it's a normal job offer this time and not some suicide mission that will attract more demons than an Ouija board convention."

"It's not in stone yet, but I think I'll be working with the Posy Unit next year."

"Oh." Josie tilted her head with a thoughtful frown. "That doesn't sound so bad."

"I guess not."

Fireworks exploded behind us over Limbo City, now a tiny sliver drenched in fog.

Josie rubbed a hand over my back. "Then shouldn't you be happier right now?"

Yeah, I should have been happier. But I was leaving Winston unattended, Horus's bracelets were stashed in a shoebox in my closet, and I had already begun the dreaded countdown of days until I would be sitting in a stuffy classroom with Craig Hogan, of all people. Hell was just what I needed right now, the Vegas of Eternity.

A wet nose pressed into the back of my knee. Coreen had turned Mr. Frog into a pitiful amputee. She whimpered at me, squishing the soggy stuffing between her teeth. Josie and I would have to do some shopping in Hell. They probably even had a pet supply store just for hellhounds. Besides, it was going to take a whole lot of shopping to take my mind off everything waiting for me when I returned.

Kevin slipped up beside Josie and wrapped an arm around her waist, giving me an unsure smile. "How's the ride so far?"

"You're doing good. How long until we get there?" I asked.

His smile widened with my compliment. "About forty-five minutes, I'd say."

"Lana's being promoted to the Posy Unit next year. Won't that be great for your training?" Josie gushed.

"Wow." Kevin gave her a playful squeeze while I tried to keep my eyes from popping out of my head.

"Don't be telling everyone! The placement proposal may not even go through."

"It's just Kevin. You know, your apprentice, who has to go everywhere you do for the next century." Josie rested her head on Kevin's shoulder.

"Don't remind me," I grumbled.

Coreen shoved her nose in the back of my knee again, harder this time. I reached down to scoop up the mangled frog and hurled it down the deck. Coreen stumbled over a napping Saul, raking her toenails along the deck floor as she vaulted after the soggy ball of fluff.

I turned back to Josie. "While you're busy spilling all my secrets, don't forget to mention that shop-talk is off limits for the duration of this vacation."

"What about the dinner with the Hell Committee?" Josie grinned.

"Don't bring it up unless Cindy does first, or the consequences could be dire," I warned them, twisting what was left of Mr. Frog out of Coreen's chompers.

CHAPTER THIRTY-FOUR

"God is a comedian
playing to an audience too afraid to laugh."
—Voltaire

Two demons met us at the gates of Hell and escorted us, after many groveling greetings, to a ferry waiting at the mouth of the flaming river of blood, Phlegethon. Charon, the Greek ferryman who usually patrolled the River Styx, reached out a skeletal hand to take our luggage. I hardly recognized him without his cowl.

"New dress code in Hell?" I asked, taking in his Hawaiian shirt.

"Casual Fridays." He shrugged, grinding his shoulders in their sockets as he examined my passport with a bored sigh.

Charon's career began in the Greek hell, Tartarus, but when Christianity tore through the land of the living, the ancient rivers refused to shrink within their new borders. They spilled outward, filling the new Hell with all their torturous glory, and saving many a pagan demon from an eternity of loitering around the unemployment offices of Hades. Charon knew the definition of job security better than most. As long as the rivers endured, so would he.

Maalik and Gabriel flew over the small gap of flaming blood while Kevin, Josie, and I waited for Charon to secure the ramp slanted off the cast-iron deck. Amy leaped the distance, giggling when she almost lost her footing as my hounds followed her on board. Two horned guards poked spears at the sooty souls howling and clawing the surface of the river with blistered fingers.

"What a perfect beginning for our vacation," Amy sighed, popping open a cherry-red umbrella.

"Yeah," Josie laughed. "Nothing like a nice relaxing boat ride down a river of flaming souls."

"I had hoped you would enjoy it." Amy grinned, not quite catching the sarcasm.

I gave Josie's hand a warning squeeze. I liked Amy, and it wouldn't hurt if she put in a good word for me with Cindy. Grim's comments on my pull within the council got me to thinking. I needed all the allies I could scrape together.

The Inferno Chateau was built on a dark, rocky cliff, overlooking a blazing lake of fire that the river Phlegethon fed into. It wasn't the Promised Land, but it was breathtaking enough. Twin towers framed an open deck scattered with little gothic tables crammed full of horned and scaled patrons sipping cocktails in their bikinis and flip flops. Beasts of the underworld grazed in a pasture beyond a Victorian iron fence lining the property next to the chateau.

Amy stood and pointed up at the spewing volcanoes to the north of her retreat. "There's where we'll be going later. It's been rated the number one volcanic hiking trail in Hell by *Demon's Health Magazine* and the *Fallen Frequency Radio Station*."

Josie raised an eyebrow and frowned at me. "No kidding?"

The ferry passed under a crumbling bridge. I held my breath and watched the monkey demons squawk and flap their webby wings at each other, hoping they were friendlier than the one who had possessed Mrs. Henderson's mailman.

Charon pulled our ferry right up against another cast-iron deck, where Beelzebub greeted us. "Cindy wished to be here herself, but she had to deliver her report to the Hell Committee first. She looks forward to dining with you tomorrow evening and has even requested that I grant you the full services of her personal tailor for the occasion. Please, take my card."

He reached into the breast pocket of his jacket and handed me a business card listing his private cell number against an artsy watermark of his nickname, Bub.

"Wow, thanks." Amy blushed at the high-ranking demon while Gabriel tried not to notice the way Bub was staring his girl down. The angel's wings flicked nervously as he stepped out of the boat and held his hand out for Amy.

Bub nodded to us. "Just call whenever you're ready." His cell phone went off in his pocket, ringing to the tune of Elvis's *Devil in Disguise*. He dug it out and gave us a wave, walking away before answering.

"What's wrong with the clothes we brought?" Gabriel grumbled and examined his tattered white pants and new flip flops.

"I'm sure Cindy's just trying to be hospitable," Amy sighed, tangling herself in Gabriel's arms as he lifted her from the boat. "Are you jealous?"

"Just a little," he admitted.

"Good, I can make it up to you later," she purred, curling her tail around his leg.

Gabriel's breath hissed out in a heady rush. "Later?"

"Or sooner." Amy reached up and ruffled his curls.

"Where's our room," Gabriel asked the luggage attendant.

Amy's idea of luxury and relaxation wasn't too demonic to appreciate. The suites at the Inferno Chateau were worth trading your soul for. Mine and Maalik's room had been decorated in shades of crimson and burnt amber. Artfully stained curtains hung in the corners, looking like golden candle wax, melting down from the ceiling. A god-size bed filled a tiered platform rising in front of a huge barred window displaying the frighteningly beautiful volcanoes I had secretly begun to worry about. Maybe I would check some death statistics before doing anything sudden. I'd been putting myself in enough danger lately.

Maalik rested his hands on my hips and pulled me back against his chest. His warm breath pooled over my shoulder, setting off fireworks in places I had been neglecting for far too long. Something of the old Maalik was slipping through. The rush of relief I felt was almost embarrassing. He brushed my curls back with his fingers and planted a lingering kiss against my neck.

I sighed, melting into him. "I wondered if I was ever going to see this side of you again."

"I had to take care of business first, but now it's playtime." He nipped at my ear.

"Aren't we supposed to be meeting up with the others for the volcanic hiking trail?" I raised an eyebrow.

Maalik grinned and then kissed his way down my neck, wrapping his arms around my waist as he went. "I slipped Asmodeus an extra coin. We'll have to go hiking tomorrow. It's going to be raining fire until later this evening."

"Raining fire? For me?" I laughed and tilted my head back against his shoulder.

He ran his fingertips up my arms and looped them under the thin straps of my dress. "Let's not waste it," he whispered.

CHAPTER THIRTY-FIVE

"Friends applaud, the comedy is over."
—the dying words of Ludwig van Beethoven

"This has gotta be some sort of practical joke." Josie winced at her reflection in the array of oval mirrors littering Cindy's dressing room. The tailor had brought in a wardrobe of frilly, outlandish costumes for us to try on. I couldn't quite bring myself to call them gowns.

Sequins spiraled over the scarlet fabric that looked like a turtleneck trying to eat Josie's face. Revealing ovals had been cut out just below the throat and around the navel of the sparkly material before plunging into a snug, floor-dragging ruffle of tulle. Josie frowned at me and placed a hand on her bony hip. "I can't decide if this thing makes me feel naked or smothered."

"This one's not so bad." I brushed my fingers along the peacock feathers clinging to my dress and tickling my knees. The blue and green sequins were a little excessive, but the simple halter-tie around my neck seemed elegant enough.

I slid Saul's crystal bands over my forehead, letting my ringlets tumble down just below my jaw. It felt strange wearing the bands outside of the Oracle Ball, but somehow appropriate. So what if Saul was gone forever, honoring his memory made me feel better. Sometimes the human thirst for spirituality really isn't that hard to understand.

"I just don't get it." Josie stomped over to the wardrobe and parted the costumes with an agitated huff. "Cindy never wears stuff like this in Limbo."

"But that's Limbo, honey." Amy waltzed out of a dressing stall and did a flamboyant twirl for us. She had chosen a black, strapless bodice and paired it with a deep red skirt that hissed like a choir of snakes along the dressing room floor. "This is Hell, the Vegas of Eternity. You know what they say, what happens here—"

"Stays here, thank God," Josie mumbled.

"Don't you mean thank Lucifer?" Amy crossed her arms. "I mean, he is the one who signed the treaty, vowing to maintain the borders of this territory. Old Jove may have thrown us out of the big house, but it's not like he has some sort of border control set up around our perimeter." Amy was sweet, even if she was a little dim at times. But at least Gabriel didn't seem to mind.

"You want some help, Josie?" I crossed the room to examine the crammed cabinet of flashy dresses.

"No, I'm only trying on one more of these monstrosities—hopefully, one without sequins." Josie sighed and pulled down a silk gown in creamy gold and orange shades bouncing off of each other. Dainty little strings tugged at the pinched material of the bust and tied behind her neck. "Now this is more like it."

"Definitely." I bit my lip and gave myself another glance in the mirrors, wondering how the Hell Committee would be dressed. I just couldn't see Beelzebub in sequins. Or Lucifer for that matter.

"Are you ladies decent?" Gabriel shouted through the door. "Dinner's in five."

"Is this decent enough?" Amy giggled as she opened the door and posed in the frame for my feathered friend—*her feathered boyfriend*. Three hundred years of friendship makes me a little possessive.

My feathered boyfriend and Kevin stood behind Gabriel. All three of them were in shiny, black robes, giving our wild dresses an even wilder appeal.

Kevin whistled and pulled Josie in for a quick squeeze. Maalik blushed at their display and wandered over to me, holding his arm out to escort me to dinner the traditional way, while Gabriel and Amy put on a steamy show that warranted a PDA trophy.

I rested my head on Maalik's shoulder and stroked his arm like a smitten schoolgirl. I couldn't help it. Why not? We were vacationing, weren't we? Of course, sparkly dresses aside, having dinner with the Hell Committee stank of work and political hoopla. I quietly prayed to Khadija to make me impervious to all political mumbo jumbo until we got back to Limbo City. I just wanted to pretend that I was a retired and carefree goddess for one night. Was that too much to ask for?

"We're in the main dining hall tonight," Amy told us excitedly, sending Gabriel's wings twitching with every thrilling breath she took. "Construction was just completed last week, and this will be the first dinner held under the domed skylight spanning the entire dining room."

The arched corridor Amy led us through glistened like a wet cave in the flickering light of burning oil dishes hanging from the ceiling by blackened chains down the hall. We came to the mouth of the passage and entered a grand room that swallowed us up.

Just as Amy had promised, a domed skylight bubbled above, giving a crisp view of the blazing night sky. Stray dots of raining fire kamikazied into the glass, bursting into multi-colored showers of sparks with a symphony-like rhythm. A glossy, black table stretched through the center of the room, looking majestic and just a bit dwarfed in a space that could easily hold the Titanic.

Tricked-out lava lamps fused with hellfire blazed down the table between dancing fire spirits, toeing the rim of their glass platforms to make soft, gothic music that sucked me into the setting. Hell had a seductive effect, as long as you weren't one of the damned.

Through an opposite passage, Cindy Morningstar and her camarilla arrived, making a grand entrance that left me feeling a bit underdressed. Cindy smiled at our gaping and slowed her pace to give a catwalk performance to the dinner table. Black leather encased her, literally, from head to toe. The stiff gown brushed the floor and soared up into a sharp collar, framing her perfectly moussed curls, in a very rock-star-meets-evil-queen sort of way. The dress still managed a gluttonous amount of sex appeal with its thigh-high slits and plunging neckline.

Beelzebub and Lucifer were a step behind Cindy, both in sharp, deep red suits that managed to look formal and casual all at the same time. Beelzebub had spiked his hair into a wild Mohawk, while Lucifer's shiny black mane hung in a loose ponytail down his back.

The rest of Cindy's camarilla had been outfitted in complementing shades of yellow and red, elegant enough on their own, but together, they looked somewhat like a McDonald's advertisement.

Through a third passage, the rest of the Hell Committee joined us, led by Iblis Shaitan, the Islamic devil, and a handful of his Djinn followers. Iblis nodded to Maalik and shot me a flirtatious grin. Maalik's jaw went rigid, and his grip on my hand tightened. Hell may have been his home, but he still considered himself a servant of Allah. The same couldn't be said of Iblis.

We gathered around the table as Cindy stilled the tiny fire dancers' music with a menacing glance. She seized the attention of everyone else by swiftly clasping her hands together. "As always, it's a pleasure to be home." She nodded to Amy. "The Inferno Chateau is quite impressive, and I am honored to dine here with you all tonight."

A cork popped, interrupting her speech. Cindy gave the horned server a wide-eyed glare. He blushed and squeezed the fizzing bottle to his chest before quickly topping off the champagne glass in his hand and scurrying out of the room, spiked tail between his legs.

Cindy's smile returned as she continued. "Before we begin the evening, I would like to congratulate Ms. Lana Harvey and her team for putting an end to Caim's tyranny over the Sea of Eternity. Also, I want to remind everyone of Coreen Bendura's valiant efforts and unfortunate death. She is with us always."

Was that a tear I saw in Lucifer's eye? Huh, who would have thought? The Devil may care.

After a guilty meal of sauced-up red meats and just as many sugary desserts, Amy dazzled us all again with her architectural expertise. Beyond a set of glass doors off the dining room hall stretched a concrete balcony over the back courtyard. A blazing stream from the lake of fire trickled around the chateau and fed into a small pond.

I shivered, despite the oven-like atmosphere. The view from the balcony was narcotic. After the bout of raining fire, a soft sprinkle of ash had begun to fall like a gentle winter snow. The ash stifled the flaming pond, forming a layer of smoky, swirling lumps over the dark waters. The pasture surrounding the pond looked like frosted grass on an autumn morning, the soft gray piercing the ruby-stained night sky.

Saul and Coreen bellowed into the void as they tumbled over the yard, sending up dusty clouds whenever they pounced on the leather ball Maalik had bought for them at Hades' Hound House. He was determined to make good on his promise to help take care of the pups. I smiled as he waved up at me from the picnic table where he and Gabriel were solemnly playing cards with the Death Deck. Neither of them seemed to be enjoying their stay. Well, that was angels for you.

Amy had run off to take care of some chateau business, and Josie and Kevin had made themselves scarce as soon as dinner was over. Most of the Hell Council had adjourned to their rooms or were puttering around the private museum inside the chateau featuring work from the latest possessed Picasso. Amy pouted when Gabriel excused himself from visiting the historic exhibit. I'd go see it with him later, without three dozen demons breathing over my shoulder, thank you. Why take the risk?

"Lovely view, isn't it?" Cindy Morningstar slid up beside me, the corners of her lips twitching at my spooked shiver. She rested her arms on the concrete ledge of the balcony and held her face up to breathe in the violent night, catching a flake of ash on her cheek.

I blushed and hugged myself, staving off the imaginary chill. "All the beauty of Antarctica cross-bred with the warmth of Hawaii. It's phenomenal."

"Yes," she sighed. "Fifty years left on my term. Daddy didn't tell me how homesick this position on the council would make me." She hung her head and then turned to smile at me. "Not that your realm isn't extraordinarily designed. I'm just partial to my homeland."

I glanced back over the foreign landscape. "I can see why."

Cindy eased closer, gliding her arms along the ledge. She lowered her voice so it wouldn't carry over the yard. "I've received your placement proposal from Horus."

"Oh?" It was all I could do not to groan.

"But before I sign it, I would make one request of you."

I tried too hard not to grimace and ended up giving Cindy a phony smile. She saw through it in a heartbeat.

"Don't look so glum. I haven't even told you what my request is."

"Well?"

"I want you to complete a two-week training course here in Hell to better prepare you for demonic encounters."

"Do what?" I stepped back as she grabbed my arm and shushed me, casting a nervous glance toward the angels.

"Look, Coreen was Grim's second-in-command. She died at the hands of renegade demons. Saul, Grim's previous second-in-command, was more than likely killed by demons too, even though Grim would have everyone believe his death was inconclusive." Cindy smirked.

"What's that have to do with me?"

"As Grim's new and improved second-in-command, you should be skilled enough to elude a similar fate. If another reaper dies at the hands of demons, things could get ugly for us down here." She sighed and shook her head. "I'm trying to live up to my title as a respectable ruler and as a woman. You should be doing the same. Just take the training course. Then, you and I can both sleep better at night."

She had lost me somewhere around "Grim's new and improved second-in-command." What the fuck? I could have cried, but I just laughed instead. Doubled-over, gasping for air, ridiculous laughter.

Cindy drew away too quickly and nearly tripped backward. I reached out and caught her arm, still wildly laughing.

"I'll do it," I said. "I'll do it, just leave out the second-in-command bit. You couldn't have possibly heard that from a reliable source."

Cindy raised an eyebrow and steadied herself before pulling her arm out of my grasp. "Reliable enough, but no matter. Take the course, and you can count on my signature."

"Everything okay?" Maalik ascended to the balcony with a worried frown.

"Fine," Cindy answered. "Lana just saved me from a dreadful fall." She cast me a pleading smile, wanting our little discussion kept private.

I wanted to tell her she could burn the proposal, but then maybe she was right. Maybe I should be reaching for more, making a name for myself.

"Are you ready to retire for the evening?" Maalik settled next to me and folded back his wings.

"I'm ready to retire for life," I mumbled as Cindy disappeared through the glass doors.

Grim and Josie were dragging me back to school. Horus was pressuring me into illegally tracking potential throne replacements. I had to keep an eye on Winston, the new boy-king. And now, Cindy wanted to turn me into a demon-proof ninja.

What had the wise Khadija said?

"This will not be your greatest challenge, and if you are strong, it will not be your last."

Khadija, grant me strength. And truckloads of it.

Catch up with Lana and company in…

POCKET FULL OF POSIES

LANA HARVEY, REAPERS INC. BOOK TWO

Available Now in Print, eBook, and Audio!

Little reaper, big afterlife.

The promise of peace in Limbo City is threatened once again, but this time the terrorists have a more specific target in mind: Lana Harvey. The up and coming reaper thought passing her classes at the Reaper Academy was going to be her biggest challenge, but when a rebel demon sends her apartment up in flames, she realizes that her victories from the previous year haven't gone so unnoticed after all…

To make matters worse, the Afterlife Council has taken notice of Lana, too. The Egyptian god Horus is blackmailing her into joining the Posy Unit so she can do an illegal side job for him, and Cindy Morningstar, Lucifer's daughter, insists that she take a two-week training course with the devilishly tempting Beelzebub, much to her angelic boyfriend's chagrin.

ACKNOWLEDGMENTS

2019 10-year anniversary update: I can hardly believe that Lana turns 10 this year! To celebrate, I asked Rebecca Frank to revamp the cover designs, my cousin Kaitlyn Beck to pose as Lana, my husband Paul to photograph her, and my editor Chelle Olson to clean up my early work that I heavily relied on English-savvy teacher pals to proofread back in the day. I also can't forget shout-outs to Hollie Jackson, the epic narrator who voices Lana in the audiobooks; the Four Horsemen of the Bookocalypse, my amazing critique group; and THE professor George Shelley, whose enthusiasm for Lana's world motivated me at times I'd almost given up on writing. All my gratitude to you wonderful mavens who make my books shine and my heart swell.

2009 peeps I thanked 10 years ago and am still grateful to: my sister Justina Roquet, who made sure my heroes had shiny black hair and not shiny back hair; Diana Kindle and Debbie Scotten, who tackled last-minute typos and grammatical errors; Brad and Tara Justice, thank you for informing me that I had a terrible short story, but a great prologue for a series.

I must also thank those who so graciously took the time to read and critique my work or to simply offer advice on the finer points of publishing: MaryJanice Davidson, Kimberly Frost, Christine Wicker, Ricia Mainhardt, Charles de Lint, Robert Fanning, Lisa Kessler, Darla Cook, Lance Carbuncle, Alex Colvin, and Jim Butcher. Friends and family, whose encouragement and enthusiasm made this whole project worthwhile: Mom and Dad, Wendi, Danetta, Danny, Nikki, Robin, Rachel, Jenni, Jennie, Jill, Candy, Bilan, Char, Ron, Mrs. Brause and her flying perfect, and all my early online readers. Thank you all so very much!

ABOUT THE AUTHOR

USA Today bestselling author **Angela Roquet** is a great big weirdo. She collects Danger Girl comic books, owls, skulls, random craft supplies, and all things Joss Whedon. She's a fan of renewable energy, marriage equality, and religious tolerance. As long as whatever you're doing isn't hurting anyone, she's a fan of you, too.

Angela lives in Missouri with her husband and son. She's a member of SFWA and HWA, as well as the Four Horsemen of the Bookocalypse, her epic book critique group, where she's known as Death. When she's not swearing at the keyboard, she enjoys boating with her family at Lake of the Ozarks and reading books that raise eyebrows. You can find Angela online at **www.angelaroquet.com**

If you enjoyed this book, please leave a review. Your support and feedback are greatly appreciated!

Made in the USA
Monee, IL
27 September 2022

14703227R00187